P9-EKC-418

DYING ON THE VINE

Other titles by Aaron Elkins

Gideon Oliver Novels

DYING ON THE VINE*
SKULL DUGGERY*
UNEASY RELATIONS*
LITTLE TINY TEETH*
UNNATURAL SELECTION*
WHERE THERE'S A WILL*
GOOD BLOOD*
SKELETON DANCE
TWENTY BLUE DEVILS
DEAD MEN'S HEARTS
MAKE NO BONES
ICY CLUTCHES
CURSES!
OLD BONES*
MURDER IN THE QUEEN'S ARMES*
THE DARK PLACE*
FELLOWSHIP OF FEAR*

Chris Norgren Novels

OLD SCORES
A GLANCING LIGHT
DECEPTIVE CLARITY

Lee Ofsted Novels (with Charlotte Elkins)

ON THE FRINGE
WHERE HAVE ALL THE BIRDIES GONE?
NASTY BREAKS
ROTTEN LIES
A WICKED SLICE

Thrillers

TURNCOAT
LOOT
THE WORST THING

*Available from Berkley Prime Crime

DYING ON THE VINE

AARON ELKINS

BERKLEY PRIME CRIME, NEW YORK

THE BERKLEY PUBLISHING GROUP
Published by the Penguin Group
Penguin Group (USA) Inc.
375 Hudson Street, New York, New York 10014, USA
Penguin Group (Canada), 90 Eglinton Avenue East, Suite 700, Toronto, Ontario M4P 2Y3, Canada
(a division of Pearson Penguin Canada Inc.) • Penguin Books Ltd., 80 Strand, London WC2R 0RL,
England • Penguin Group Ireland, 25 St. Stephen's Green, Dublin 2, Ireland (a division of Penguin
Books Ltd.) • Penguin Group (Australia), 250 Camberwell Road, Camberwell, Victoria 3124, Australia
(a division of Pearson Australia Group Pty. Ltd.) • Penguin Books India Pvt. Ltd., 11 Community
Centre, Panchsheel Park, New Delhi—110 017, India • Penguin Group (NZ), 67 Apollo Drive,
Rosedale, Auckland 0632, New Zealand (a division of Pearson New Zealand Ltd.) • Penguin Books
(South Africa) (Pty.) Ltd., 24 Sturdee Avenue, Rosebank, Johannesburg 2196, South Africa

Penguin Books Ltd., Registered Offices: 80 Strand, London WC2R 0RL, England

This book is an original publication of The Berkley Publishing Group.

This is a work of fiction. Names, characters, places, and incidents either are the product of the author's
imagination or are used fictitiously, and any resemblance to actual persons, living or dead, business
establishments, events, or locales is entirely coincidental. The publisher does not have any control over
and does not assume any responsibility for author or third-party websites or their content.

DYING ON THE VINE

FIRST EDITION: December 2012

Berkley Prime Crime hardcover ISBN: 978-0-425-24788-4

An application to register this book for cataloging has been submitted to the Library of Congress.

PRINTED IN THE UNITED STATES OF AMERICA

10 9 8 7 6 5 4 3 2 1

ACKNOWLEDGMENTS

As always, it took a number of people to help me over the rough spots and keep me out of trouble in *Dying on the Vine,* and it's a pleasure to express my appreciation to them.

Capitano Roccangelo Tritto and *Luogotenente* Roberto Conforti treated me most cordially at *Carabinieri* headquarters in Florence and took time to answer my questions there. For many months afterward, *Luogotenente* Conforti patiently continued to answer them by e-mail.

Also demonstrating commendable patience were my Italian friends Vincenzo Panza, Alberto Venanzetti, and University of Ottawa Professor Cristina Perissinotto, who uncomplainingly answered every one of the many questions I posted to them on Italian culture, language, and mores. I apologize to them for bending a few things in the interest of storytelling.

As usual, J. Stanley Rhine, professor emeritus at the University of New Mexico, was my go-to person on matters anthropological.

Dr. David L. Black, clinical assistant professor in pathology, microbiology, and immunology at Vanderbilt University and president of

Acknowledgments

Aegis Sciences, was extremely helpful in the area of forensic toxicology, even going so far as to plan a murder with me (and solve it as well).

And my thanks to Martin and Ryan Johnson, proprietors of the Ruby Magdalena Vineyards in Zillah, Washington, for their hospitality and friendship during an early research trip to the Yakima Valley wine country. I learned a lot from Marty and had fun doing it.

DYING ON THE VINE

ONE

IT had long been the unvarying custom of Pietro Cubbiddu, following that of his father back in Sardinia, to take a *mese sabatico*, a solitary, monthlong sabbatical each fall, at the conclusion of the arduous September grape crush. In recent years, on the advice of his physician, he had begun taking it at the beginning of the month instead, to escape the stress that went along with the harvesting and crushing. During this time he rested, he thought deep thoughts, and he pondered plans and decisions for the ensuing year. That no other major winemaker in Tuscany did likewise was of no concern to him. Pietro Vittorio Teodoro Guglielmo Cubbiddu was every inch (all sixty-four of them) a patriarch: of his family, of the Villa Antica winery, and—although many would argue the point—of the winemaking fraternity of the Val d'Arno, the Arno River valley between Florence and Arezzo.

As large as Villa Antica was today—the fourth largest of the valley's seventy-plus wineries—it was still very much a family affair, but with Pietro himself firmly at the helm. And Pietro's every act was guided by the wise old adages of his forebears, very much including *Quando il gatto non c'è, i topi ballano.* *When the cat's away, the mice will dance.* Thus, it was also his custom to gather his three sons before he left on his sabbatical, to issue detailed instructions for running the business in his absence, to resolve differences with Solomon-like decrees, and to deal with issues that might arise while he was gone. For the last several years he had found it helpful to have Severo Quadrelli, his lawyer, confidante, and oldest friend, as part of this group as well.

It was for this reason that Quadrelli, along with Pietro's offspring, Franco, Luca, and Niccolò, had been gathered with him for the last hour around one of the tables on the porticoed, vine-shaded back terrace of the ancient villa, originally a fifteenth-century convent, where they munched almond biscotti and sipped from tiny, thick-walled cups of tooth-dissolving espresso, both of them made by the housekeeper according to Pietro's exacting specifications.

The *padrone* set his cup down in its mini-saucer with a clack that would have broken a lesser vessel. "Okay. So. What else we got to talk about?" His gaze went around the table and settled on his old friend Quadrelli. "I can see you got something on your mind, Seve. Spit it out."

"Well, yes, I do, as a matter of fact," said the lawyer after one of his lengthy, harrumphing throat-clearings. "About this Humboldt matter. Don't you think we ought to tell them *something* before you run off and disappear into *casus incommunicado*?" The use of Latin—frequently rather suspect Latin—was also typical of signor Quadrelli.

2

Pietro glared at him. "No! What for we got to tell them something?"

He had grown up in the mountains of Barbagia, the remote and primitive interior of Sardinia, where the dominant language was still Sardu, rather than Italian. Indeed, he had spoken virtually no Italian until he came to mainland Italy ("Europe," as he called it) as a married man in his thirties. And in the two decades since, he had never lost the thick Sardu accent or the brusque speech constructions that sounded so coarse to mainland Italian ears. Whether he still spoke this way out of shrewd business calculation (*"Ey, signore, I'm just a dumb paisano right off the boat, what do I know?"*) or because he couldn't help it or simply because he liked talking that way, was a question that even his family had never resolved to its satisfaction.

"Well, you see, Pietro," Quadrelli said, lifting a placating hand, "the thing is, I don't know how much longer we can put them off. There are a great many other wineries they could go to, you know."

Pietro's round, balding head came up. His response, delivered with flashing eye and a whack of his hand on the table, was like the snap of a whip. "But only one Villa Antica!" This was followed by a bark of laughter: *Ha-ha, I've got you there, my friend!*

The matter at hand was an offer from the giant Humboldt-Schlager Brewing Company to acquire Villa Antica. The Dutch-American beer conglomerate was eager to get its foot into the premium-wine market, and it thought that Villa Antica would be the perfect entry. Last week they had upped their offer from an already stunning €3 million to a staggering €5.5 million, more than enough for Pietro to move back at last to his beloved Sardinia, where he would be able to retire in great luxury, far from his old enemies in the mountains, to the swank Costa

Smeralda, where he'd live on the beautiful coast, right in there with the opera singers and rock stars. Maybe with his wife, Nola, at his side. Maybe not. What to do about Nola would be one of the many things that would occupy his mind over this next month.

"Of course, Pietro, that goes without saying," Severo was saying. "I'm merely—"

"They don't want to wait, they're in such a big hurry, *let* them go somewheres else." Then, as a muttered afterthought: "They don't like it, they can go to hell."

"Yes, but what do we tell them if they want a definite answer?"

"You tell them what I just say. I have not yet made up my mind. What is so hard about this?"

Franco, the eldest, who thought of himself as a natural peacemaker and arbiter (he was neither) intervened. "*Babbo*, all Severo is asking is that you make your decision before you leave for your vacation. Surely—"

"Is no vacation." Pietro told him sternly, not for the first time, "Is *un mese sabatico*. I think about this thing on my *mese sabatico*. *Then* I make up my mind."

But his voice had lost some of its authority. He was being evasive, even untruthful. The Humboldt-Schlager offer had a catch. Naturally. (*Non c'è rosa senza spine. There is no rose without thorns.*) The catch was known only to Pietro and Quadrelli. When the company had increased their offer they'd also changed the original provision that called for Franco to become the winery's chief operating officer and for Luca and Nico to continue in their present positions. Now they'd decided they had no use for any of them; they wanted all of them out and gone the day the deal closed; out of the winemaking operation and gone from the living quarters. Otherwise: no deal. To Pietro, it would once have been unthinkable: family came first, above everything. But times had changed, and Pietro had changed with them—at least a little—so more recently, it had become, well, thinkable. Besides, with the money he would get from the sale, he would make ample— very ample—provision for their futures. So, there was nothing for him to be embarrassed about, anybody could see that. But then why had he not told them?

"*Why* do I make my *mese sabatico* now, this minute?" he went on with a ferocity that stemmed from shame. "Because this is when I take. Just as the vines must have their set time to rest and replenish, so must the mind." He glanced at the inexpensive Casio watch on his stubby wrist. "Now, if nobody got nothing else—"

"I have something," said Niccolò, at twenty-six the youngest of the brothers by a dozen years.

Pietro, who had begun to rise, sank down again and looked suspiciously at him. "Well? Nico?"

"It's something I really think you need to think about before you leave, *babbo*."

"Wha-a-a-t?" It was as much a warning growl as a question. Pietro Cubbiddu didn't care for being told what he "needed" to do, even when it came from his handsome, charming rascal of a baby boy, who was granted indulgences that his older brothers didn't get. Besides, he thought he knew what Nico had on his mind, and he didn't want to hear it.

"Well, it's not about the winery, it's about your will. I know you're upset with Cesare, and I agree with you, he has it coming, but don't you think he deserves at least—"

Just as he'd thought. "Don't tell me what Cesare deserve or don't deserve," he snapped. "My will is my business, not yours. I got every damn right to change it any damn time I feel like."

Every right and every reason. Cesare was his wife Nola's child by her murdered first husband, Eliodoro. He had been an infant when she and Pietro had married; a few months younger than Nico. It was Cesare, even more than Nola herself, who was the source of the tightness, the hollowness, that now never left his chest. Pietro had joyfully welcomed the child into his family, treating him as his own and lovingly introducing him even as a boy to the rudiments of wine and winemaking. Cesare had taken to it like fleas to a dog. Like his stepbrothers, he had been sent off to the United States when the time came, to the famous "enology" program at the University of California. And, like the others, he'd lapped it up and been given an important role to play in the winery.

And how had Cesare repaid him? By betraying him. With his years of priceless training and experience at Pietro's expense, and with no warning to Pietro, two months ago he'd announced that he'd accepted the position of assistant cellar master at Tenuta Vezzi, a rival winery only a little smaller than Villa Antica, and just fifteen kilometers to the north, near Rignano sull'Arno, halfway to Florence. There was no doubt in Pietro's mind, and no surprise either, that Agostino Vezzi—spiteful, envious, old geezer that he was—had offered the boy the job for no other reason than to get Pietro's goat. But that Cesare had accepted—and accepted without even having had the decency to consult with him—that had been a blow that had laid him low.

Pietro had responded in the way honor demanded. He had thrown Cesare out on his ear (incredibly, the boy had expected to continue to live at Villa Antica) and had made it clear that he was no longer to consider himself the son of Pietro Cubbiddu. At Pietro's instructions, Quadrelli was now drawing up the formal papers for disowning and disinheriting him. Signing them would be Pietro's first order of business on the day he returned from his *mese sabatico*. It was not what he would have wished, but it had to be done.

As might be expected, all this had done nothing to improve his deteriorating relations with Nola, who had shrieked at him like a fishwife for an hour, been silenced only by the mute threat of his raised and quivering fist, and had sulked ever since. The road trip to his cabin in the Casentino mountains wasn't going to be a pleasant one, and for the first time he wished that he'd learned to drive, rather than having to depend on others to get him anyplace. For years one of the boys had taken him, but since Nola had learned to drive a few years ago, the task had fallen to her. On the first day of September, Nola, who was uncomfortable at Villa Antica in his absence, would take him to the isolated cabin, then continue north to spend a quiet month with her spinster aunt near Bologna, and then return exactly one month later to pick him up on the way home.

He'd thought about asking one of the boys to drive him up instead, but Nola was no fool. If he suddenly declined to ride with her, she would conclude—correctly—that something was up. And that he did not want; it was necessary that she behave as she normally would.

Nico clamped a hand over his heart, pretending fright. "Okay, *babbo*, okay! I didn't mean to wake the sleeping giant."

Pietro laughed. Even when he didn't understand what Nico was saying, the boy could always make him laugh.

Franco raised a bony finger. "There's one more thing, *babbo*. I need to know whether to keep the rotary fermenter or not. We only have another week to commit. I think we should do it."

A rough shake of the head from Pietro. "The what?"

"The rotary fermenter? From Cosenza? Three years old? Twenty thousand euros? It's an excellent buy. We've had it on approval for almost a month now. Galvanized frame, access catwalk—"

"And what is it that such a thing does again?" This was asked partly because he'd forgotten the details, but mostly for the simple pleasure of irritating his increasingly officious, impatient, eldest son.

"It macerates the—"

"It *what*?"

Franco pursed his lips. Clearly, he knew he was being had, but he also knew that Pietro would trust his judgment in the end, as he always did when it came to things that didn't engage his father's interest—such as modern production methods and sophisticated equipment. "A rotary fermenter," he said through only slightly clenched teeth, "will assure consistent contact between the must-cap and the juice, not only shortening the total fermentation time, but eliminating the labor-intensive—"

He was interrupted by Luca, the middle son. "Rotary fermenters," he said disgustedly, "those cement-mixers you love so much— damn it, Franco, can't you see they rob the grapes of their individual character, of everything that separates the soil of *our* vineyards from every other vineyard in the Val d'Arno? No, better to take a little longer and let the wine macerate naturally into what it was *meant* to be, not something some machine made it into."

Pietro unconsciously nodded his head in agreement. When it came to wine—when it came to just about everything—the old ways were best. If they weren't, would they still be around after all these centuries?

But Franco shook his head sadly. "Ah, Luca, you're living in the past. Today, the manufacture of wine—"

"*Manufacture* of wine?" Luca's eyebrows jumped up. "Did I hear that right? Since when do we *manufacture* wine? Are we the Villa Antica wine factory now? Do we produce our wines on an assembly line, producing a thousand bottles a day of perfectly uniform, identical wine . . ."

It was an old, ongoing argument between the two, and Pietro's mind drifted. How different they were from each other, these sons of his. It wasn't that Franco was without merit. He was smart, he was a hard worker, and he was single-mindedly dedicated to Villa Antica. Much of the winery's growth had been due to his ingenuity and foresight. He knew everything there was to know—far more than Pietro did—about the science of winemaking.

But, and it was a big *but* . . . for Franco it was *all* science—all polymerization, micro-oxygenization, anthocyanin extraction. In evaluating a wine, Franco would trust his Brix hydrometers and his protein precipitation meters before he'd trust his own palate. He had the head of a winemaker, yes, but not the heart; there was no feeling in him for wine, no passion. For Pietro, wine was a wonderful gift from God, and to be privileged to devote one's life to making it, nurturing it from vine to bottle, was an even greater gift.

Uncork a fine bottle of wine—a 2003 Villa Antica Sangiovese Riserva, for example—on a gray winter's night with snow swirling outside, and your nose was immediately filled with the aromas of the rich loam from which the grapes had sprung and with the warm, dry air of early autumn. You could practically feel the sun on the back of your neck. And then the first taste, taken with the eyes closed . . .

But Franco? Did he even *like* wine? Once when they were tasting to decide if a bottling was ready for release, Franco was going on and on about acetate esters and phenols. Pietro, finally losing patience, had asked him whether he *liked* it or not.

Franco had looked at him with honest incomprehension. "What's liking got to do with it?"

Pietro had just shaken his head and mouthed a silent *mamma mia*.

Luca was as different as different could be. Luca had for wine the same deep affection that Pietro did. More important, like Pietro he respected it for what is was. He understood the soil and the seasons and the life cycle of the grape itself. But, somewhere along the way, he had lost interest. Possibly, this was a result of frustration. Luca being the middle son, he'd had to take a back seat to Franco in winery matters. In Villa Antica's unofficial hierarchy, Franco was the chief operating officer, Luca the head winemaker. (As for an "official hierarchy," Pietro was the boss; that was about as official as it got.) It would have been better had Luca's and Franco's positions been reversed, Pietro knew, but what was a father to do, ignore the rightful claims to primacy of the first-born son? Not likely for most fathers, highly unlikely for Italian fathers, impossible for a Sardinian father. As a result, although he trusted Luca's opinions more, he deferred to Franco's whenever it was feasible.

Surely, that must have soured Luca's attitude toward the winery, and the knowledge that it would be Franco, the eldest, who would eventually inherit it could not have helped either—but whatever the cause, Luca's enthusiasms had swung away from wine and toward food. Already he and his unconventional, unpredictable American wife were talking about the restaurant in Arezzo that they would one day own.

Well, that was all right too, Pietro supposed. A chef, a real chef, was nothing to sneer at. A man could be proud of having a great chef for a son, especially a chef who truly knew something about wine.

And he had no doubt that Luca would make a fine chef. Still, it wasn't what he'd hoped for.

And Nico? Nico liked wine, all right—a little too much, in fact—but he had never been serious enough to learn and retain something about it. Nico had never been serious enough about anything. Even now, he took no interest in the argument between his brothers, but only sat there drumming his fingers and staring smilingly into his own thoughts. Of the three, only Nico's role in the winery had nothing to do with the production of it. Nico was their connection to the industry and to the dealers. He spent half his time on the road, like a traveling salesman. And he was extremely good at it. This very afternoon he was off to a winemakers' conference in Hong Kong. Whoever heard of a winemakers' conference in Hong Kong? And yet, there was no doubt in Pietro's mind that he would come back with a suitcase full of orders. A good kid: smart, handsome as a movie star, fast with the ladies, quick with words, a born salesman. But a businessman? No.

All these considerations had played into his decision to accept the offer from Humboldt-Schlager. He was left, as he saw it, with little choice. Tradition, of course, required that in his will, he leave the winery to Franco. But Franco was no different than anybody else; he would never change. (*Chi nasce tondo non muore quadro. He who is born round does not die square.*) With Franco at the helm, the Villa Antica that Pietro had poured so much of himself into would die with him. Once Pietro himself was gone, and without Luca's tempering influence, Franco would turn it into something cold and passionless: a scientific laboratory, its wines perfectly uniform from bottle to bottle, made—"manufactured"—by the cold dictates of chemists and food scientists.

And so Pietro had concluded that if his own tradition of wine-making wasn't going to survive him anyway, what was wrong with hurrying its demise along a little—and pocketing €5.5 million from it? About his sons he felt little guilt. Franco, Luca, and even Nico were grown men now, and it was time—past time—for them to strike out on their own. They were all mature, capable men now. Hadn't he provided them with fine educations and years of highly marketable experience? Besides, as he'd told them, with the money from the beer maker he planned on giving each of them a generous stipend of €5,000 a month for the next five years, a total of €300,000 apiece. Yes, they would find it a shock when they learned that they would be out of jobs and their home, but if €300,000 wasn't enough to make a place for themselves in the world, what was? He had started Villa Antica with less than a hundredth of that. With the advantages they had, the advantages he'd given them . . .

When he surfaced again, Luca and Franco were still going on about rotary fermenters. Nico had stopped drumming his fingers long enough to pour himself another glass of wine.

Pietro silenced the two older brothers with a weary wave. "Enough. Don't order the damn thing; let it wait. It's not the last whatever-you-call-it in the world." *Let Luca win one for a change. What difference did it make now?* "Okay, I got to get going. Any minute, Nola, she gonna be here to drive me. So, if nobody got anything else—"

The mere mention of Nola, Pietro's second wife, was enough to cause a stiffening around the table. The prickly, uncomfortable relations between stepmother and stepsons were, if anything, worse than they'd been twenty-five years earlier when she'd made her first appearance in their lives. For a while Pietro had tried to smooth things between them, but patience was not his strong suit, and eventually he'd given up. And the truth was that by now he had plenty of smoldering grievances of his own against her. Grievances, doubts, suspicions . . . he hardly knew what she was thinking anymore. He hardly knew *her.*

The shy, plump, young widow he had married back in Sardinia had been full of gratitude to him. She'd been a simple, dutiful wife, and for the first five hard years in Tuscany she had worked shoulder to shoulder with him, planting vines, building trellises, culling and harvesting grapes until their fingers bled. But things changed when a noted wine critic more or less accidentally visited Villa Antica in 2009 and tasted the 2001 Pio Pico, then raved about it in his blog: "elegant yet rustic, assertive yet balanced, subtle yet bold, this big-hearted wine . . ."

What made it truly astounding was that what the famous critic was blathering about wasn't one of Franco's fancy, meticulously engineered varietals, but the simple, down-to-earth wine Pietro made primarily for their own everyday drinking, the same blend of Carignane and Nebbiolo that his father and grandfather had made back on the farm in Sardinia.

Nevertheless, the review put them on the enological map; their fortunes took a sudden, huge jump; and things were never again the same with Villa Antica. Unfortunately they had never been the same with Nola either. Now that she was part of Tuscan royalty, she changed overnight from a Sardinian to an Italian: first the relinquishing of her kitchen duties to a newly hired housekeeper, then the driving lessons, the "diction" lessons, the fashion magazines, the hairdresser in Milan, the endless diet regimens, the flaunting of her middle-age body in shamefully revealing new clothes. At home and with the winery staff, she had become domineering; in public, vulgar and whorish—

"I don't have anything else, *babbo*," Luca said.

"I don't have anything, *babbo*," Nico said.

Franco, sulking over the rotary fermenter, was silent.

"All right, then," Pietro said, getting up. "Don't blow up the winery while I'm gone. Franco, you're in charge."

Franco stood up to shake hands with his father. "We'll take care of everything. I'll see you at the end of the month."

"If God wills it," Pietro grunted. "*Che sara sara.*"

TWO

RESPONDER: "One-one-two, emergency response. What is the nature of the problem, please?"

CALLER: "I don't know if this is the number I should be calling. I—I—"

RESPONDER: "Just tell me the problem, signore. Speak slowly."

CALLER: "Well, I just saw two dead bodies."

RESPONDER: "Give me the address, please, signore."

CALLER: "There is no address. I was hiking. I'm in the mountains, in the Casentino National Park near Mount Falterona. But I have a GPS. The coordinates are, ah, 43.87983 and, ah, 11 .758633. Yes, that's right, 8633."

RESPONDER: "And can you see these bodies right now?"

CALLER: "Not exactly. They're on the other side of a big boulder, maybe five meters from me. I'm at the bottom of a cliff. If I remember right, there's a path up there along the edge, and it looks to me like they fell off it, but I don't—"

RESPONDER: "Signore, you are certain they're dead?"

CALLER: "Oh, yes, definitely."

RESPONDER: "Are you sure? Have you checked their pulse? Their breathing?"

CALLER: "No, but—"

RESPONDER: "It may be that they're still alive. We—"

CALLER: "If they are, it'll be the first time I ever saw skeletons that were still alive."

RESPONDER: "Skeletons? Did you say skeletons? But are you're sure they're human? There are many animals in the park, signore. Goats—"

CALLER: "Well, if they're goats, it'll be the first time I ever saw goats wearing clothes."

RESPONDER: "I see. Signore, the authorities will be there shortly. We request—"

CALLER: "I'm not sure they'll be able to find the place, even with a GPS. Tell them to drive into the park on SS67, and maybe two kilometers after they come to a tiny village—Campigna, it's called—there's a gravel road on the right. It's not much of a road, it has no number, it's rough, you have to drive slow. But it they take that a few kilometers through the forest, they'll come to a clearing—it looks like maybe they were going to build something there, but there isn't anything. Well, that's where I am, and the skeletons are right—"

RESPONDER: "Signore, we request that you kindly remain at the site."

CALLER: "Oh no, I don't think so. I've done my duty. This doesn't concern me."

RESPONDER: "But may I have your name, please?"

CALLER: "No, no, I don't think so, no."

Telephone call terminated

CAPITANO Roberto Marco Conforti, commander of the Operations Department of Florence Province's *Arma dei Carabinieri*, read the transcript for the second time, while his secretary, who had brought it to him, awaited his instructions.

"Cosima," he said, with a sigh of resignation that few people besides his longtime aide would recognize for what it was, "please tell *Tenente* Gardella I would like to see him."

As Cosima left, the captain rose from his teak desk and walked to the arched window of his airy office. Ordinarily the view down Borgo Ognissanti, an ancient street of ancient churches and stately, gray palazzos (of which Number Forty-eight, *Carabinieri* headquarters with its great interior stone courtyard, was a classic example), pleased and calmed him, but not today. Beribboned, bemedaled (by the president of Italy, no less), and famed within the corps for his unflappability, Captain Conforti was not a man to be intimidated by anything, least of all by the prospect of an interview with a member of his own staff. With one exception. From the day the young lieutenant had been transferred from Palermo four years earlier, Rocco Gardella had displayed an unmatched knack for raising the captain's blood pressure.

"Come!" he called on hearing the quiet tap at his door. When it opened, he turned reluctantly from the window to look dourly at his subordinate.

"You wanted to see me about something?" Lieutenant Gardella asked.

Well, there you were. The conversation hadn't even begun, and already the lieutenant had managed to get under his skin. "Upon entering the presence of a superior officer, *Tenente*, it is customary to salute," he said coldly.

"Oh yeah, right, sorry about that," was Gardella's affable reply, accompanied by a vague gesture in the general direction of his forehead, a motion somewhere between a wave and a flap.

The captain, erect as always despite his fifty-four years, returned this halfhearted gesture, but did it one hundred percent by the book, shooting it back with stiff, snapping precision. Not that he thought the lesson would take; not with Gardella. Still, it was his obligation to try. "It is also customary to address senior officers either by their rank or by 'sir.'"

"Sir," Gardella said, following it with a closed-mouth grin, as if happy to go along for the sake of form with a custom that they both knew to be ridiculous.

With a discreet roll of his eyes, Conforti returned from the window to sit behind his desk, indicating with a curt dip of his chin that Gardella was to take the chair across from him. Gardella fell into it and settled comfortably back. A small, fit, compact man, he sprawled like a teenager, more or less on the bottom of his spine, not easy to do in a government-issue visitor's chair, and not at all suited to the beautifully tailored uniform he wore, and even less to the two silver stars on each shoulder tab. Just *looking* at him was enough to make Captain Conforti grind his teeth.

If he were a raw twenty-five-year-old, it would be one thing; he would still be moldable. But this baby-faced Gardella was nearing forty; he'd been in the corps for over ten years. He would soon come up for *luogotenente*—senior lieutenant; a position of considerable responsibility—and would no doubt pass the test with flying colors, as he had passed all his tests. But how had he lasted this long without running up against a senior officer with less patience than the forbearing and tolerant Conforti? How did he ever get to be a *carabiniere* in the first place? Why had he ever *wanted* to be a *carabiniere*?

On the other hand, it wasn't the man's fault, really; it was simply the way he was made, something in the blood. Rocco Gardella was half-American, a dual citizen born in the United States to an American mother and an Italian father. Through his teens, he had spent his summers in New York with his mother's family, and unfortunately the American half had come to dominate. Not that the Italian half was anything to write home about; his father was from Sicily, after all. Lieutenant Gardella was overly casual, bordering on irreverent, in his attentions to the glorious history and traditions of the *carabinieri*, overly informal in dealing with his superiors, frequently on the edge of insubordination—but never quite actionably over the line—and infuriatingly cavalier in matters of rules and deportment. He spoke Italian with an American accent, and, so it was said, English with an Italian accent.

But he was also the finest investigative officer Conforti had under him, maybe the finest he'd ever had, and that made all the difference in the world. And the public—he knew how to get along with them.

In his decade with the corps he had received a dozen commendations from citizens and not a single complaint. No, it was only here, within the hallowed ranks of what was, after all, an elite military organization going on two hundred years old, that his incurable Americanness proved so grating on the *capitano*'s nerves. At the same time, it had to be said, Gardella was hard not to like; always innocently cocksure and blithely unaware of his offences. Which naturally made him all the more infuriating.

"Here," Conforti said gruffly, sliding a sheet of paper across the desk. "Something for your attention. This is a transcript of a 112 call that was made half an hour ago."

Gardella took the transcription and read it with interest, pausing only to utter a snort of laughter at one point, no doubt at the reference to goats wearing clothing. Even that displeased Conforti— understandable it might be, but decorous it was not, considering the situation. Nevertheless, the captain contented himself with no more than a recriminatory rumble from deep in his throat, of which the lieutenant predictably took no notice.

"Casentino National Park," Gardella mused. "You think it could be that winery couple, the . . ."

"The Cubbiddus, yes," Conforti responded. "Those coordinates, they're less than half a kilometer from Pietro Cubbiddu's cabin. A remote and difficult area. I think we may have found them at last." He proffered another sheet. "A map of the area with the coordinates shown."

Gardella studied it, nodding. "You could be right."

Conforti scowled. Well, there it was again. *You could be right.* Technically, there was nothing wrong with what Gardella had said; it was a statement of fact. But "You *could* be right?" Was this the way to address one's superior? "I would like you to handle the investigation, *Tenente*," Conforti said mildly.

"Me? Well, who headed up the task force when they first disappeared?"

"That was the late, unlamented *Maresciallo* Galli," the captain said. "But even if he were still among us, I would be assigning the responsibility to you. That is, of course, if you wouldn't mind."

But sarcasm bounced off Gardella like raindrops off a mallard. "All right, no problem. I'll see that it's taken care of for you," he said as if bestowing a favor. "I'll give it to Martignetti. Tonino's a good man." He folded the sheets in two and (without being dismissed) rose to leave.

"No, I want you to lead the investigation personally," Conforti said.

"Me, personally? Why?"

"Because this may well turn into a high-profile matter." Was it possible to *feel* one's blood pressure rising? Conforti was sure he could sense his arteries tightening. "Because there may be foul play involved. I want a commissioned officer in charge from the beginning, not a *maresciallo*. I have chosen you."

"But I barely know the case. I hardly—"

"Nevertheless you will be the investigative officer." He spoke through clenched teeth. His patience continued to fray.

"But—"

Conforti glared at him. Had the man ever, even once, accepted an order without a *but*, an argument, a question? A *why*? "*Tenente*!" he said sharply. "I have given you a direct command. I do not wish to be questioned further."

"But—"

"I do not wish to be questioned *at all*. You will go to the site now. Take Martignetti with you. The crime-scene van is on its way. Representatives of the prosecutor's office and the *medico legale* will meet you there. You will give an account to me when you return, even before making out your report. Is all this clear?"

"Well, sure it's clear. I just—"

"Dismissed."

"I only—"

"Dismissed."

Gardella, totally unfazed by his captain's growl, got up with an amiable shrug and made for the door. "You're the boss. I'm on my way." He pulled open the door and stepped into the hallway.

Conforti began to call sharply after him. "On *leaving* the presence of a superior officer, *Tenente,* it is customary . . ." Mid-sentence, he threw up his hands. His final muttered words were addressed to the walls.

"Ah, ma va all'inferno."

Ah, the hell with it.

THREE

THE city of Florence, like the rest of Tuscany, was slogging its way through another humid, sweltering August, so the prospect of spending the afternoon in the mountains was a welcome one. Rocco Gardella had gratefully changed out of his uniform and now had on light, tan summer jeans, a short-sleeve blue sport shirt, and sockless sandals. Traveling east on SP556 with Rocco driving and the equally casually dressed Martignetti in the passenger seat, it didn't take long before they were climbing out of the heat haze, through the tiny stone villages of Ponte Biforco and Montemezzano, and up onto the cool, forested, green flanks of Mount Falterona. He turned off the air-conditioning, opened the window at his side, and leaned his head out, lapping up the wind like a dog. This was terrific, and only forty minutes out of Florence. Why didn't he get up here more often?

Rocco remembered a little about the Cubbiddus' disappearance a year earlier, but not much more than what he'd seen in the newspapers. However, Martignetti had pulled the old case and had it on his lap. As they drove he browsed through it, reading the background aloud to Rocco.

Pietro and Nola Cubbiddu had migrated from Sardinia twenty-five years earlier. In the time since, starting with a half hectare of decrepit vineyard that had produced its last wines fifty years before, they had built one of the largest wineries of the Val d'Arno.

A year ago, Pietro had been spending a few quiet weeks at his vacation cabin in the Casentinese, and Nola was supposed to have come to pick him up in her car and drive him back home to the villa, but they'd never shown up there. The family had called the police that night. There had been an extensive search of the area over the next few days, which had produced the wife's parked car not far from the cabin, but nothing else. The investigation that followed had led to dead ends. Today's telephone call was the first thing that sounded as if it might be a real lead.

The last few kilometers to the location were on an unmarked road—a pair of ruts, really—that even Rocco's GPS didn't know about, and they had to concentrate to keep from wandering off it onto even vaguer pathways. Still, Rocco's mind was working on the case. It was too early to arrive at any hypotheses, of course—it had yet to be determined whether these were or weren't the Cubbiddus—but he couldn't keep a couple of speculations from rattling around his brain. First, whoever they were, he thought that foul play probably *was* involved. One person falling accidentally to his death from a mountain path; that was possible. But two people? Unless they'd been caught in an avalanche, highly unlikely. Second, and this wasn't so much a hypothesis as an archaic word that he couldn't get out of his mind: *faida* it was in Italian, and though the deadly, senseless—but undeniably romantic—institution was a thing of the past on the mainland, it was still alive and well in the remote, mountainous interior of Sardinia, from which the Cubbiddus had come.

Vendetta.

THE unique and particular chunk of earth identified by its coordinates as 43.87983, 11.758633 turned out to be a flat rock, most of which was hidden from view at the moment by a smiling fat man sitting cross-legged on it, like a statue of Buddha, with his hands folded in front of his belly. He was chewing contentedly on a stick of red licorice. Beside him was an ancient black physician's bag, its leather so cracked and peeling it looked like alligator hide.

"I'd say it's about time you two got here," said Melio Bosco, Florence Province's senior police physician. Bosco, well into his seventies, had first started contracting with the office of the *medico legale* thirty-seven years ago. Rocco had been two years old at the time.

"Hello, Melio. Crime-scene crew isn't here yet?"

"Not yet."

"The public prosecutor?"

"No sign of him. Perhaps he's gotten lost."

"From your lips to God's ear," Martignetti said. In Italy, all police agencies, including the *Carabinieri*, work under the close supervision of the public prosecutor, commonly referred to as the magistrate. And every one of them chafes at it. The two men were pleased to have their initial look at the scene without having a magistrate looking over their shoulders.

"So?" Rocco said. "What do we have?"

"We have the skeletal remains of a man, and we have the skeletal remains of a woman."

"And?"

"And after careful analysis I am ready to certify that they are both deceased."

Despite the age difference, the two men had become friends. Like Rocco, Dr. Bosco took the hidebound formalities of the criminal justice bureaucracy with a golf-ball-size grain of salt. And he had a sense of humor, not something in great supply within those precincts.

Rocco looked around the wooded surroundings. There were a lot of boulders, most of them big. "Which ones are the skeletons behind?"

"Oh, I don't know that I'd call them *skeletons*, exactly. The animals have been at them, you see. Wolves, bears, marmots . . ." He frowned. "Perhaps not marmots. Are marmots carnivores?"

"I don't know, Melio. It's something I've always wondered about."

"I don't either." Dr. Bosco chewed, smiling and inscrutable.

"Martignetti," Rocco said, "write this down: 'Find out if marmots eat meat.'"

"At once, *Tenente*, immediately," Martignetti said, yawning and scratching behind his ear.

Maresciallo Antonio Martignetti was five years older than Rocco and had been eight years longer in police work. He and Rocco had been working together for two and a half years and over that time had built a comfortable, easygoing relationship. They understood each other.

"So what do you say, Melio?" Rocco asked. "You planning to tell us where they are?"

"Do you see that boulder over there, the biggest one, right up against those trees?" He used the licorice stick to direct Rocco's attention. "Go and look behind it, and see what you see."

What they saw was pretty much what you'd expect a couple of corpses to look like after they'd fallen off a cliff, then lain out in the rain, snow, heat, and cold for the better part of a year, in an area well supplied with meat-eaters: two mostly skeletonized, moldy, greenish-brown things with a dissolved, out-of-focus look, as if they were on their way to melding with the soil (which they were), and if the dividing line between earth and bodies had been blurred. Both of them were clad in jeans and leather jackets, much soiled and discolored.

If the caller was right (and Rocco thought he was), they had fallen from the cliff that towered some sixty or seventy meters above. Apparently, they'd landed on the sloping scree at its base and rolled (or bounced) down a few more meters into some woods until they'd been stopped by the immense boulder, one jammed against the boulder itself, the other jammed against the first. Both were on their faces or what would have been their faces. The one directly up against the rock had its arms and legs splayed out at crazy angles that no living body had ever assumed; the other, pressed close against it, was crumpled up almost into a fetal position. The two of them looked like a couple of moldy old scarecrows tossed onto a refuse pile, torsos caved in and only one foot, shod in an ankle-length boot, visible between them. The body against the boulder had lost its hands too. As for the other, the arms were wedged beneath it, so it was impossible to tell if the hands were there or not. Only about half its skull was still present; the rear half was pretty much an open hole.

Ligaments and hardened bits of soft tissue could be seen here and there on the bony surfaces of the bodies. They were long past the stench of decomposition, and now emitted a milder and less stomach-turning odor of decay; a musty, mushroomy kind of forest smell that wouldn't have troubled you, had you not been aware of its source.

Rocco stood looking at them for a few moments, his hands on his hips. He'd have loved to start poking around in the human wreckage, but—as he'd learned the hard way—better to wait for the crime-scene van and that goddamn ever-present prosecutor before touching anything.

"You smell something funny?" Martignetti asked.

"I do," said Rocco, who hadn't noticed it until then.

They walked the ten yards back to the doctor.

"Hey, Melio," Martignetti said. "Something smells funny back there."

"Is that so? An odor emanating from a couple of rotting corpses? Gentlemen, you amaze me."

"Ha-ha," said Rocco. "No, something else, something sharper. I can still smell it."

"You have a good nose. It's alcohol spray. I thought it best to spray it into the male's skull."

Rocco's brow wrinkled. "Why?"

"Because I preferred not to get stung. There's a wasp's nest in there, and it was buzzing away."

"No kidding. Does that happen very often?"

"Often enough for me to carry the spray. Sometimes you find a family of mice nesting happily in one. Cute little things. Those, I don't kill. I always hate to disturb them."

Martignetti shrugged. "Live and learn. Something new every day."

"Which one's the man?" Rocco asked.

"The one with the broken head."

As Rocco nodded his response, he caught sight of two vehicles inching their way over the rough gravel toward them: a familiar, boxy blue van and a black, sleek, private sedan. "Here they come." He peered at the sedan. "Oh Christ, the prosecutor's office has sent Migliorini. That's all I needed. What can you tell me before he gets here and starts issuing orders?"

"Not much, my boy. I didn't want to disturb the scene before your people were able to have a look. I'll tell you more after I get the remains to the mortuary, of course, but for now . . ." He stood up and turned so that he faced the cliff wall that rose behind them at about a sixty-degree angle. "From the looks of it, both of them fell from up there."

"That's what the caller thought," Rocco said. "Me too. That makes three of us."

"Four," said Martignetti, peering upward. "That would be, what, sixty meters?"

Bosco nodded, sucking on the licorice stick. "Mm, sixty or seventy."

"The woman must've come down first," Rocco mused. "Since she was right up against the rock and the man was up against her."

"My gracious, nothing much gets by you people does it?"

Rocco was craning his neck toward the top. "What's up there? Do you know?"

"No roads, if that's what you mean. I picked up a topographical map at the visitor center in Poppi. It indicates that there's a hiking trail along the rim. The nearest structure would appear to be the Cubbiddu cabin about half a kilometer away."

"Any ideas about cause of death?" Rocco asked. "Do we have a homicide here?"

Slowly, sadly, Bosco shook his head. "Ah, Rocco, you grieve me. You simply cannot keep it straight, can you? You mean 'manner of death.' There are an infinite number of *causes* of death, but homicide is not among them. There are, however, five and only five possibilities as to *manner* of death: accident, suicide, natural, undetermined . . . and homicide."

Rocco rolled his eyes. "Oh, excuse me, signor *dottore*. Can you offer us any preliminary hypotheses concerning the *manner* of death of the deceased?"

"Oh, it's homicide, all right. But as it happens, I believe I *can* also supply you with the cause. That blown-apart skull the gentleman has? It was a bullet that did that, entering at the left temple and exploding out the right side. A similar cause for the woman. A clear-cut bullet entry wound in the skull. No exit wound visible now, but I suspect we'll find one when we clean it up a little. We'll learn more when we get them on the table and cut their clothes away."

"So we've got ourselves a double murder here?" Martignetti said.

"That, or a murder-suicide. Or, for that matter, a double suicide."

"I'm guessing double murder," Rocco said. *Vendetta*, he was thinking.

Bosco, Buddha-like on his rock with his hands folded in front of his belly, smiled. "We shall see," he intoned, "what we shall see. Ah, good afternoon, signor public prosecutor. How nice to see you."

IN the event, Rocco's guess turned out to be wrong. Eight days later, the following article appeared in the Val d'Arno's leading newspaper:

DYING ON THE VINE

Corriere di Arezzo, Tuesday, 30 August 2011

PUBLIC PROSECUTOR ENDS CUBBIDDU INVESTIGATION

Ending a mystery that has gripped the Val d'Arno for the last month, Deputy Public Prosecutor Giaccomo Migliorini said yesterday that his office had concluded its investigation into the deaths of Villa Antica founder Pietro Cubbiddu and his wife, Nola, whose skeletonized bodies were found in a remote part of the Casentino National Forest on 22 August.

"It has been established that Cubbiddu killed his wife and then himself," *avvocato* Migliorini told assembled reporters, reading from prepared notes at the offices of the Public Prosecutor. "This tragic incident took place in September of last year. Since prosecution is obviously impossible, we do not feel that the situation warrants a continuing investigation. Thank you."

When questioning followed, additional details came to light. The deceased had each sustained a single gunshot wound to the head. The shootings occurred on a mountainside trail. The bodies then fell some sixty meters to a rocky area below. The weapon involved was a Beretta M1935 semiautomatic pistol, using .32 ACP ammunition. This pistol, which was originally produced for the military, had been in signor Cubbiddu's possession for many years, and was found under his remains. Signora Cubbiddu, who was also born in Sardinia, had been Cubbiddu's second wife. They had been married for twenty-five years.

The Cubbiddu family declined to be interviewed but issued the following joint statement through their Arezzo attorney, Severo Quadrelli: "We appreciate the professionalism shown by the

Carabinieri and the public prosecutor in their investigation, and find no fault with their efforts. However, we maintain the unshakable conviction that our beloved father, Pietro Cubbiddu, did not commit these horrible acts." Cesare Baccaredda Cubbiddu, Nola's son from her prior marriage, had no comment.

Motive for the tragedy remained in doubt.

Well, yes, but in Rocco's opinion, not a whole lot of doubt. Interviews with the family had made it clear that Pietro suspected Nola of having an affair. For an old-school Roman Catholic Sard like Pietro, what further motive was needed? Being cuckolded would have been unendurable; the most humiliating fate imaginable. And divorce was out of the question. Thus . . .

But where was the good in pursuing it now, or even making it known? With the killer dead, what difference could it make? Where could it lead, except to more anguish for the family? It was Deputy Prosecutor Migliorini's decision to bury these details, and for once Rocco agreed with him.

FOUR

The following week, Tuesday, September 6, 2011

THE church of Santa Maria Novella is one of the great treasures of Florence. Built in the fourteenth century, this immense basilica boasts tranquil Romanesque cloisters, venerable statuary, and works of art by Renaissance masters like Vasari, Giotto, and Masaccio. No travel guide to Italy fails to rave about it, and it is an obligatory stop for even the most sore-footed, art-weary tourist.

But there is one wing of the church—a monumental wing, half the complex, in fact—that tourists do not see and that guide books either ignore altogether, or sidle by with no more than a curt "Closed to visitors." This is the aptly named Great Cloister, the most ancient and historic part of the church. For two centuries now, in one of history's more peculiar marriages of church and state (courtesy of Napoleon Bonaparte), this tranquil quadrangle, along with the four low buildings that enclose it with their gracefully arched and frescoed porticos, has been the property of Italy's national gendarmerie, the *Arma dei Carabinieri*. For the last two decades it has been their Warrant Officer and Brigadier Training School.

During this particular September, it was more or less on loan, serving as the venue for the Fourteenth International Symposium on Science and Detection, a week of seminars for mid-level law-enforcement personnel from all over the world: Indian sub-inspectors, Russian *militsiya* majors, Japanese NPA *keishi-sei*, Romanian commissars. In the vaulted, richly frescoed "Pope's Room" a lecture was currently in progress that would have singed the ears of the fifteenth-century Pope Eugenius IV when he administered the papacy from this very space. (No doubt the lecturer would have found himself more thoroughly singed soon afterward.)

The subject was human evolution, and the lecturer was Gideon Oliver, known throughout the world of forensic science as the Skeleton Detective. But in his own mind, he was first and foremost a professor (currently the Abraham Goldstein Distinguished Professor of Anthropology at the University of Washington), and at this moment he was in his element: a full classroom, a lectern to lean on, and a captive audience.

"What you have to remember," he was saying, "is that 'survival of the fittest' doesn't mean survival of the biggest, or strongest, or cleverest, or any other such thing. No, natural selection simply favors those best adapted to the existing local conditions, by weeding out those *least* able to adapt to them. For example, sometimes being large—and therefore intimidating and powerful—is obviously a survival advantage; but at other times—as when food has become hard to come by or speed is more valuable than strength—it can be a disadvantage. You know that old joke about the two hikers and the bear?" he asked, shutting down the laptop he'd used for his Power-Point presentation on post-cranial blunt-force trauma.

Only the two Americans in his audience indicated they'd heard it, responding with groans. Strictly a New World joke, apparently.

"Okay. Two hikers are out in the woods when, fifty feet down the path, a huge grizzly bear rears up on its hind legs and roars at them. Ralph immediately starts to struggle out of his backpack, getting ready to run for it. 'Thank God I wore my running shoes,' he says. Rodney stands there, frozen stiff. 'What's the point of running?' he groans. 'You can't outrun a bear!' 'I don't have to outrun the bear,' Ralph yells back, already thirty feet down the path. 'I just have to outrun *you*.'"

There was an obligatory murmur of laughter. Gideon waited, and then, as expected, a louder, longer wave followed. This was one of the things you had to get used to when giving lectures to multilingual audiences. English was the official language of the conference, so anyone attending was required to have a grasp of it. But grasps varied, and many attendees took a little time to process what they heard. Humor apparently took more processing than most things. It was unsettling at first—your immediate reaction was that your jokes fell flat, but eventually you got used to it and learned to wait.

He continued as the chuckling died away. "Well, to me that's a great metaphor for the way natural selection works. Ralph didn't have to be the fastest man alive, he just had to be fast enough to be the one to survive on that particular day. Now . . . fast-forward fifty years, and there's Ralph, the faster one, sitting there at a family barbecue—well, a family dinner. He's a white-haired old grandfather now, and he's surrounded by his family—say he had two children and each of them had two children—he'd have six descendants, and all six would be carrying his genes, including, perhaps, whatever genes might have made him a little faster than Rodney that fateful day.

"And what about Rodney? Ah, poor Rodney's but a dim memory. He's been gone these fifty years now, and his genes with him. So in the gene pool as a whole, the ones he was carrying are a little less well represented than they used to be, while Ralph's now have a bigger share—those six descendants. Well, assuming that those 'fast' genes keep providing a survival advantage—however slight—every generation will have more people carrying them and fewer and fewer of the 'slow gene' people. The genetic makeup of the population as a whole would change. *But . . .* they wouldn't necessarily become as fast as it was humanly possible to become, they'd just need to be fast enough to get away from the bears. Well, that's the way natural selection works. The results don't have to be perfect, they just have to be good enough to get by."

One of Gideon's many admirable traits was his ability to deliver a coherent, fully formed lecture on the spur of the moment. One of his less attractive ones was his tendency to deliver them at the drop of a hat. Like most good professors, he was convinced that the subject matter that fascinated him must likewise fascinate everyone else. He was, of course, more often wrong than right, and this was one of those times. It took a while, but eventually the glazed, concussed look on a growing number of the sixteen faces in front of him got through to him. He'd done it again, slipped right off their radar.

And no wonder, he thought guiltily. They were there to learn how knowing something about bones might help them solve homicides. The subtle, slow-moving machinery of natural selection was not a high priority, or any priority at all. He cut himself off in the middle of a sentence. "We seem to have wandered a bit off the subject here. Clive," he said with mock severity, "kindly try not to take us off-course again."

This was directed to Clive Devlin, a scholarly, well-spoken chief inspector from Gibraltar, whose innocent, half-joking remark had started Gideon off. "Here's what I wonder," the chief inspector had said. "If natural selection is as wonderful as it's cracked up to be, and it's been working away to weed out the weakest among us all these millions of years, how is it that we still have so many diseases? One would think our bodies would have been perfected by now."

"Please accept my apology, Professor Oliver," Devlin said smoothly now. "I promise not do it again."

"Apology accepted." Gideon smiled back, stalling for time. *Now,* he thought, *where the hell were we?* "Umm . . ."

He was saved by Lieutenant Rocco Gardella, one of five Italian *Carabinieri* officers in the class, who, easily reading his expression, supplied the answer. "So, you were asking if anybody here might have some skeletal materials the class could use for, like, a case study." The cocky, outgoing Gardella was a compact, oily-haired guy in a black leather bomber jacket who reminded Gideon of a young Mafia wannabe from a 1950s teenage gang movie—a Gino or a Guido, say. Well, or a Rocco, for that matter. And his brand of perfectly fluent English went along with the image, singing more of Manhattan's Little Italy than of Mother Italy. "I think I got one for you," he went on. "The one I was talking about yesterday? The murder-suicide that laid out in the snow and rain and everything all year? Well, the husband's already been cremated, but the wife—that is, the wife's bones—should still be available."

"That'd be great," Gideon said, "could you bring them in?"

"No, that I can't do. Technically, they're not ours anymore. They've been released to the family. But they're still in a funeral home down in Figline, this little town I used to live in. Not far."

"*Where?*"

"Fee . . glyee . . . neh," Rocco repeated, stressing each syllable, thinking Gideon had been stumped by the Italian pronunciation, typically not so easy on American tongues.

"I know the place," Gideon said. "Figline Valdarno. I've been there."

"You been to Figline?" Gardella's thick black eyebrows—*eyebrow* would be more accurate—rose. "*Why?*"

"Oh, come on, it's not such a bad place, Rocco. Look, are you saying it'd be all right to have a look at them if we went to the funeral home? If Figline Valdarno's the place I'm thinking of, it's just twenty kilometers or so south of Florence."

"Yeah, that's the place. I could call my cousin; he owns the funeral home—well, he's almost my cousin, and he doesn't exactly *own* it yet—and we could probably do it right now, if you want."

Gideon looked at his watch. One ten. The seminar ran till four. Time enough, if they got going right then. He addressed the class as a whole. "Okay, let's do it. How many cars do we have?"

Four hands went up: enough room for everybody. Gideon motioned the group up out of their seats. "Let's pile in."

Rocco pulled out his cell phone. "I'll tell Alberto we're coming."

FIVE

BUT the lieutenant had been unable to get through to almost-cousin Alberto, the almost-proprietor of the funeral establishment. As a result, Alberto Cippollini was understandably startled when three imposing midnight-blue *Carabinieri* vehicles—two Alfa Romeo 159 compact executives and one Iveco VM 90 van, plus one not-so-imposing two-seater, an aptly nicknamed *ovetti* (little egg) that looked like the cockpit of a helicopter (minus the helicopter)—pulled screeching into the parking area of Onoranze Funebri Cippollini and fourteen burly men (and two burly women) piled out of them. A tentative, nervous little man in a too-tight black suit and tie, he came to the glass doors looking a little sick.

Blinking, he opened one of the doors enough to stick his head through. "*Che . . . che cosa . . . ?*"

"It's all right, Alberto," Rocco yelled back to him in Italian, his hands lifted placatingly. "This is nothing official. We just want to look at that skeleton you got the other day. It's for our school."

"You mean right now? But . . . but there is a memorial service in progress in the chapel," he whispered. "I can't have you . . . marching through . . ." His hands were fluttering in front of his chest. Gideon expected him to start wringing them, and a second later he did. "The mourners . . ."

"Well, let us into the workroom through the back door, then. We won't go anywhere near the chapel. They'll never know we're here."

"You're not going to take the, the remains away, are you? The cremation is tomorrow. It's all been arranged by the son, and I don't want—"

"I'm Professor Oliver," Gideon interrupted in Italian. His command of the language was good enough to put together grammatically correct sentences (as long as they were in the present tense), and to comprehend a good deal more. "I'm in charge of the class, and I promise you that we won't disturb the remains in any way. All we need is an hour, and we'll leave everything as we find it."

"Of course, yes, I see. Now, I . . . I haven't done anything with them, you understand. That is to say, I haven't prepared them, other than to clean them up a little—"

Rocco laughed. "Alberto, they're bones. I don't think anybody expected you to embalm them."

"Well, that's certainly so, ha-ha." He cleared his throat and lowered his voice even more. "Come around to the back then. I'll get them out for you." He hesitated. "And Rocco—perhaps you could see to it that these police cars are moved out of sight to the parking area in back? It doesn't look so good to visitors, you know?"

AS forensic scientists went, Gideon Oliver was a celebrated wuss. He didn't like working with dead bodies, and the more violent the manner of death or the fresher the bodies, the queasier they made him. What he did like working with, what intrigued and motivated him, were skeletons: the cleaner, and drier, and older, the better. Early Pleistocene remains were about right, and they constituted his main area of scholarly research. He didn't like autopsy rooms, he didn't like dissection labs, and he didn't like mortuary embalming rooms. As a result, the preparation room at Onoranze Funebri Cippollini came as a pleasant surprise. When the door was opened and signor Cippollini stepped out of the way to let them in, Gideon steeled himself for the expected odor (a combination of innards and formaldehyde, like a high-school lab where frogs and fetal pigs are dissected, only worse). Instead, what greeted him was a welcome wisp of lavender. And the room itself was almost jolly, with multicolored wall tiles randomly placed among the white ones. Even the bases of the two work tables were faced with colorful tile mosaics.

And no bidet-like conveniences for flushing away the bodily fluids and other nastinesses that came out of corpses. None of the other medieval-torture-chamber implements he'd expected either—the tongs, the knives, the alarming hypodermics. Of course—he'd forgotten: Italians by and large didn't practice embalming. Rooms like this were used for little more than a washup, a little cosmetic work if necessary, and a proper fitting-out for viewing at the memorial, which usually took place within a couple of days, for obvious reasons.

There were two standard zinc work tables in the room, though, on one of which Cippollini placed the remains, enclosed in a three-foot-long box of heavy cardboard; a child's cremation container, Gideon assumed.

"Let's get at it," he said when Cippollini reluctantly left them to it. "Rocco, this is your treat, so if you'll remove the bones one by one, I'd like everyone to work together getting them laid out as near as possible to their anatomical relationship. And I'll just watch from back here and keep my mouth shut."

"Don't bet on it," muttered a big Hawaiian with an affable, easy laugh.

"Hey, when I say something, you can take it straight to the bank," Gideon said, smiling back.

John Lau was his closest friend, an FBI special agent out of the Seattle field office. They had worked together more than once, and the two of them with their wives got together regularly back home. John had taken a similar seminar from Gideon years ago, when the symposium had convened in St. Malo, France, but science, as does everything else, changes with time, and he, like two of the other attendees, was back for a refresher. Gideon and John had both come with their wives and had been seeing Florence together in their off-time, so it had been as much pleasure as work. And then when the seminar ended the following day, the four of them were off to a winery out in the Tuscan countryside, where the two women had signed up for a five-day cooking class.

Rocco had barely gotten the skull out of the box when John was proved right. "Whoa, hold it, what do we have here?" Gideon exclaimed.

"Ha," observed John in quiet triumph.

Rocco handed over the skull, and Gideon peered hard at the

frontal bone, running his fingers over an area in the center of the forehead, where the hairline would be on a living person. "Well, this is something you don't see every day," he murmured.

"Oh, I can tell you what that is," Rocco said. "We figured that out pretty fast."

"I'm sure you can, but let's see what the rest of us come up with, okay? Anybody got a flashlight?"

Someone handed over a penlight attached to a key chain, and Gideon stuck it in the opening at the base of the skull to light up the interior. "Huh," he said, "that's what I thought. Interesting." He handed back the penlight, turned the skull right side up, and held it in both hands just above the tabletop so that the area he'd been so interested in was uppermost. At that spot there was a sort of escarpment; an inch-long ridge of bone rising from the flat, curving plateau of the skull, looking for all the world as if there had been an eruption below the surface.

"Ideas, anybody? What do you suppose this could be?"

"Would it be a genetic thing?" someone asked.

"Nope."

"Some kind of bone disease?

"Nope."

"Brain disease?" This from John.

"Uh-uh."

"Some kind of trauma?"

"Good man. Trauma it is; blunt trauma. What we have here, you see, is an unusual kind of depressed fracture—what I think of as a *reverse* depressed fracture." He explained that a depressed fracture was a fairly common kind of cranial injury that jams a segment of bone inward, so there is (usually) a sharply defined indentation in the bone.

For example, a blow with a ball-peen hammer can leave a dent the exact shape and size of the hammer's ball, sometimes even reproducing its irregularities closely enough to permit identification of the specific weapon. The area on the underside of the dent, of course, is necessarily forced inward, frequently causing grave damage to the brain.

"You're losing me, professor," someone said. "This part here"—the speaker fingered the ridge—"isn't dented *in*, it's sticking *up*."

"Exactly," Gideon replied. "Which is why I call it a depressed fracture in reverse—the force came from inside the head and pushed *outward*."

This produced the expected murmurs of incredulity. "How can that be?" someone said.

"Ah," said Gideon, "that is for me to know and you to find out—shut up, Rocco—which I have no doubt that you will do in the next few minutes. But for the moment, go ahead and continue laying out the bones. I'll just stand here and keep perfectly quiet." He leveled a quick forefinger at John as his friend opened his mouth to speak. "Watch it."

John raised both hands to profess innocence of intent, and Rocco got back to work unloading and laying out the bones.

The two-and-a-half-day forensic anthropology seminar was midway through its second day, so there had been time for only a few hours of training in the basics of bone identification. Nevertheless, they did pretty well. Gideon was pleased; apparently they'd been paying attention, and perhaps had even gone so far as to study the handout materials in the evenings. Inside of fifteen minutes, they had what was left of the skeleton laid out on its back: skull, mandible, pelvis, scapulas, vertebral column, arm and leg bones, one collarbone, and most of the ribs. The hands, right foot, left collarbone, and some of the vertebrae were missing, probably carried off by car-nivores, and the facial skeleton, mandible, and leg bones had been gnawed. The bones of the left foot—un-gnawed—were in a clasp envelope, with "bones found in left shoe" written on it in Italian. Gideon told them not to worry about identifying those individually. (Distinguishing between the five metatarsals and fourteen phalanges of the human foot—let alone telling left from right, and distinguish-ing the metatarsals of the foot from the metacarpals of the hand—took a lot more than a few hours' training.) There were also a lot of broken fragments, most of which the group had correctly identified as crumbling chunks of vertebrae.

"How'd we do?" they wanted to know.

"You did a good job," Gideon said, surveying the result.

"You mean we even got the ribs right? Amazing."

"Don't be amazed. I said 'good,' not 'perfect.' You didn't get them all." He did some deft, rapid rearranging while he spoke. "This goes here, this goes here, this goes . . . here. And you got the clavicle upside down and backward—and on the wrong side. It goes here, like this. And the fibulas are on the wrong sides too. But look," he said, respond-ing to the grumbles and the accusatory *Didn't I tell you that*s that fluttered around the group, "you're cops, not anthropologists. No reason for you to know all that. I don't care if you can't tell a right clavicle from a left clavicle or which side goes up, I'd just like you to be able to say that's what it is when you see one lying out in the woods—a clavicle, a human clavicle, and not some bone from a rabbit or a fox. The forensic specialists can take it from there. So I'm telling you: you did well."

A final look at the arrangement and a nod of approval. "Okay, we know this is a female because Rocco told us so yesterday. But you should be able to tell even without that. Anyone care to tell me how? We talked about it in yesterday's session."

Among others, John raised his hand, but Gideon called on a ruddy-cheeked Swiss *oberstleutnant* whose hand had shot up before the question had been finished. Helmut Waldbaum was a good, eager student, but his English, while more than sufficient for him to understand things, was close to impenetrable.

He grinned when Gideon called on him. "Za ghrule oaff tzoom," he said proudly.

Gideon, who had gotten used to the accent, nodded. "Right. The rule of thumb."

This referred to the fastest and simplest approach to sexing a skeleton, and a fairly reliable one, although not so reliable as was once thought. What you did was to place your thumb—or imagine placing your thumb—into the sciatic notch, the indentation that separated the ilium of the pelvis from the pubis (the upper from the lower half). If it was so narrow that the fit was snug, then it was a male you were looking at. But a female's sciatic notch was wider, with plenty of wiggle room. Often you could fit two fingers into the notch.

"Now here's something interesting to think about: why would this particular difference between the sexes exist? And once again, natural selection provides the answer. Since childbearing requires more of a bowl-shaped container for the growing fetus, the biomechanical forces of evolutionary development . . ." He caught himself with a laugh. "There I go again. Strike that from the record. Let's move on."

He turned the skull upside down again so the bottom faced up. They found themselves looking at a caved-in skull base. A good third of it—much of the rear half—had been thrust a half inch inward (upward in a person standing erect), cracking a ragged-edged disk of bone two to three inches in diameter. In the center of the disk, as in the center of a CD, was a smooth-rimmed hole, the foramen magnum, the opening through which the spinal cord emerges from the brain.

"Is this another depressed fracture?" someone asked, fingering the collapsed bone. "Only this one goes the right way, pushed in, not out."

"Right," Gideon said.

"But that's huge," Rocco said. "What the hell caused that?"

"You don't know?" Gideon asked.

"No, I don't," Rocco said defensively. "Look, I never actually saw the skull before, all cleaned up like this."

"But your *medico's* report didn't say?"

Rocco shrugged. "It said a lot of the bones were busted. Was I supposed to memorize them or something?"

"Hey, relax, Rocco. I just thought he might have made a special point about it."

"Well, he didn't."

"Then he missed something pretty significant," Gideon said, laying the skull back on the table. "This is what is known as a basilar ring fracture. It's not very common, and it tells us something important about what exactly happened here."

"What?" asked someone.

"Well, let me give you a chance to figure the whole thing out for yourselves first. It'd be a better exercise if we didn't know what the circumstances were and what had actually happened, but Rocco's already told us, so—"

"No, he told us what the *Carabinieri* concluded had happened," somebody said archly. "That's a different thing."

Rocco pulled a face. "Thanks a lot, pal."

"Actually, that's a good way to look at this whole exercise, if you like," Gideon said. "Your job is to review the police findings on these bones and see if you agree or disagree. Murder-suicide, both deaths by gunshot, and so on—did they get it right? And just concentrate on the trauma, don't worry about the other things we've talked about—race, age, occupational indicators, height—just the trauma. I'll give you"—he looked at his watch—"twenty minutes, plus another five minutes to write up your report on the dry-marker board over there."

"What if we all don't agree?" someone asked.

"Then indicate that in the report. Okay, folks, the clock is running. Better get on with it."

While John and the others went to work, Gideon and Rocco sat on stools next to the other table, with Rocco back in a good mood and telling dumb-*carabinieri* jokes. Apparently there was no shortage of them.

"So this village station commander—a *maresciallo*, a marshal—is sitting in his car, and he calls one of his *carabinieri* over. 'Martino, take a look at my rear turn lights, will you, and tell me if they're working right.' The *carabiniere* goes to the back of the car and watches, while the commander holds down the turn-indicator lever.

"'Yes, *maresciallo*,' he says after a second, 'they work fine. No, wait, they don't. No, wait, they do. No, wait, they don't. No, wait . . .'"

Gideon smiled, which encouraged Rocco. "Why do *carabinieri* always work in pairs?

"Beats me."

"One to read and one to write." Rocco laughed.

"I gather there are a lot of these?" Gideon asked.

"Millions. In real life, though," Rocco said, turning serious, "the *Carabinieri* are a pretty selective outfit with some really stiff standards. Hell, my own brother applied, but they turned him down. You know why?" He waited for Gideon to bite, but Gideon wouldn't, so Rocco supplied the answer. "He scored too high on the intelligence test."

They were only a few feet from the work table, so the others had no trouble hearing them, and most grinned at the jokes every now and then. But a *Carabinieri* major from Rome, the highest-ranking officer there, had been glaring over his shoulder at Rocco for a while, clearly unamused.

"Um, Rocco . . ." Gideon began.

"Hey, do you know why *carabinieri* trousers have those red stripes down the sides? So they can find the pockets, hee-hee."

The major continued to glare. "Rocco, I think maybe . . ."

"Okay, wait, this guy lives halfway up a narrow mountain road. So one day he sees this *Carabinieri* car driving backward up the mountain. 'How come you're driving backward?' he wants to know. 'Because we're not sure if there'll be a place to turn around at the top,' they tell him. An hour later, here they come back down the mountain . . . backward again. 'So why are you still driving backward?' he asks. 'Because we found a place to turn around after all.' "

When Rocco paused to think up the next one, Gideon was finally able to break in. "Rocco, I think you might be annoying the stern, important-looking gentleman over there at the foot of the table," he said quickly, hoping to head Rocco off.

Rocco glanced up. "Major Grimaldi?" he whispered back. "He's been listening? Oh Christ, that's all I need. Come on, let's get some fresh air. I need a smoke."

"Are you in trouble?" Gideon asked when they'd stepped outside into the rear parking lot and gotten under an eave to avoid the misty rain that had begun to fall. Gideon had gotten a soft drink, a *limonata*, from the vending machine next to the door, and he pulled back the tab and took a couple of gulps.

Rocco, in the meantime, flipped open a box of Marlboros, pulled one out with his lips, lit up, and blew out a long breath. "Nah, not trouble, exactly. But I know Grimaldi. He'll report it to my captain, who won't be happy. Ah, don't worry about it, no big deal."

"*Carabinieri* jokes are a no-no?"

"Everything's a no-no, Gideon, everything that doesn't make the *carabinieri* look like God's gift to the world. You know what this general told us the day we graduated from the academy?" He tucked in his chin and lowered his voice to a magisterial bass. " 'From this day forward, no longer are you Paolo, Mario, or Giovanni. You are a *carabiniere*. Everything you say, everything you do, is a reflection on the republic which we are honored to serve, and the glorious history of the body of which you are now a part.' And God, did he mean it."

Another long pull on the Marlboro. "One time, when I was still on patrol, I was eating my lunch in the car, relaxing, noshing on a *panino*, you know? And this call comes in. There's a knife fight in a bar less than a block away from where I'm sitting, and somebody's gonna get killed. So I drop what I'm eating, jump out of the car, and run over there, and, sure enough, there are these two guys having at it, and they are seriously trying to hurt each other. I get in between them, which is when I got this"—he held out his hand, showing a thin white scar running diagonally along the heel of his palm—"and manage to get them apart. One guy was totally whacked out on something, and I had to get him down on the floor and cuffed before he calmed down.

Anyway, I called it in, got them arrested, went to the hospital to get stitched up, and was back at headquarters in an hour to write up my report. What do you think I got for my trouble?"

"Not an award, I'm guessing."

"A reprimand. Because why? Because I appeared in public without my cap." He grunted a laugh. "Can you believe it? Jesus H. Christ."

"Rocco, I have to say—are you sure the *carabinieri* are a good fit for you? You don't quite seem . . . well, cut out for the life."

The lieutenant was shocked. "Are you kidding me? I *love* the corps. It's fantastic. I'm proud to be on it. It's just that they can be a little . . . tight-assed sometimes, about things that seem pretty petty to me. I guess my problem is that I'm a *carabiniere*, yeah, but underneath, I'm still Rocco. Unfortunately."

A few moments passed with Gideon silent and Rocco morosely smoking away.

"We'd better get back in, I think," Gideon said. "They should be finished by now."

Rocco nodded, took another pull, flipped the cigarette away, and they headed back. "I guess I'm just going to have to learn to toe the line a little better," he said, but as the door swung open, the edges of his mouth curled into a cherubic little smile, and he put a hand on Gideon's forearm to stop him.

"Hey, how many *carabinieri* does it take to screw in a lightbulb?"

IN the preparation room, the others were still writing up their report on the board and arguing out the last of their differences. Gideon used the time involved to have his first uninterrupted, solitary look at the remains. He went through them slowly, turning this bone over and over in his fingers, lifting that one to his eye and scanning it at an angle, the way you'd examine a pool cue to see if it were straight. By the time he was done, the report was finished, written with red marker on the glossy white board, in the exuberant, loopy script of a sergeant major from Nigeria:

"In examining the skeletal remains presented to us for our analysis, the following traumatic injuries to the skull have been identified: a ballistic entrance wound in the center of the back of the skull, just below the occipital protuberance, and what appears to be an incomplete exit wound at the front, in the form of a 'reverse depressed fracture.' We believe that this GSW was the cause of the victim's death, which was probably instantaneous.

"Trauma to the rest of the body includes fractures of both tibias and fibulas, both femurs, both sides of the pelvis, and numerous thoracic and lumbar vertebrae. Many of these bones suffered multiple breakages. In addition, there were fractures of the bones of the left foot. These injuries are all consistent with a fall from a height. There were also many signs of animal gnawing.

"Our findings: The victim was killed by a fatal gunshot to the head. Her body then fell some distance, sustaining much additional damage. We also attribute the basal ring fracture of the foramen magnum to this fall.

"In conclusion, we conclude that the findings presented by Lieutenant Gardella are supported by the evidence."

"Thank you, thank you, thank you all," said Rocco, taking bows all around.

"Good job, everybody," Gideon said. "You've all been working hard. Let's take five minutes for a break. Rocco, can I talk to you for a minute?"

"What's up?" said Rocco as the others wandered off in twos and threes. "They did a great job, don't you think? It took our *medico* two days to get it right."

"Well, yeah, they did a good enough job, but the thing is, they didn't get it right. And neither did you guys. I wanted to talk to you about it before I made my comments. I wouldn't want to make you look bad in front of them, and—"

Rocco lifted his hand. "Don't give it a thought, Gid. Those weren't our findings, they were the *medico's* findings. Everything I know about skeletal trauma I learned from you in the last three days. Anyway, it was the public prosecutor who made it all official. He's the boss. We just do the grunt work." He followed this with a sudden grin. "And I have no problem at all with making Migliorini look bad; pompous, self-important twit that he is."

"Okay, then."

"But what exactly did they get wrong? She *wasn't* shot in the head?"

"No, she was shot in the head."

"She *didn't* fall off the cliff?"

"No, she fell off the cliff."

"So then what am I missing here?" He spread his hands. "What else is there to get wrong?"

"They're starting to filter back in, Rocco. May as well wait till everybody's here."

GIDEON stood on one side of the table while the cops gathered in a standing half circle on the other side, a few feet back. "You did a fine job," he began. "You only made one mistake, but it's a zinger. A big one," he emended, seeing from a number of frowns that *zinger* wasn't in everybody's vocabulary. "Now, you got the basics right: she was shot in the back of the head. The hole near the occipital protuberance is the entrance wound, and the defect in the forehead, that 'reverse depressed fracture,' is indeed a partial exit wound. By the way, Rocco, did you find the bullet? Was it still in her skull?'

"It was, just rattling around in there."

"Okay, so we can consider it definitely established that, for whatever reason—maybe it was old, maybe it was the wrong caliber for the gun, maybe the charge had gotten damp or wasn't big enough, maybe something else—whatever, the bullet didn't have enough oomph to make it all the way through. But since it did make it to the inside of the *front* of the skull, we know that it had to have passed right through her brain, back to front. All the same, I think we can safely say that it didn't kill her."

A tentative hand went up; the formal, scholarly chief inspector from Gibraltar. "I certainly don't mean to question your judgment, Professor Oliver, but I served as a paramedic in Afghanistan, so I know something about head wounds. And—no offense, sir—but a bullet that took this trajectory would necessarily destroy so much vital brain tissue that . . . well, in my belief, death would have been, well, certain . . . and instantaneous."

"I agree with you, Clive. And remember, a bullet destroys a lot more than what lies directly in its trajectory, because the energy it generates hollows out a cavity much wider than the bullet's actual diameter. And the brain is the softest organ in the body, more like jelly than any other human tissue, so it pulps very easily. And then don't forget that the bullet carries pieces of bone and tissue along with it, and that messes up things too. So yes, that bullet would have killed her, all right. And almost certainly, it would have been instantly."

"Hey, wait a minute, Doc," John said. "Didn't you just say—?"

"I didn't say it *wouldn't* have killed her, I said it *didn't* kill her." To himself Gideon somewhat shamefacedly admitted that he was having fun. The boggling of policemen's minds was one of the innocent little vices of the forensic set.

"And there's a difference?" someone finally asked.

"Ah, well, there we have—"

One of the two women, a *polizeihauptkommissarin* from Vienna, lifted her hand. "Professor, I regret to interrupt, but we run a bit late. Already it is four hours twenty, and there are five o'clock section meetings for some among us, so—"

"So we'd better wrap up right now. All right," he said, "go ahead and get the remains back in the carton—carefully—and we'll head back to Florence. We'll finish this up tomorrow morning."

Rocco was frowning hard. "Wait, wait, wait, at least tell us—"

Gideon shook his head. "Tomorrow." He was a longtime believer in the Creed of the Artful Professor:

Always leave 'em wanting more.

SIX

ROCCO, John, and Gideon all drove back to Florence in different vehicles; the same ones they'd come in, but when the cars pulled into the *Carabinieri* parking lot alongside the Great Cloister, Rocco was waiting for him. He was still scowling. "Listen, Gid, I can't figure out what to make of what you were telling us back there. If the shot didn't kill her, what did?" This was the second time that Rocco had called him Gid, and Gideon resisted the impulse to ask him to knock it off. For whatever reason—he didn't know himself—it annoyed him to be addressed by diminutives or nicknames—he liked his own full name—and he didn't hesitate to say so. He had only one friend, none other than John Lau himself, who was granted the privilege. John had been calling him Doc since the day they'd met, and Gideon had had no choice but to go along with it. Gid was even worse than Doc, but somehow, coming out of Rocco's mouth, it couldn't have been more natural. It fitted with his brash, wise-guy manner in a way that the prissier Gideon wouldn't have. So now there were two who were allowed to get away with it. He was mellowing with age.

"The fall is what killed her," he said.

"The fall?" The scowl deepened. "The *fall*?"

"The fall."

"But . . . I don't get it. The cop from Gibraltar, Clive, he said the bullet would have killed her then and there, and you agreed with him. I agree with him, for that matter."

"I do agree with him. A .32, back to front, right smack through the middle of the head? It should have killed her, it would have killed her—well, it would have if she hadn't already been dead."

"What do you mean, already dead?" John had come up behind them. "Why shoot her if she was already dead? And how do you know that, anyway?"

Rocco was equally bewildered. "Gid, stop messing with us, will you? What exactly are you telling us here?"

"What I'm telling you, Rocco . . . John . . . is that the fall came first, *then* the bullet. She was already dead—from the fall—when he shot her."

Rocco, hands spread, looked to one side, then the other, as if searching for someone to explain it to him, but no luck. "Gid, she fell sixty *meters*—that'd be, uh . . ."

"Almost two hundred feet."

"Yeah, two hundred feet. That's a lot of feet. So what the hell would be the point of shooting her after that?"

"Beats me, Rocco."

"Take a guess," John said.

"All right, all I can think of would be that he was taking out some insurance. He wasn't positive that the fall had done it, so he came down and finished the job. Administered a coup de grace. That's all I can think of, but I have to say I'm not real confident about it, considering that she fell off the equivalent of a twenty-story building onto a rocky surface and must have looked it. But it fits the facts. Sort of."

Rocco was suddenly irritated. "Okay, tell me something, Mr. Expert—"

"That's *Doctor* Expert to you, buddy."

Rocco was unmollified. "How the hell *do* you know which came first? I mean, I swear to God . . . you 'experts' . . . that's just the kind of thing . . ." He jerked his head, muttering to himself.

"Fun, isn't it?" John said, grinning. "I always love when he does this."

"Well, good for you. I don't."

"Rocco, what are you getting worked up about?" Gideon asked. "Does it really make any difference exactly when he shot her? Obviously, it doesn't change the outcome."

"Yeah, it makes a difference. It's weird, it's inconsistent, it's . . . well, it's a loose end, it doesn't fit."

Gideon laughed. "If you ever run into a murder case where everything's consistent with everything else—no conflicting eyewitness testimony, no loose ends, no ambiguities, no unanswered questions—please let me know, will you? We'll write it up for the journals."

"You can say that again," John agreed.

But Rocco stuck to his guns. "It doesn't make sense to shoot someone if they already fell off a goddamn mountain. That alone throws the scenario our guys put together out of whack, and it worries me. If it's true. It *should* worry me. What kind of a cop would I be if it didn't?" Meaningful pause. "*If* it's true."

Gideon considered himself well and deservedly rebuked. "Rocco, you're absolutely right. I've been treating this as a class exercise, no more. I kind of forgot it's a real case with real human beings."

"Oh, it's a real case, all right. And there's one other minor little point. If . . ." He sighed. "John, you keep checking your watch. What, I'm boring you guys? You gotta be somewhere?"

"Yeah, as a matter of fact, we do," John said. "We're supposed to meet our wives for dinner at six, and we don't know how far the restaurant is from here. We don't even know where the hell it is, exactly."

"What restaurant?"

"Umm . . ."

"L'Osteria di Giovanni," Gideon said. "Do you know it?"

"Yeah, it's a ten-minute walk from here. A good place. Come on, I'll walk you over partway. We can talk while we walk."

"Sure," Gideon said, "but listen, if you're free, why don't you join us for dinner while you're at it?"

"Hey, I'd love to," Rocco said, his testiness of a moment ago gone as abruptly as it had come, "but I can't. I have to pick up *my* wife back at the train station at six-twenty. Come on, it's this way, down Via degli Avelli."

Florence's Via degli Avelli—the Street of the Tombs—is not the gloomy passageway the name suggests. In fact, it is one of the city's livelier, trendier thoroughfares, with wall-to-wall restaurants, sidewalk cafés, and upscale hotels lining one side of it. The other side, however, runs for more than a hundred yards along the outer wall of Santa Maria Novella's narrow, old cemetery. This wall consists of a long row of twenty-foot-high, horizontally striped, Moorish stone arches that protect upscale wall-to-wall shelters of a different sort: the ornate, aboveground stone burial vaults of Florence's fourteenth- and fifteenth-century elite, all bearing intricately carved reliefs of their family crests and insignias of rank.

Rocco gestured at them as they walked past. "Bet there'd be some bones in those things that'd perk your interest."

Gideon laughed. "I bet there would. So what's this other minor little point, Rocco?"

"Only that *he* fell off the cliff too—after shooting himself up there—so he must've been twice as dead as she was when he hit the bottom, right? Which would have made it a little hard for him to administer that coup de grâce down below, wouldn't you say?"

"He shot himself at the top?" Gideon echoed, frowning. "No, you're right, that complicates things. How sure are you that it worked that way, that he didn't kill himself down below, after he shot her?"

"Pretty sure, considering that he left most of his skull up there, with some of the rest of it scattered along the way down, while he was bouncing off the rocks. Our guys took most of a day picking them out of the cliff. His skeleton was every bit as busted up as hers was. He took one hell of a fall too, no question."

"That's puzzling," Gideon said. "It would seem to mean he shoved her off the cliff, then climbed down and shot her just to make sure she was well and truly dead, then climbed all the way up *again*—two hundred feet—shot *himself*, and then fell off the cliff too. How would you explain that?"

"How would *I* explain it? Sheesh, you came up with it, how would *you* explain it?"

"Yeah, how would you explain it?" John contributed, but then he came up with a question of his own. "What's that cliff like, Rocco? I mean, is it really, like, a *cliff*—straight up and down—or more like sort of a hill?"

"Well, I guess it's not technically a cliff. You can get up it without a rope and pitons, if that's what you mean, but it sure as hell isn't what anybody would call a *hill*. I mean, I made it to the top okay myself, but there were some dicey spots along the way. I had to use my hands a lot, and I was breathing pretty hard by the time I got there."

"So how likely would it be," Gideon asked, "that a man of Pietro's age—"

"Almost sixty," said Rocco. "And, from what I understand, he wasn't in the greatest shape in the world. A whole lot of years working in those damp wine cellars had screwed up his lungs."

"So it wouldn't be too likely, would it, that he'd climb back up a cliff like that unless he had some really good reason? Since he could have just shot himself right down there with her."

"That's the way I see it," said Rocco.

They walked a few paces, heads down, thinking, and then Gideon said: "Could there be anything special about that particular cliff? Does it have any kind of history or reputation? You know, is it a place people come to commit suicide? Lovers' Point, Suicide Mountain, something like that?"

"Not that I ever heard of."

"Well, maybe it had some special significance, some personal significance—emotional, symbolic—to them. Could that be?"

"Yeah, I suppose so," Rocco said with a shrug. "I guess that could be."

Gideon laughed. He didn't think much of the idea either. "All right, tell me this: How did you establish that *he* killed *her*? How do you know it wasn't the other way around? She killed him and then shot herself?"

"How could she? According to you, she was already dead from the fall when she was shot. Pretty damn hard to shoot yourself in the head when you're dead."

"Never mind 'according to me.' How did you establish it in the first place, during the investigation?"

"Oh God, a lot of things. First, the way she was shot: back of the head, execution style. You saw that in the class. The bullet entered in the lower back part of her skull and then ran slightly upward, hitting the inside of her skull pretty much in the middle of her forehead. Which—as I'm sure I don't have to tell either of you guys—is the path you get if the victim was kneeling, with her head bowed. Well, how many suicides have you run into where the person shot himself in the back of the head that way? Not many."

"No," Gideon said, "but there are some who do."

"That's true," John said. "In fact, you can't come up with any part of the head that some suicide hasn't shot himself in: the nose, the eye, the ear, the top of the head, the back of the head, the teeth . . . almost any part of the body, in fact: the crotch, the armpit—"

"Well, you guys are lucky," Rocco said. "You get to look at a lot more gunshot deaths than we do over here, so I can't argue with you. But I've seen a few suicides and I never saw one that did it back-to-front. I mean, why would they? It's harder. It can't happen very often."

"Well, yeah," John agreed, "that's so . . ."

"Yes, it is," said Gideon, "and your execution-style killing idea was pretty good thinking at the time, but—well, sorry, but it's not correct. She was already dead when she was shot."

"Yeah, so you keep saying." Rocco rolled his eyes. "Jesus, did we get *anything* right?" His hand flew up. "Don't answer that."

"Well, it's understandable. You didn't know then what you know now—that she fell off that cliff first, before—"

"No, *you* know that. I don't know that, and I'm waiting to hear something that convinces me. I mean, no offence, Gid, I know you're this great expert and everything, but I need a little more than your word here."

"Give me a minute, Rocco, I'll get there. But for the moment just assume I'm right. Now think about it. Here's this woman. She's just taken this horrendous fall. She's about as dead as she can get. Half her bones are broken. Now, for whatever reason, he wants to shoot her. So how—"

Rocco held up his hand again. "Yeah, I see the problem. How is he supposed to get her into a kneeling position?"

"That's it. What he did do, I'm guessing, was to shoot her where she lay, right on the ground. Prone. Not execution-style at all. The bullet trajectory would have been exactly the same."

John hunched his shoulders. "I'd say that's a pretty good guess."

"Thanks, but it's actually more than a guess. Remember this afternoon, when I tossed out a couple of reasons why the bullet might not have made it all the way through her skull? Well, there was another reason I didn't mention, because I didn't want to muddy the waters at the time—"

"But now you do," Rocco grumbled.

"I'm a scientist, Rocco. I have to say what I find."

"That's what he always says when he does this," John said cheerfully. "Every single damn time."

"Okay, so what's this other reason?" Rocco asked reluctantly.

"It's something that happens when the spot where the bullet would ordinarily exit is up against something firm, so that the bone is shored up and kept from exploding outward. So the bullet can't get out either, and it just bounces off and stays inside."

Rocco nodded his acceptance.

"So if I'm right and she was lying facedown on the ground, and he just leaned over and plugged her, then the earth, or rock, or whatever that was under her head would have kept the bullet from exiting."

"Well, she was laying on her stomach, all right. Oh boy, I'm starting to think maybe we're going to have to reopen this whole can of worms after all." He shut his eyes. "God help me."

"What about the husband?" Gideon asked. "How was he shot? Was it compatible with suicide?"

"Oh yeah, I'm pretty sure we're on safe ground there. Couldn't have been more compatible. Right out of the books. The classic spot for a handgun suicide." He raised his left hand and jabbed his forefinger at his temple. "Bang. And please, don't give me any more crap about shooting yourself in the armpit. You know damn well this is where they do it nine times out of ten."

"I don't know about your statistics," Gideon said, "but generally speaking, yes."

"And righties shoot themselves in the right side of the head and lefties shoot themselves in the left side of the head—"

"But not always," John put in.

"Oh, come on, you guys, give me a break. What, it's only ninety-five percent of the time?"

Gideon had to smile. There had been a recent study of just this question, based on an examination of confirmed suicides. The answer: 95 percent.

"And he was shot straight through the left temple," Rocco continued. "Wanna guess whether he was a lefty or a righty?"

Gideon laughed. "Well . . . this is just a hunch here, but I'm going to take a chance and guess he was a lefty."

"Bingo. Okay, your turn, Mr. Expert—pardon me, Dr. Expert. Now you're gonna go ahead and tell me what's wrong with our theory—why he couldn't possibly have committed suicide, right?"

"Hey, Rocco," John said approvingly, "you're a quick learner."

"I don't see anything wrong with it," Gideon said. "You're right. Sounds like a suicide to me."

Rocco staggered and clapped a hand to his heart. "I'm shocked . . . shocked." They stopped walking to let Rocco draw a Marlboro from a pack with his lips and apply a lighter to it.

"Rocco," Gideon said, "what were the other things that made you so sure he killed her and not the other way around? You said a minute ago that there were a lot of them."

"Well, two of them, anyway," Rocco said in a choked, constricted voice while he pulled in his first lungful of smoke. He held it there a moment with his eyes closed and then let it out in a long *hoosh.* "The other thing was the way their bodies were lying—hers right up against this big rock and his up against hers, which means she would have had to come down first, so how could *she* have killed *him?*"

"Well, what about this?" John asked as they began walking again. "Someone else killed them both and tried to make it look like a murder-suicide. You know, rearranged the bodies and all."

Rocco took two meditative drags. "Look, John, anything's possible, but there's just nothing, nothing at all, that points in that direction." And then, in a muttered afterthought, "Until today, anyway."

John shrugged. "Okay." He didn't think the idea held water either.

"You didn't come up with any other suspects?" Gideon asked. "At all?"

Rocco bristled. "What do you mean, 'at all?' Like we didn't do a thorough enough investigation or something?" But on reconsidering his words he cooled down. "Well, we didn't, that's true. We didn't do a whole lot of searching. I mean, sure, we interviewed his family, the people who knew him best, and we looked into things, but it was all so obvious. . . . Hell, it *seemed* obvious. . . . The facts spoke for themselves, you know? He killed her and then he killed himself. Why would we go hunting for other suspects?"

"Yes, I can see that it would have seemed like a waste of money and manpower."

"Anyway, no, there weren't any other viable suspects. Oh, wait, there was one other thing: we found the gun. It came down the cliff with him, and it was his, all right. A wartime Beretta. Had it for forever."

"Any prints?" John said, then jerked his head. "No, what am I talking about? There wouldn't be, not after all that time out in the weather."

"As a matter of fact there were. It wound up caught in the opening of his jacket, sort of wedged into his armpit. And it was a good leather jacket, so it was pretty well protected from the elements. So, yeah, we did manage to lift a couple of partials off it."

"And?"

"And they're his. I mean, I wouldn't want to go to court on it because, as I said, they're only partials. Besides, his prints aren't on file anywhere. But we found prints that matched what we had on the gun all over his things at home . . . hundreds of them. I don't know, maybe thousands. On his shoes, his eating utensils, his toothpaste tube, everything. We took prints of his family and the winery staff, and there's definitely no match there. Our tech guy says the odds are ninety-nine out of a hundred they're his."

"You're right," John said. "Good odds, but they wouldn't cut it in a courtroom."

"There's something that seems a little hinky to me here, Rocco," Gideon said. "Am I the only one who thinks it a little, shall we say, unusual that the gun stayed with him all the way down and never bounced away anywhere where you couldn't find it? That lady we looked at today sure did some bouncing, so I presume he did too, since he took the same route."

"Well—" Rocco began.

"And then the gun just happened to end up in the very best possible place to preserve any fingerprints that happened to be on it?"

Rocco shrugged. "Sometimes we get lucky. It happens."

"It happens," John agreed.

"Yeah," said Gideon, but he wasn't satisfied.

"Rocco, you got a motive?" John asked.

"Uh-huh. He thought she was having an affair. This was what you might call an ultratraditional kind of guy, a real dinosaur, and that was all the motive he would've needed: she deserved to die, and he couldn't stand to live. And fossils like him, they don't do divorce."

"And was she?" asked Gideon. "Having an affair?"

"Who knows? We were satisfied he did it, and he was dead. No reason to follow up. What would be the point? Just make more misery and unhappiness for the family. Enough said, case closed." He threw a wry glance at Gideon. "Only now along comes the great Skeleton Detective with his gaga theories and screws up the works."

"Whoa," said John, "that's the first time I ever heard anybody say that about you, Doc."

"Well, now, how exactly did I screw up the works? Tell me that. All I did—"

"All you did was tell us first she fell off the cliff and *then* she was shot."

"Well, I know that complicates things a little—"

Rocco snorted a laugh. "Nah, not really. This guy shoves his wife off a two-hundred-foot cliff, then he runs down and pops her one, just in case a fall that broke every bone in her body didn't do the job. Then, instead of killing himself right there and making it easy on himself, he climbs all the way to the top again—this fifty-eight-year-old guy with bad lungs—so he can shoot himself right on the edge, the very same spot, and fall down on top of her. Oh, yeah, nothing wrong with that picture."

"Rocco, we're getting ahead of the story here. All I can tell you for sure is that she was alive when she fell off the cliff, which I know because—"

"Oh, yeah, I wondered when you were gonna get around to that," Rocco grumbled

"—because she was conscious when she fell, and if you're conscious, it's a pretty safe bet that you're alive."

"*Conscious?*" Rocco practically shouted. "Damn, Gid . . ." When words failed him he just shook his head.

"Yes, conscious. Sure. You see—"

"Hold it, hold it, hold it. What hat did that get pulled out of?

Don't you ever stop? First you know she was alive, now you're telling me you know she was *conscious*?"

He had stopped walking so abruptly that a daydreaming man walking behind him had to stop himself from stumbling into him. Catching himself just before contact, he made an exasperated noise and gave Rocco the finger, a gesture as readily understood in Florence as in New York.

"Screw you too, pal," was Rocco's nonchalant, over-the-shoulder response, in English, before he returned his attention to Gideon. "What are you gonna tell me next, what she was thinking about?" Still shaking his head, he flipped his cigarette into the gutter.

"Believe me, if I could I would, but all I can tell you is that she was conscious."

"Aw, man, give me a break. How the hell can you possibly know something like that?"

"I know because—"

Rocco glanced at his watch and did a quick mental calculation. "Nuts, I gotta go if I'm gonna make it back to meet the train. Jesus, Gid, you sure know how to turn a simple case into a, a—" He shook his head and pulled out a business card on which he scribbled something. "This is my cell number, my personal phone. Give me a call later and tell me what you were gonna say, will you? But no mumbo jumbo. If I'm gonna go anywhere with this, I'm gonna need some solid evidence—facts—to convince Captain Conforti. He's a tough nut to crack." And then to John: "If you think reopening a closed case is tough in the Feeb, you oughta see the *Carabinieri*. Don't forget, red tape was invented right here in Florence. Thank you, Machiavelli."

"I'll call if you want, Rocco," Gideon said, "but there's no need to interrupt your evening. I'll be going over it all in class tomorrow morning. In detail."

"Yeah, except I'm not gonna be there. I gotta be in court, available to testify on another case. So call me later? Tonight, I mean?"

Gideon took the card. "I will."

"In an hour would be good. So look: You can cut across the piazza right here. That street on the other side is Via della Scala. Left on that for two blocks and turn right on Via del Moro. The Osteria's just a block down." Another look at his watch, a momentary chewing of his lip. "Ah, what the hell, I can go a little more with you. I can always run back to the station."

"Or just flag down the first car you see and jump in," John suggested and growled: "'Police business.' That's what we do in America. Don't you watch any movies?"

"Yeah, right. Okay, Gid," he said as they started across the Piazza Santa Maria Novella, "you know she was conscious because . . . ?"

"Well, go back to the bones we were looking at this afternoon, to all those fractures. Did you notice any kind of pattern in the damage?"

That brought roll of the eyes from John. "Oh, honest to God, you can't just tell us? We really have to do this Socratic thing?"

"Hey, I'm a professor, John. It's what I do."

"Tell me about it," John said grumpily.

"Pattern in the damage . . ." mused Rocco. "Gimme a minute . . . Most of the injuries were to the lower half of her body, is that what you're driving at?"

"Yeah, that's right," said John, "her legs were a mess. Her arms weren't so bad."

Gideon nodded. "Correct. More specifically, every single one of the six bones in her legs was broken, whereas not a single one of the six bones in the arms was damaged. And the one foot we have has more splintered bones than I had a chance to count. The pelvis is mashed too. But above the waist, the only injuries are some crushed vertebrae—not fractured, but *crushed*—and her skull. Well, how would you account for a pattern like that?"

"She landed on her feet?" John suggested as they started moving again. "I guess."

"And you're right, she landed on her feet, and the fact is that the bodies of dead people—or unconscious people for that matter—don't do that. If a nonconscious body falls from a great enough height—and two hundred feet is way, *way* more than enough—then it tends to align itself in the air, so that it lands horizontally. It's a function of the state of uniform motion of a falling object."

"The state of . . . ?" Rocco's brow furrowed.

"Not important," Gideon said dismissively. "Now—"

"Meaning he doesn't know what the hell it means either," John told Rocco.

"Pretty much, yes," Gideon agreed. "Physics never was one of my strong points. But the point I'm making here is: people who are *conscious* during a fall, they—"

"Land on their feet." This from Rocco.

"Exactly. Well, with some qualifications. If it's from a low height—ten, twenty feet—they won't have time to change their alignment, so a lot of times they hit with their hands or forearms, trying to protect their heads. Or suicides might land head down on purpose. Otherwise, yes, they almost always land on their feet. And this one very definitely did. You're frowning."

"Yeah, I'm frowning," Rocco said. "I got a problem with this."

"Which is?"

"Which is, you seem awful sure of yourself, but when I listen to the words, what I hear is 'tends to' and 'almost always' and 'most often.' That doesn't exactly convince the hell out of me, and it wouldn't convince a court either, you know what I mean?"

"I do, and it's a good point. But in this particular case there's no *almost always*. I *know* she landed on her feet . . . and I know it from her *skull*."

John and Rocco puzzled over this—Rocco was talking to himself—as they made their way through the great square that fronted the church's beautifully maintained façade. The piazza itself, however, had seen better days. For more than three centuries the grand event of the Florentine year, the Palio dei Cocchi, had been held here. Now it was a scruffy lawn area, more sandy dirt than grass, on which they had to pick their way between the young and not-so-young backpackers who sprawled, picnicked, and slept, oblivious to the many pedestrians using it as a shortcut.

Beside one of the two stone obelisks that had once marked the turning points for Palio's chariot races, John paused, eyes narrowed, and leveled a finger at Gideon. "I know you, Doc. If you're waiting for us to go, like, 'Whoa! How the hell can you tell somebody landed on their feet from their *skull*?' forget it."

Gideon laughed. "Actually, that would be very much appreciated. I'm not getting paid for this, you know, so how about at least giving me some enjoyment out of it?"

From Rocco, a threatening growl. "How about just telling us?"

"You guys sure know how to take the fun out of it, but okay. Do you—"

"Damn it," Rocco interrupted, "I really better get out of here.

Tell me about it when you call. This is Via del Moro, you turn here. Jesus, Carlotta's gonna kill me." He jabbed a finger at Gideon. "No mumbo jumbo. Just facts." He started off, moving fast.

"Hey, Rocco!" Gideon called after him.

Rocco slowed without turning. "What?"

"So how many *carabinieri* does it take to screw in a light bulb?"

Now he turned around and grinned. "Four. One to climb up on the chair and three to turn the chair."

SEVEN

"SO, okay," John said relatively patiently as they turned the corner. "How do you *know* from her skull that she landed on her feet?"

"Well, you remember that basilar ring fracture in her skull?"

"Where the bottom got all pushed in?"

"Mm-hm. Well, there aren't many ways you can cave in the skull base like that, but impacting on your feet after a two-hundred-foot drop is one of them. The force is so great that it not only fractures your lower limbs, it drives the spinal column up into your brain—"

John grimaced. "Yeesh."

"—taking the bottom of the skull partway with it, because the vertebrae are wider than the opening of the foramen magnum. It's also likely, by the way, to drive the leg bones, the femurs, up into the pelvis and punch holes through it on either side—which also happened here—and to crush and dislocate . . . well, you get the idea."

"I do," John said thoughtfully. "And so you think—tell me if I have this right—in a nutshell, you figure she had to have been shot after she fell and not before, because no way could she be alive, let alone conscious, *after* taking a .32 ACP slug right through the middle of her head."

"Let's just say it would be highly unusual."

"But what could be the point? I still don't understand that. I mean, okay, say she was alive when she went over the edge, she'd be dead as hell once she hit the bottom, right? All those injuries she had?"

"Oh, definitely. There would have been massive internal damage, organs torn from their moorings, probably a snapped spine. And the basilar ring fracture alone—"

"Okay, then, so why shoot her?"

Gideon shrugged. "John, I honestly don't have an answer for you, but don't you think this is all starting to get just a little circular? Anyway"—he pointed over John's shoulder—"we're here. Let's go in."

L'OSTERIA di Giovanni was in a sixteenth- or seventeenth-century palazzo, relatively modest by Florentine standards. Through the modern glass doors they could see a dining room that managed to be both trendy (well-lit, with abstract art on the walls, and widely spaced, white-clothed tables) and yet distinctly Tuscan (honey-colored, roughly plastered walls, red terra-cotta floor tiles, ancient stone accents peeking through the plaster here and there). At this early hour (by Italian standards), there were few diners.

At the door they were spotted from the rear of the restaurant by a rotund, jolly fellow in a grubby green T-shirt, who came toward them at a trot. This rumpled, convivial personage turned out to be Giovanni himself, who seemed pleased to find that they were Americans, but spoke little English himself and turned them over to the part-Asian hostess. ("This my daughter, Caterina," he told them."She speak French too.") Caterina led them to a table in an interior room. This space was cozier and more traditional—an old copper-hooded fireplace with a family crest, stone pillars anchoring the ceiling arches, tables closer together so it was almost like communal dining. More crowded too, and the noise level suggested the diners had been at it long enough to down a few glasses of wine.

"Your waiter will be Bruno. I hope you enjoy."

Within seconds the busy, balding, smiling Bruno was bobbing at their side—"*Buona sera, signori* . . ."—setting down ice-frosted flutes of pale, sparkling wine and a fragrant, red-and-white cloth-covered basket. "*Complimenti della casa*," he declared. John peeled back the cloth to have a peek. "Chicken McNuggets?" he crowed, as incredulously delighted as a kid finding a live, saddled pony waiting for him in the middle of his backyard.

The ingratiating smile dropped off Bruno's face. He drew himself up. "Is no' Chicken McNug'," he told John, oozing grievance. "Is *coccolini*. Special pasta. Fry."

"Okay, *amico*, *no problemo*. But they look like, *mismo* like, Chicken McNuggets, chicken *mcnuggo*, *pollo mcnuggeti*, that's all. *Capisce*?" John's forays into foreign languages were rare, but when they occurred they were always surprising, usually multilingual, and, at least to Gideon, highly entertaining.

Bruno stood even taller and frowned even harder. "I speak English. Is no' necessary—"

"*Grazie*, Bruno," Gideon said. "*Sembrano deliziosi*."

Bruno huffed something and stomped off.

"Well, they do," John moped. "What's the big deal? What's so terrible about Chicken McNuggets?"

"Can't think of a thing. What do these taste like?"

John tried one and lit up. "Not bad! Greasy, salty, crunchy . . . wow. We better finish 'em before Marti gets here, though," he said, reaching for another.

Marti Lau, John's wife, was a nutritionist at a Seattle hospital, and although she knew better than to try to impose on her husband the same saltless, fatless, sugarless, meatless regimen she inflicted on her captive clientele, John, an enthusiastic trencherman, found it more enjoyable to do his cheeseburger-chomping and milkshake-slurping when she wasn't around. She herself lived by dietary rules almost as stringent (she permitted herself cheese and dairy products—sparingly) as the super-healthy regimen she imposed on her hospital population and looked it: a five-foot-ten beanpole, healthy as a horse, and, other than her dietary strictures, a lively, funny, laid-back woman who was a terrific fit for John.

Gideon tucked in too and helped the morsel down with a swig of the wine, a fizzy, lemony prosecco. "They *are* good. I could make a meal of these things."

"Probably wouldn't be the first time somebody did," John said. He used his fork to pluck another from the rapidly emptying basket and more or less flipped it into his mouth, to be quickly followed by one more. When Bruno bobbed up again with menus, Gideon told him they were waiting for two ladies and would order after they arrived. Bruno's shoulders lifted and fell with acceptance and resignation, as if Fate itself had decreed that these two difficult *americani* were to be his burden for tonight.

"Hey, Bruno," John called after him, holding up the basket. "We could stand another order, *un altro ordero*, of these things. My buddy here, *mi amigo*, has pretty much gobbled them up, *tutto*."

Bruno came back and snatched the basket out of his hand. "Will be cost," he told them, as if expecting an argument.

"*Va bene, amigo, no problemo*," John told him with an expansive wave, but then turned seriously to Gideon. "Doc, you can see that you've got Rocco thinking about getting the whole case reopened, can't you?"

"Well, maybe he should. Something's weird."

"Yeah, but you have to understand, it's not just a question of him going to his boss and saying, 'We should reopen this case.' It's a lot more complicated, a lot dicier, than that."

"Dicier? Why?"

"Because egos are involved, man. When you close a file, especially on a high-profile homicide—in the *Carabinieri*, or the FBI, or the Podunk PD—a lot of people—prosecutor, judge, the cop that was in charge—have put their reputations on the line by signing off on it, on whatever the conclusions were. Believe me, they are *not* happy when some underling comes along wanting to open it up again. So Rocco knows he's probably gonna get crucified when he brings up the idea. *If* he brings up the idea. He needs some solid ground to stand on."

"And you don't think what I've been telling you is solid enough."

"Well, let me ask it this way. How sure are *you* about what you've been saying?"

"About which part?"

"About the weird part; that the fall came first, that she was already dead before she was shot."

"Well—"

"No fancy explanations, no lectures."

"No mumbo jumbo," Gideon said with a smile.

"Right. Just how sure are you? Say on a scale of one to ten."

"Come on, John, I can't do that. Look, when I say that if you're conscious when you fall, you're going to land on your feet, I'm making a generalization. You realize that, don't you? I don't know that it works that way every single time. How could I know? How could anyone? And even when we say that a bullet traveling through the middle of the brain *always* produces instant loss of consciousness, how could we possibly know something like that for a certainty? And when we say—"

John tossed back his prosecco in a single impatient gulp. "God-damn it, it never fails. It's exactly what my boss says about you. You come on the scene, you throw a monkey wrench into everything, but then, when we want to act on it, the first thing you do is cover your rear end. 'Gosh almighty, folks, I'm just making a generalization here, don't hold me to it.' "

"That's not fair, John. I can tell you what I find and what I conclude from it. I can't tell you what I don't know. I'm not going to make stuff up."

John shrugged. "Okay then, tell me what you do know. What are the statistics? What percentage of conscious people land on their feet, and what percentage don't? Because you can damn well bet it's gonna get asked in an Italian court if this ever gets there, so give me some figures. Something Rocco can work with."

"John, you can't—"

"You don't have any percentages, do you? There aren't any, are there?"

Gideon leaned back with a sigh. "Boy, in your next career, you know what you ought to be? A defense lawyer. You sound like the kind of gorilla-for-hire that comes after me in cross-examinations. 'Can you tell the jury, *Doctor* Oliver, *exactly* what percentage of proximal tibial epiphyseal unions are complete by age twenty-two and one half among Hispanic females with one non-Hispanic maternal grandparent, as compared to that among Hispanic females with—' "

John cracked a smile. "Okay, okay, but seriously, *are* there any statistics? I'm just asking you: do you think Rocco should go back and stir this kettle up again unless you're pretty sure it needs it? I mean, even if he reopens it and it goes nowhere—*especially* if it goes nowhere—he'll still have a bunch of important people ticked off at him."

"Let me put it this way—"

"Statistics," John demanded.

With a sigh, Gideon leaned back in his chair. John had a point, but what he wasn't taking into account was that forensics didn't have the advantages of the experimental sciences. You couldn't push a thousand conscious people off a cliff to see how they landed, and then shove a thousand more unconscious ones over the edge to find out how the two groups compared. All you had to work with were the suicides, murders, and accidents that happened on their own, without your help—and of those, only the ones that happened to come your way or happened to get written up, which the great, great majority of them didn't. And even in those you were familiar with, you could only rarely be *certain* that a supposed suicide really was a suicide, or an accident an accident. Not after the fact.

Bruno returned with another basket of *coccolini* and even two more proseccos (without additional cost, presumably). John happily busied himself with them.

True, Gideon thought, there were experiments in which dummies or pig cadavers had been dropped from cranes, and those were instructive, but dummies, even anthropomorphic ones with weight distributions precisely like people's, weren't people. The upshot was that your forensic conclusions were often grounded on a shockingly small database, a compilation of your own experiences and those of a few others, along with an intuition that (you hoped) was based on years of subliminal information-processing But there wasn't any point in going through all the *ifs*, *buts*, and *maybes* with John, who'd heard it all before anyway. "If what you're asking me is, could I prove, to the certain satisfaction of a judge and jury, that she was still alive when she fell, still conscious, then my answer has to be no. Nobody could prove it because it's unprovable one way or the other. Do I *believe* she was? Yes, definitely, and I've got some decent scientific backing for my opinion. But would I bet my life on it? No way."

John shook his head. "Oh, that's just great."

Gideon pondered for a moment longer, gaze turned inward, finger to his lips. "*Your* life, maybe."

That won a laugh from John. "Okay, so what do you think? Is there enough there to suggest that maybe this was a double murder, not a murder-suicide? Or let me put it this way: if it were you, would *you* push the buttons to get the case reopened? Considering that, if it didn't come to anything, you'd be in the doghouse for the next five years."

Gideon leaned back. "Well, before I did, what I'd really want would be to have a look at the other skeleton, the husband's skeleton. See if it's got anything to say for itself. But—"

"Rocco said it'd been cremated."

"That's right, he did. But wait a minute." He put down the prosecco he'd been sipping. "There's bound to be a report of some kind from the *medico:* an autopsy or something like it."

"An autopsy of a bunch of bones? Be pretty short, wouldn't it?"

"Probably, but you never know what you might find. You know, I think I'll ask Rocco if he can send me a copy." He searched for and found Rocco's card and flipped his cell phone open.

As he began to dial, the sound of a welcome voice floated over his shoulder. "Well, you two weren't very hard to find. We just followed the words 'skeleton' and 'murder,' and here you are." She grinned at the woman standing next to her. "Do we know our husbands or don't we?"

Gideon looked up laughing, but with a catch in his throat too. It was ridiculous, really; almost a decade of marriage, and the unanticipated sound of Julie's voice, the sight of a smile—just for him—on that lovely face, still squeezed his heart and sent a surge of gratitude for his good fortune through him. He jumped up.

"Julie, hi! Marti, how's it going? How was your day? Did you make it to the Bargello?"

The Museo Nazionale del Bargello was one of Florence's smaller art museums and a little out of the way, but a real gem, housed in an especially beautiful fourteenth-century palazzo, with airy, high-ceilinged, evocative old chambers and sculptures by the likes of Michelangelo, Donatello, and Cellini. Best of all, unlike the perpetually jam-packed Uffizi, there was plenty of room to wander, and no need to elbow anybody out of the way to get close to the art. It was Gideon's and Julie's favorite museum in Florence, and Julie had been looking forward to showing it to Marti.

"Oh, we got there, all right," Julie said.

"All the way to the door," Marti put in. "Which was closed, and on which a little sign was pasted. In English, sort of: *Museum close, becowse on strike.*"

"Too bad. Will it be open tomorrow? We'll still be here in the morning."

"That information," Marti said, "was not forthcoming."

"But we did get to the Pitti Palace and the Boboli Gardens," Julie said, "so, all in all, it was a good day."

John gestured to the two unoccupied chairs. "So, join us. We promise, no more talk about skeletons and murders."

Marti began to sit down, but Julie stopped her. "I wouldn't count on that, Marti. I'm looking forward to a nice, long, two-hour Italian dinner, and I don't know about John, but I doubt that Gideon can go that long without skeletons creeping into the conversation. Let's go freshen up and let them get it out of their systems."

"No, really—" Gideon said.

Marti shook her head. "Nup, Julie's right. You two were right in the middle of something. At least finish that. Anyway, I need a touch-up. We've been out all day."

"Well, I might as well finish getting that call to Rocco out of the way, then," Gideon said as the women left in search of the restroom. "Shouldn't take long."

Rocco picked up at once. "*Pronto.*"

"Rocco, it's Gideon."

"Hello, Gid. Look, we're just about to eat. Could I maybe call you a little later?"

"Sure, but this'll just take a second. I'd really like to have a look at any medical reports that were made on the husband's skeleton. Would it be possible for you to e-mail me copies down in Figline Valdarno?"

"Yeah, it'd be possible, but it'd take about a year to get the clearance to do it. If you could come back into Florence, you can look at them here."

"Can't. Class until one, and then we head straight for Figline. How about the day after?

"Thursday's not so good for me, I'm kind of tied up. Unless you could be here before things start, say eight o'clock?"

"Will do. I'll be there at eight A.M. sharp. I expect John'll be there too." He threw an inquiring glance at John, who responded with a shocked "Eight A.M., as in eight o'clock in the *morning*?" John was not known as an early riser. "Are you kidding me?"

"He says he's greatly looking forward to it," Gideon said. "Where do we come?"

"Regional headquarters. Borgo Ognissanti 48. It's not that far from Santa Maria Novella, not even a ten-minute walk."

"Thanks, Rocco, see you Thursday. Sorry about interrupting your dinner."

"No problem," Rocco said, and then, mostly to himself: "Just let me jot this down. P. Cubbiddu report for—"

Startled, Gideon jerked upright. "*What* did you say?"

"I didn't say anything. What'd you think I said?"

"*Cubbiddu.*"

"Oh. Yeah. I know, it's a weird name—Sardinian. These people—"

"We know these people," said Gideon. "We know these people. That's where we're going tomorrow, to the winery, to Villa Antica. That's how come I know Figline Valdarno."

"You're kidding me! Why didn't tell me that before?"

"Now, how could I tell you that when you never told us—"

"Okay, okay, you're right, but how do you come to know them? Oh, jeez, I really gotta go. I'm gonna get my head handed to me if the food gets any colder. Tell me about it later." And he was gone.

Marti and Julie had returned while Gideon was on the phone.

"Who were you talking about the Cubbiddus to?" Julie asked as she took her seat.

"Rocco Gardella. A lieutenant in the *Carabinieri*."

"A *carabiniere*? Has something happened in the case? Have they found them?"

"Yes, both of them, Pietro and Nola. Their bodies."

They waited for more, but Gideon just sat there, abstracted, hands steepled in front of his mouth, and it was John who had to fill them in on the afternoon's events.

Julie had been watching her husband. "Gideon? What's wrong?"

"Oh, nothing, really, it's just . . . well, it's kind of . . . I don't know, disconcerting . . . disturbing . . . to suddenly find out that the bones you've been handling so casually and treating like . . . like specimens of some kind, belonged to someone you know, a person you've talked to and dined with. It just brings you up short." He smiled. "Don't worry, I'm fine. Just a brief funk."

Julie nodded her understanding. "I know." She waited a moment for him to come all the way out of it. "Gideon, why do you suppose Linda didn't even let us know they'd been found?"

She was referring to Linda Rutledge, an old friend of theirs who was married to the middle son, Luca Cubbiddu, and who was the reason the four of them were heading down to Figline Valdarno the next day to spend the rest of the week at the Villa Antica.

"Well, the investigation was wrapped up only a few days ago. We're not really that close to them, and I guess she figured it could wait until she saw us. After all, it's not as if anybody thought they could still be alive after all this time."

Bruno showed up with a fresh basket of *coccolini* and two proseccos for the newcomers, and menus for all. The arrival of two attractive women at his table had brought a fresh smile to his face. "*Complimenti della casa*," he announced, with a far deeper bow than he'd given Gideon and John. Even his voice was a richer, more seductive purr. With a flourish he peeled back the checkered cloth like a magician revealing a wonderful surprise. "*Coccolini*." And waited for his applause.

Julie accommodated him. "Mm," she said, trying one. "*Meraviglioso*."

Bruno dipped his chin in gratitude and backed away a few steps before turning and going into the kitchen. Naturally enough, Marti wouldn't touch, let alone eat, anything deep-fried, but—thank goodness—she wasn't one of those people who went out of her way to make you feel guilty for indulging. She simply ignored them. She sipped her prosecco, though. With wine she had no quarrel.

There were more questions now, and when Bruno showed up again to take their orders, John and Gideon were still explaining. Not having had an opportunity to examine the menus, they asked Bruno for his recommendations. Julie and Gideon took them: the antipasto platter, followed by ravioli stuffed with porcini mushrooms and black truffles, and then veal chops with roasted cherry tomatoes. And a liter of the house red, a Carmignano rosso from nearby Brucianesi. No dessert. Gideon then interpreted for Marti, whose hold on Italian was even shakier than John's. Tuscany, of course, is justly famous for its beef and meat dishes, so finding something for her on the menu wasn't easy.

He requested the minestrone for her, a dinner-sized portion. Bruno nodded, writing on his pad. He approved, but not wildly.

"But can she get it made with vegetable stock, not chicken stock?" Julie asked in Italian.

Bruno was shocked. "*Ma certamente non*!" But then he got it. He gestured at Marti. "*Ah, vegetariana?*"

She responded with a vigorous nod. "*Si.*"

He waved a magnanimous hand. All would be well. "I take care of. You leave to me. You will like very much."

"Thank you, Bruno. That sounds wonderful. *Mera . . . meraviglioso.*" She expressed no reservations or caveats about salt or fat. When dining out, she very sensibly allowed herself considerable leeway.

Bruno, pleased, turned to John. "Signore?" He tried a little levity. "Sorry, no more Chicken McNug', ha-ha."

"Ha-ha," said John.

Gideon knew that John was longing to try Florence's famous *bistecca alla fiorentina*, a reliably gigantic slab of prime porterhouse served ultra-rare and usually simply flavored; nothing more than salt, olive oil, or butter, and perhaps a little rosemary or lemon. But with Marti there, even though she would make no comment, it would dent his pleasure with a tinge of guilt. "I'll have what they're having," he said, making his request clear by gesturing at Julie and Gideon.

As Bruno, pleased with his tableful of *americana* after all, hurried to the kitchen to place the orders, Gideon's cell phone emitted its soft *bip-bip*, the least intrusive sound he could find on its ringtone menu. When he opened it, Rocco was at the other end. "Hey, Gid, I was thinking more about all this. You said you're going to be spending some time with the Cubbiddus the next couple of days?"

"Right. We'll be staying with them till Sunday."

"Well, look, let's keep all this stuff to ourselves for now, okay? I think it'd be better if they didn't know about these questions that have come up. In fact, I think it'd be better if nobody knew."

"If you mean our wives, I'm afraid you're a little late."

"Well, tell them to shut up about it too if they know what's good for them."

"Oh, right. We'll do just that."

"Slap 'em around a little if they don't like it."

"Yeah, right, excellent idea, I'll make a note of that." He closed the phone and slipped it into a pocket. "Rocco's asked us not to mention any of this to the Cubbiddus."

"He's planning on reopening the case, then?" John asked.

"Thinking about it, I guess. He didn't say."

Bruno returned with the wine and poured a little for everyone. They clinked glasses and settled back.

"You know, I think I'm going to give Linda a quick call while we wait," Julie said, clicking buttons on her own phone.

"But—" Gideon began.

"No, not to talk about Pietro and Nola, just to touch base and make sure we're all still expected. What with the bodies having just been found, and this police determination of murder-suicide . . . Linda?" she chirped. "Hi, this is Julie. . . ."

Linda Rutledge was their connection to Villa Antica and to the Cubbiddu clan. Julie and Linda had met more than a decade earlier when they were both nineteen-year-old students enrolled in culinary arts programs. (Linda had been interested in wine and food even then; Julie had been going through a hotel-management phase before switching to a multidisciplinary degree program in wildlife studies, psychology, and national-park management.) To cut costs they'd shared a hotel room at a hospitality-industry exposition in Chicago and had become fast friends, a relationship that continued even after Julie married and Linda remained single. A couple of times a year, Linda had flown from her home in Tennessee to spend a few days with the Olivers, and every once in a while, Julie had returned the favor to go on some kind of brief jaunt with her old friend, who was by then the food and beverage director at a big Memphis hotel.

Then, a few years ago, Linda had met two of the Cubbiddu sons—Luca and Nico—at a winery conference in Basel. Luca and Linda had fallen head over heels in love, and six months later she was married and living happily with her husband in Tuscany, in one of the spacious "noble apartments" of Villa Antica. Since then, Julie had heard less from her, but a year ago, when she and Gideon were on an Italian vacation, they'd accepted her invitation to visit her there; it had been only a month or so before Pietro and Nola's disappearance. Expecting to stay only overnight, they'd wound up canceling their other reservations and remaining for a week. They'd gotten to know and like Luca, and they'd met the others at the mandatory (by order of Pietro) daily family luncheons; noisy, spirited repasts of five or six courses, mostly simple, hearty Sardinian or Italian fare built around a main dish of spit-roasted rabbit, goat, or lamb that had been turning over a charcoal fire all morning. And always there were bottles of the same hearty, rustic wines that Pietro's father and grandfather had made back on the farm, wines that Pietro had been drinking every day of his life since the age of five, and that were still closest to his heart.

They'd enjoyed themselves immensely, and this time around, being more or less in the neighborhood, they had pretty much invited themselves back. Linda and Luca's response had been gratifyingly enthusiastic. It would be at the tail end of the annual Val d'Arno Wine Festival, put on by the valley's winery consortium, the program committee of which was chaired this year by Linda in her role as Villa Antica's public relations manager. So, it would be a busy time, but a lively one.

And the very next day, Villa Antica itself would be putting on its third annual *Vino e Cucina* program, a four-day course, conducted in English, that was primarily a cooking class, but was richly leavened with material on Italian wines and culture. The program would be led by Luca, who had founded it.

Although John and Marti had never met Linda, she had invited all four of them to attend the program free of charge. Julie and Marti had accepted but had insisted on paying the €500 fee (they were, after all, already being put up at the villa for the better part of a week), while John and Gideon had politely and unsurprisingly declined. They would find other things to do, and Thursday morning was already allocated: they would be at Borgo Ognissanti 48 in Florence.

When the antipasto plate came, they automatically adopted the gastronomic division of labor they'd become accustomed to when the four of them ate together: John, Julie, and Gideon tucked into the salami, prosciutto, and paté, while Marti no less happily went after the olives, the roasted peppers, and the marinated artichoke hearts and eggplant.

"Well, everything's on, and they're expecting us," Julie said, slipping her iPhone into her bag. "Linda told me about finding Pietro and Nola, and about the police investigation and all. It was a little awkward pretending we didn't know anything about it, but . . ." She shrugged. "Anyway, we're supposed to meet Linda and Luca at the wine festival tomorrow afternoon. At three, if we can make it. It's in the main square of Arezzo."

Gideon nodded. "That'll work. Seminar'll finish up at one."

"Oh, and she's taking us up on our offer to help out at the festival—your offer, anyway," she said to Gideon. "They want you to be a judge."

"Do they now? For a wine tasting?" Gideon, who thought rather more of his wine expertise than was strictly warranted, was flattered.

"Um, not exactly. For the grape stomp."

"Grape stomp," Gideon repeated suspiciously. "And what is a grape stomp?"

"It's a contest. Teams of people take off their shoes and socks and stomp around in barrels of grapes to see which team can squish them and produce the most juice. Being a judge is an honor," she added but she couldn't help laughing.

Gideon's visage remained somber. "What do they need judges for? Wouldn't it be easier just to measure the amount of juice?"

"Well, yes, and that's what they do, but you've written books, you've been on television. You're a celebrity."

"Only one of my books has been published in Italy, and its sales were in the low three figures. And I've never been on Italian television, so how am I a celebrity?"

"Oh, don't be such a grump. Linda said you'd add gravitas to the situation. You'd be a cultural ornament. You'll do it, won't you?"

"Great," muttered Gideon. "A cultural ornament."

"Oh, come on, Gideon, you *will* do it, won't you?" Julie prompted. "All it takes is giving the awards to the winners."

"Giving the awards to the winners, boy, I don't know, that sounds pretty hard. I'm not sure I'm up to—urp."

She had speared one of the ravioli on his plate and jammed it into his mouth. "Here, have a ravioli. It'll improve your mood."

He chewed and swallowed. "That's *raviolo*, for your information. There's no such thing as *one* ravioli."

"Or maybe it won't," she said, and they all laughed and clinked glasses again.

John joined in, but he was still mulling over Thursday's appointment with Rocco. "Eight o'clock in the frigging *morning*," he grumbled. "Honest to God."

EIGHT

FLORENCE proper has a population of four hundred thousand. Include its surrounding sprawl, and you get a metropolitan area of a million-and-a-half. Arezzo proper, by contrast, holds fewer than a hundred thousand souls. And being a walled city, there is essentially no sprawl, no "metropolitan area." What you see is what you get. You can walk from one end to the other in half an hour. Try that in Florence.

Despite its disadvantage in size, it has no lack of artistic and architectural splendors, among which is the elegant, sloping, thirteenth-century Piazza Grande, with its striking trapezoidal shape, its grand fountain, and the beautiful old palazzos, towers, and loggias that surround it. In Etruscan days it had housed the central market; in Roman times the staid, august offices of provincial government. But when Gideon and Julie arrived there after finding a parking space (not easy), it was anything but staid. A flapping red, green, and white banner stretched between fifteen-foot posts proclaimed *FESTIVAL DI*

TUTTI I VINI DEL VAL D'ARNO in giant letters. Behind it, the square was crisscrossed with the multicolored tents, tables, and umbrellas of vendors. The happy, patently bibulous crowds made it clear that the winemakers had been unstinting with their tastings.

They'd been shooting for an arrival time of three o'clock, the start of the grape stomp and of Gideon's "ornamental" responsibilities, but with the parking difficulties they'd run into they were late. John and Marti, traveling in a separate rental car, were doing a little touring on the way to Figline and were skipping Arezzo altogether. They planned to show up at the Villa Antica a little after six. In the US it would have been rude to arrive at dinnertime, but in Tuscany in late summer, dinner would still be an hour or two—or three—off.

"Gosh," Gideon said, as they hunted for the stomp, "I sure hope we haven't missed it."

Julie responded with one of her looks. "Yes, I know you'd be just devastated."

They didn't have to search long to find the signs for *La Gran Pigiatura Dell'uva Del Val D'arno*—the Great Valdarno Grape Stomp—which was under way in a downslope corner of the square, where six contestants drenched up to their hips in purple liquid were stomping away in half-barrels full of grapes that had been set up on a stage, with the resulting pulpy fluid flowing sluggishly through hoses into ten-liter jars. Over a loudspeaker someone was accompanying them with a jazzy, Dean Martinesque version of the drinking song from *La Traviata* interspersed with jokey, encouraging comments. As they watched, a bell sounded, and each stomper gave way, as in a relay race, to a replacement who had been standing in back of him or her. In front of the stage were two dozen rows of folding chairs, most of which were empty because the audience was on its feet, cheering on their favorite teams with much noise and gesticulation.

"They're awfully excited about this, aren't they?" Julie said as they stood at the rear of the viewing area.

"I'm guessing there's a little wagering going on," said Gideon.

"And your guess," said a voice behind them, "is, as usual, on the mark." They turned to see an apple-cheeked, pleasantly plump, merry-eyed woman beaming delightedly at them.

"Linda!" exclaimed Julie with a happy little squeal, and much hugging all around ensued.

"Sorry I'm late for the stomp," Gideon said. "I was looking forward to judging."

"Amazing man," Linda said to Julie. "He managed that with a perfectly straight face." And to Gideon: "Don't worry about it. Nico's come to the rescue. I asked him to take over for you."

"A wise decision. He's more ornamental than I am."

Linda smiled. "Well, maybe a *little* more, but you make up for it in gravitas."

"That's true," Gideon agreed.

Nico was the baby of the Cubbiddu family, a movie-star-handsome twenty-six-year-old. And now Gideon spotted him at the microphone to the rear of the stage. It was Nico who was doing the singing and the patter. That he sounded like Dean Martin came as no surprise; he was cut from similar cloth: effortlessly charming, happy-go-lucky, ridiculously good-looking (if just a tad lounge-lizardy), totally laid-back, and perhaps a little too fond of the *vino*. A lock of black, oily hair even dipped roguishly down over his forehead—possibly on its own, but more likely with a little help.

"Nico's got this well in hand," Linda said, "and I could use a break. I've been working our booth since noon. What would you say to some coffee?"

She walked them up the slope to the long, colonnaded stone porch of the famous Vasari loggia at the top of the piazza, where the food vendors had set up. There were pushcarts offering *panini*; pizza; plates of sausage, peppers, and onions; and various sweets: *arancini*, cannoli, gelato. At one end of the porch was a permanent-looking espresso bar with half a dozen tables in front of it. It wasn't getting much business, and the white-coated barista stood with his arms folded, his chin on his chest, and his mind seemingly a million miles away.

"*Un cappuccino, per favore*," Gideon said, giving him Julie's request, "*e due espressi.*"

It was like watching one of those "living statues" that one sees on the streets of big cities, who stand utterly motionless until a dollar is put in their offerings box, whereupon they spring robotically into action for a minute or so. The barista jerked to life at the splendid, gleaming baroque apparatus of polished levers, spouts, and tubes that was his espresso machine. Julie's cappuccino came first. Levers were pulled, hisses were heard, and the air was filled with the thick, smooth aroma of good Italian coffee as jet-black espresso sluggishly flowed from a spout into a bowl-sized cup, covering the bottom by an inch or so. A seemingly unmeasured splash of milk was more or less flung into a metal pitcher, held under another spout, and jiggled and rotated until it was heated to a steaming froth, then poured into the cup, which it filled precisely to the point at which the stiffened froth was higher at the center than at the rim but was kept from overflowing by its surface density.

The barista looked sharply up at Gideon. "*Cioccolata?*"

"*Si, per piacere.*" For Julie a cappuccino wasn't a cappuccino if it didn't have chocolate on it.

With a flourish that would have done credit to a circus ringmaster, the barista sprinkled powdered chocolate onto the froth and went to work on the two espressos, which were briefer, simpler operations, but no less grandly handled. All three were placed on a tray and handed to Gideon.

"They look great, thank you."

The barista replied with a dignified half bow and Italy's fits-all-purposes response: "*Prego.*" He then used a cloth for a quick polish of the equipment and sank once again into reverie and immobility, awaiting his next customer.

Gideon smiled as he brought the tray to the table. There wasn't any shortage of espresso bars back in Seattle, but if you wanted the full-scale spectacle, the true drama and excitement of coffee-making, you had to come to the mother country itself: *la bella Italia.*

Linda dealt with her espresso in the Italian manner, dumping a spoonful of sugar into the little cup, stirring, and then throwing her head back and tossing the three ounces down in a couple of gulps, the way a thirsty barfly handles a double-shot glass of whiskey. Gideon preferred his straight and drank it more slowly, four sips in all. Julie, as usual, made more of production of her cappuccino, holding it up to her nose and inhaling, sighing, stirring the foam and chocolate into the coffee, lifting the cup to her mouth with both hands and taking one minuscule sip at a time, her eyes closed with pleasure.

While she drank, Linda talked a little more about Nola and Pietro. "It was a relief when their bodies were finally found, of course, but none of the boys have really accepted that it happened the way they said—that *babbo* killed her. I mean, nobody's criticizing the *Carabinieri*—the lieutenant, Gardella, his name was, did a really thorough job; they all did—but the boys simply can't make themselves see their father as a murderer."

"I'm having a hard time myself," Julie said.

Gideon said nothing. He'd have liked to tell Linda that he had his own doubts, having examined Nola's bones himself, and that he had the lieutenant rethinking things as well. But Rocco had specifically asked him not to discuss that, so he kept it to himself.

Rocco hadn't, however, asked him not to talk about the case in general, and after all, the three of them were old friends who had shared a good many confidences, so . . .

"What about you, Linda?" he asked.

"What about me what?"

"Do you see Pietro as a murderer?"

She thought about it. "Well, there were some rumors about Nola's having an affair, and *babbo* was, you know, very Italian, very . . . theatrical. Not exactly cool-blooded. Sometimes life with him was like living in a Puccini opera, nothing small-scale about it. He didn't get mad often, but when he did, boy, you didn't want to be anywhere within range. And—and this is the main thing—he was an extremely, and I mean *extremely*, old-fashioned male, straight out of the nineteenth century. It took him years to get over the fact that I wanted to keep my maiden name and not become signora Cubbiddu. Heck, I'm not sure he ever really did get over it."

She smiled. "And you notice I'm calling him *babbo*, not Pietro. When I first got here I tried calling him by his first name, but that sure didn't last very long—not coming from a daughter-in-law and a foreigner as well. It was a slur on his honor—those were his own words. He had his rules about how the family should act toward the *padre*, you see, and you had to follow them if you knew what was good for you."

She paused, remembering. "So if he found out she was cheating on him? Then yes, I could see him killing her. And himself too, for that matter, yes. A normal person would maybe choose divorce, but *babbo*? Not an option. 'Family above everything, except honor,'" she said. "That was his motto." And then, in an acid undertone: "Or so we used to think."

"Were they true?" Julie asked. "The rumors?"

Linda shrugged. "I doubt if anybody really knows. Honestly, Julie, the whole thing was so awful that everybody just wanted it to be over. I don't think anybody wanted to know. What would be the point?"

Interesting, Gideon thought. The same words Rocco had used when asked the same question.

Linda's expression, sober for the last few minutes, suddenly brightened. Seeing it happen was like watching the sun break through on a gloomy day. Her face was transformed. "Well, well. Here's my hubby," she proclaimed with transparent pride as Luca came charging up the steps to the portico.

Like Nico, Luca was a good-looking guy, but in a different way: a bigger-than-life type, expansive and spontaneous, more rough-cut than either of his brothers, and, in general, much like their father in personality. He was earthy, generous, opinionated, blunt, honest, and always ready to laugh, which he did loudly and lengthily. There had been times when Gideon had expected him to break into the big dance from *Zorba the Greek* at any minute, but so far he never had. Luca was great fun to be with for a few hours, but any more than that and Gideon needed to get away to someplace where Luca didn't suck up all the air and take up all the space. Now, as he strode toward them with a giant grin plastered on his face and his arms spread wide, Gideon thought for a moment that he was going to try to gather Julie and him in at the same time in one of his bone-crushing hugs, but he settled instead for two separate ones, first Gideon, then Julie. Gideon's was accompanied by a wince-inducing back-thumping, which he returned in full measure, but Luca got the best of it. He was an immensely powerful man, about an inch shorter than Gideon's six-one, but far thicker in the chest and shoulders. Then on to Julie.

"Luca, honey," Linda suggested sweetly as her husband wrapped his arms around Julie and swayed back and forth with her, "you might want to let her go now. It's possible she might want to breathe."

"Ah, she loves it," Luca said, "and why wouldn't she?" He finished with an explosive vacuum cleaner of a kiss to her cheek: *mmwaaak!* Julie, who wasn't really that keen on being engulfed by large males (happily, she made an exception for Gideon), smiled politely. There wasn't much else you could do when Luca Cubbiddu decided he was going to hug you.

He had barely signaled to the barista for an espresso and sat down when Nico showed up as well, fresh from his grape-stomp responsibilities. Brushing back that Superman forelock from his forehead (to which it immediately bobbed back) and giving them his raffish but inarguably appealing grin, he welcomed Julie and Gideon. "Hey, pallies, long time no see. How's it going?"

Like his brothers', Nico's English was first-rate: fluent and casual. That had been their father's doing. Pietro had never learned English himself—even his Italian was rudimentary—but he'd understood that if the boys were to compete in the increasingly globalized business of wine, English would be a necessity. He had seen to it that they learned it as children and learned it well. Since then their travels—trade shows, expositions, conferences—had given them an idiomatic ease with the language. To Gideon they all seemed as comfortable in English as they did in their own tongue, and he'd heard them chatting in it even when there were no Brits or Americans around.

"Fine, pally," he said amicably, "how about you?"

"Can't complain."

"Hey, who's tending the booth?" Linda asked.

"Gianni and Ettore are there now," Luca said. "We just wanted to say hello. We'll go back in a minute and give them a hand wrapping up. There won't be that much to load back up in the truck. We moved a *lot* of wine."

"Yeah, it helps when you're giving it away," Nico said and went to the bar, coming back with Luca's coffee and for himself a glass of Moscato, a golden, mellow, afternoonish kind of wine.

"No, I mean we sold a lot too," Luca said. "It was a good festival."

Nico sat, took a long swallow, sighed, and stretched, looking worn out. "Lot of work, though. I'm beat."

"*You're* beat," Luca said. "How do you think I feel? And about three hours from now, *Vino e Cucina* gets going. Whew. It's like it never ends."

Linda laughed. "You know you love it, honey."

"I thought the class started tomorrow morning," Julie said.

"The class, yeah, but there's an opening reception at seven tonight. You two will be there, I hope. And your friends."

"Actually," Gideon said, "John and I haven't signed up, Luca, so—"

"Oh, please, tonight's different. No cooking demonstrations, I promise. No lectures. Just some good wine and a few simple appetizers, and a chance for people to mingle. And a few introductions. I'd really appreciate it if you came, Gideon. You'd be a—"

"Cultural ornament," Gideon said. "I know."

"Well, that too, definitely, but I was thinking more of an extra body to help out in the kitchen with the heavy labor." As it often did, a burst of bluff, hearty laughter followed his comment.

"Oh, well now, that's different, Luca. Of course I'll be there."

Nico stood up and finished his wine with a single gulp. "Luca, my man, what do you say we head back to the booth and flog another case or two of Villa Antica plonk to the unsuspecting masses?"

Luca responded in kind. "Watch it, baby brother, you're speaking of what I love most in the world."

Linda cleared her throat, loudly and meaningfully.

"Second most, that's what I meant to say," Luca amended. He bent to plant a kiss on her forehead. Eyes closed, smiling, she tilted up her face to receive it.

"We'll see you two later," Luca said to the Olivers.

"Ciao, pallies" Nico said.

"I'll be along in a while," she called after them, and then to Julie and Gideon, with a long sigh: "I really love that man, did I ever tell you that?"

"Really? You're kidding us," Gideon said. "I would have thought from those flushed cheeks and shining eyes that you couldn't stand the guy. Hey, I'm going to get a cappuccino for myself. Watching Julie drink one always makes me want one of my own. Linda?"

"You bet. Don't tell anyone, though. Having a cappuccino at any time of the day other than with breakfast incurs the wrath of the purists."

Julie declined, holding up her cup to demonstrate that it was still half full.

Gideon went back to the counter, put the barista through his motions again, and returned with the brimming cups. While he'd been getting them, Linda had gone to one of the colorful little push-carts and brought back a cardboard carton of *zeppole*, the sugared, donut-hole-like fritters originally from Naples, but now a fixture at every Italian street fair from Rome to San Francisco. She lifted the lid as he set the coffees down in their saucers, bit into one, and offered them around.

Julie took one. "Linda, a couple of minutes ago you said you *used* to think Pietro put family above everything. What was that about? If it's none of our business, just—"

"No, no, that's okay." She and Julie had shared many confidences over the years and, in any case, she was one of those cheerfully open, talkative people who didn't need any coaxing when it came to retailing inside information that more guarded people would keep close to the vest.

"Well, here's what happened. Last summer, a couple of months before he died, *babbo* got this *amazing* offer from Humboldt-Schlager to buy the winery, lock, stock, and barrel. We're talking megabucks here."

"Aren't they a beer company?" Julie asked. "Are they into wines too?"

"This was going to be their entry. Well, *babbo* liked the idea—he was thinking about retiring anyway—and even if the rest of us weren't crazy about it, we weren't dead set against it either. According to their offer, Humboldt would stay out of the internal management of the winery for at least two years with Franco as chief operating officer and also a member of the corporation's board of directors. The rest of us would stay on in our present jobs at the same salaries we were getting from *babbo*. And we could keep on living here. Not a bad deal, really."

"But," said Gideon.

" 'But' is right. *Babbo* took his time about signing, and Humboldt had second thoughts. About a week before he's going to go up to the cabin, they change the terms. No jobs for the boys or for me, and no place to live either—we'd even have to clear out of our living quarters. No financial settlement either, just good-bye and good luck. And they weren't open to negotiations. Take it or leave it." She polished off her fritter and licked the sugar off her fingers.

"Yikes, that must have caused a little consternation," Julie said.

"Well, it would have if we'd known, but we didn't. As blunt and straight-talking as *babbo* was, apparently he didn't have the nerve to tell us. We only found out a couple of months later when the whole deal went south for good and Severo finally let us in on it. He felt bad about keeping it from us, Severo did, but he'd been honoring *babbo's* request. I don't blame him. It's a good thing *babbo* was already dead, though, or one of the boys probably would have killed him." She began to laugh but cut it off and sobered. "Whoa, that was just a stupid joke. Not for one minute do I think any one of them would ever—I mean, those boys *loved*—"

"We understand," Julie said smiling.

"Figure of speech, not a statement of fact," said Gideon.

He was also smiling, but his mind was chewing over what she'd said. Rocco had said they hadn't come up with any tenable motives for anybody but Pietro himself. Here, all of a sudden was a lulu of a motive, and three people—four, counting Linda—who shared it.

There was a time when he'd have felt guilty and been embarrassed about having such thoughts about friends, but sad experience had taught him not to discount them. It didn't stop him from hoping (and believing) that there was nothing to them, but Rocco would need to hear this all the same.

"They wouldn't have wanted to, anyway," said Linda, still a little defensive. "*Babbo* was making up for it by giving them big stipends, more than enough to live on when the sale went through—which it never did, of course—so nobody would have been exactly poor. Even Cesare was going to get one, the same as the other three."

Julie frowned. "Who's Cesare?"

Linda frowned back. "Who's Cesare? Cesare, Nola's son . . . Luca and Nico's stepbrother. And Franco's. You know."

"No, I don't know. I didn't know Nola had a son," Julie said. She glanced at Gideon, her brows knit: *Did you know?*

Gideon hunched his shoulders. "News to me."

"How could you not know about Cesare?" Linda demanded, as if they'd been remiss in their study of Cubbiddu history.

"I don't know how we'd know unless you told us," Julie said, "and you never told us."

"You mean you didn't . . . Oh, wait a minute, that's right; you didn't meet him when you were here last time. He'd moved out by then, and there was no particular reason to talk about him." She hesitated. "He . . . well, he wasn't all that popular, to put it bluntly. He didn't get along with the brothers very well, and he had . . . issues with Pietro too. I mean . . . you know."

Gideon didn't know, but he was suddenly interested. Issues with Pietro? "Like what?" Motives seemed to be popping up all over the place.

"Oh, it wasn't anything that—"

"Come on, Linda, I'm curious too," Julie said. "A step-brother—how does he fit into the picture?"

"Oh, all right," said Linda, lighting up at the prospect of opening up another skeleton closet. She dabbed powdered sugar from her lips and paused a moment to order her thoughts. "Okay, now, you remember that the two of them, Nola and Pietro, came from Sardinia, which is another world to begin with, but you probably don't know that the particular region they come from is Barbagia, which is the part—"

"The central interior," Gideon said. "Nuoro Province, basically. Mountainous, isolated, poor. Depending on how you look at it, very traditional or very backward and primitive."

"That's the place. Interestingly enough, the name—Barbagia—is supposed to mean 'barbarian'—"

"It does," Gideon said. "From '*bárboros*,' ancient Greek for the way foreigners were supposed to talk."

"Right," Linda said with a slight arching of one eyebrow in Gideon's direction. "Anyway—"

"It's because, to their ears, other languages sounded like *bar-bar-bar-bar*—babbling, in other words. They used the term a lot when they were naming places and peoples."

Linda made a growling noise. "Hey, who's telling this story?"

"The Barbary Coast, for example, although some authorities seem to think that's because the Barbary pirates were Berbers, but—"

"Is he always like this?" Linda asked.

"Pretty much, yup," said Julie. "He can't help himself. Apparently, it's in his DNA. You just have to ride it out. If you wait long enough, he runs out of gas. Or out of trivia; one or the other." She smiled sweetly at him.

Gideon laughed. "All right, I can take a hint. And anyway, I'm flush out of both. It's all yours, Linda."

"We'll soon see," Julie murmured.

"Well, the reason I mentioned the name at all is because it's still pretty barbaric in some ways. It's the only place in Italy where there are still honest-to-goodness, old-fashioned bandits in the mountains, and the only place—"

"Where *vendetta* still exists," said Gideon. "It—" He winced. "Sorry, sorry, sorry, won't happen again."

"All right, then," Linda said a little suspiciously. "Well . . ." She threw a wary eye at him to make sure he was really giving up the floor. When she saw that he was, she settled happily back into her chair with another *zeppola*. "Now, if you ever want to hear a real-life Romeo-and-Juliet story, this is it. . . ."

Pietro Cubbiddu and Nola Baccaredda had been born in the neighboring ancient stone villages of Nuragugme and Dualchi. The two families had been involved in an on-again, off-again vendetta going back to the 1950s that had begun over confused back-and-forth accusations of sheep-stealing. There had been three murders over the years and at least a half dozen attempted murders. According to Pietro, when he had been christened, the priest had consecrated six bullets and put them in with his swaddling clothes for use in avenging his family's honor, a not-uncommon practice in Barbagia at the time.

But the feud had died down about then, flaring up only occasionally in minor altercations, until 1985, when Nola's then-husband, Eliodoro, had been ambushed and assassinated on his way to deliver a load of cheese to Nuoro, the provincial capital.

Soon after, Pietro's older brother Primo had been shotgunned to death while tending his goats in their winter pasture. The Cubbiddu clan had made it clear to Pietro that it was now his solemn duty to put some of those six bullets to use, but Pietro had no wish to continue the feud—primarily because he had gone over to the dark side; he had met and fallen in love with Nola.

In 1986, they had shocked both families by announcing their upcoming marriage. Pietro was in his mid-thirties with three young sons. Nola, four years younger, had one child, Cesare, who was then an infant.

It was the couple's hope that their wedding, like a union between foreign royals in old Europe, would end the bad blood and even bring the two families together. As a gesture, one of Pietro's wedding gifts to Nola was the six bullets, still in the padded box in which they'd come from the priest. But it was not to be. Most members of both families—including the couple's parents—stayed away from the church, and muttered threats hung in the air. And when Pietro's oldest son, Franco, narrowly averted a nighttime roadside ambush (a row of flaming garbage cans suddenly blocking his way at a country crossroads, and two cars, each with several men in them, waiting alongside the road), Pietro and Nola concluded that it was time to leave. The family headed for Tuscany, the only place in mainland Italy with which they had any familiarity at all.

As it happened, Pietro had had a huge windfall a few months earlier: a government bulldozer had cut across his land without permission, wrecking his vineyard and much of his small, century-old olive grove. Fearing a suit, the government had quickly settled on 5 million *lire* for him—at the time the equivalent of three thousand euros. It was a fortune, ten times more money than he'd ever seen at once, and most of it went to buy an abandoned fifteenth-century convent, dilap-idated and war-damaged, that he'd seen in the Val d'Arno, thirty kilometers south of Florence. It had been converted to a winery for a while in the early years of the twentieth century, and it came with a half hectare of withered, moribund Malvasia grapes. But the soil was fertile and the climate conducive to grape growing; this was Tuscany, after all. They had had to set to work at once, and work like dogs they did, joined by Luca and Franco, who were then in their teens.

Gideon and Julie had heard this part of the story before, but Linda was rolling along in high gear, and they didn't have the heart to stop her. Besides, they both liked listening to her smooth, gentle Tennessee accent.

The Cubbiddus had plowed their earnings back into the vine-yard, and with time success had come. The enterprise had blossomed (Villa Antica was now the fourth largest of the valley's seventy-something wineries), their sons thrived and grew into four healthy young men, and they lived without the fear of *faida* hanging over their heads, since no one in Barbagia knew where they were.

Yet all was not well in the Cubbiddu household. At the time of the marriage, Franco and Luca were still grieving for their mother, who had died from a kidney infection a few weeks after bearing Nico, and Nola's intrusion into the family in her place was deeply resented. Nola, for her part, made an effort to win them over, but, like Pietro, she wasn't endowed with much in the way of patience, and she soon gave it up, settling for the mutual disaffection, deep but in general peaceably constrained, that continued to the end. This rift had created an ongoing strain between husband and wife, and, to a lesser degree, between father and sons as well.

But it was Nola's son, Cesare, who'd had the toughest time of all. When she and Pietro had married, Pietro's two older boys were fifteen and sixteen. Cesare was a squalling infant, not yet a year old; the teenage Cubbiddu boys couldn't have had less interest in him; at best, he was simply another intruder, but one who commanded a great deal more than his share of attention. And although Pietro treated the boy with kindness and generosity—he adopted him, he did his best to treat him no differently from his own sons—the underlying paternal pull was simply not there. Cesare had no doubt felt his isolation and by the age of four or so he had become a needy, manipulative, totally self-centered child. To Luca and Franco, by then into their young manhood, he was nothing but a hindrance and a pest.

"To Luca and Franco," Gideon said. "Not to Nico?"

"That's right. Well, you see, Nico is quite a bit younger than his brothers too, so as a kid he didn't have much in common with them either, although of course the love was always there. Blood, you know; this is Italy. But Nico and Cesare—at the time, they were only a few months apart—well, they still are, of course, but as children, they couldn't play with Franco or Luca, but they could play with each other. And they had no memory of ever *not* being brothers, which also wasn't the case for the older boys. So there was a connection there that nobody else had with Cesare. You understand, I wasn't there for any of this. Basically, I'm telling you what Luca's told me."

"Of course," said Julie.

"Nico was the older one, the more secure one, so he sort of took Cesare under his wing, spoke up for him, took his side, that kind of thing. Made excuses for him. Baby brother playing big brother. And he still does; he still sees himself as Cesare's protector. I have my doubts about how Cesare feels about Nico these days, but I do know that there's still a genuine love there on Nico's part. You wouldn't think so from that loosey-goosey way of his, would you, but Nico's a deeply affectionate guy. He's never given up on trying to bring Cesare more into the family." She shook her head fondly. "It's kind of touching, really."

"But apparently it hasn't worked," Julie said. "Bringing him more into the family."

Linda paused to let another *zeppola* go down before continuing. "That's right, Franco despises him, and Luca's not exactly crazy about him either. Neither am I, for that matter. And this I can tell you from my own experience: 'manipulative' and 'self-centered' still fit him to a *T*. He's always . . . I don't know, *hatching* something for his own benefit, if you know what I mean. As far as I'm concerned, I'm glad we don't see the little worm that much."

She paused, hesitating, but decided she might as well finish the story. "And it doesn't help any that he's been into and out of drugs since he was fourteen. Marijuana at first, then other junk, then cocaine. *Babbo* paid for him to go to rehab three, four times, but it never took. His best friend died from it, from mixing cocaine and booze—"

"A lethal combination," Gideon said with a shake of his head.

"And that stopped him for a while, but then he started thinking, 'Well, I guess I better give up one of them, but do I really have to quit both?' Unfortunately, it was the booze he gave up. He doesn't even drink wine any more, which is pretty unique around here. But now he's back on coke. Nico says it's all because of stress, because Pietro threw him out, and maybe it is, but I don't know. . . ." She shook her head. "It's all just too damn bad."

"He injects it?" asked Gideon

"According to Nico, he snorts it. He thinks it's less harmful than injecting, less addictive."

"About harmful I don't know, but about addictive he's probably right. You get a more immediate, more intense high from delivering it straight into the bloodstream."

"Nico keeps thinking he can get him to quit, but . . . well, good luck to him, but I think it's way, way too late. He's already lost his cellar-master job. Doesn't have a job at all, as far as I know. Lives on *babbo's* will."

"That's really sad," Julie said.

Linda nodded. "Yes, it is. But trust me, he'd still be a creep even if he wasn't stoned half the time." She drank the last of her cappuccino and set the cup down with a satisfied sigh. "Well, that's pretty much the story, and I'd better head back to the booth to help out. Things are winding down here." She gestured toward the piazza, in which the crowds had indeed thinned out. A general sense of fatigue now hung over it. Several of the booths were already being dismantled.

"Can I help?" Gideon asked. "Need some muscle?"

"No, thanks, we've got everything under control." She pushed herself to her feet. "You know how to get to the villa from here?"

Gideon nodded. "SR69 to the A1, and then straight up to Figline."

"Right. You're in the same apartment you were in last year. Key's in the door. Reception's at seven. Totally informal; what you're wearing is fine. With the weather so nice, it'll be outdoors, on the garden terrace. Remember where that is?"

"Oh, I think so."

"You won't have any trouble finding it. Things haven't changed since you were here last."

"Wait, one more question?"

Linda paused. "Okay, shoot, but I need to run."

"You mentioned *issues* with Pietro. Anything serious?"

Linda studied him for a moment, wondering why he was interested. "Well, not really, not until last year. Cesare took an offer to become assistant cellar master at this big winery right here in the valley—an old enemy of Pietro's. It was a few months before you came the last time. From *babbo's* point of view—after all the things he'd done for him, all he'd taught him about wine, yada yada—it was nothing short of treachery. He threw him out of the villa the day he found out about it, which is why he wasn't here anymore when you showed up.

"How did Nola feel about that?" Julie asked. "Throwing out her son?"

"How do you think? But if anything, she was madder at Cesare than she was at *babbo*. I think down deep she thought the kid had gone out of his way to screw up a pretty decent situation—which he had—and what he got was what he deserved. At the same time, well, he *was* her son, and she and Pietro had some pretty good dustups about it. You could probably hear them in Florence. But there was only one *padrone* here, and it wasn't Nola."

"So Cesare must have been pretty ticked off at both of them," Gideon said.

"Not as ticked off as *babbo* was at him. *Babbo* cut him out of his will, disowned him. Or rather, he was *going* to. It was the first thing he was going to do when he got back from the mountains. 'You are henceforth no longer the son of Pietro Cubbiddu.'" She shrugged. "But of course, he never did get back, so Cesare wound up getting the exact same share as the brothers got—from the will, I mean. Which is a damn shame, in my opinion. *Babbo* probably turned over in his grave. Or he would have if he'd had one at the time."

"Well, how—" Gideon started.

"No, I really have to go. Luca and Cesare will screw everything up without some responsible adult supervision. Talk to you later. Bye-bye."

Julie and Gideon, still seated at the table, watched her leave. Then Julie looked at Gideon curiously. "Are you thinking what I think you're thinking?"

"I suspect so. One more person with a reason to murder Pietro—to murder both of them, really."

"That's what I was thinking you were thinking, all right. I was thinking it too."

"Great minds," said Gideon. "Well, I'll tell Rocco about all this tomorrow. I'm not sure how happy it's going to make him, though. What do you say, shall we go?"

"Let's take what's left of the *zeppole* for John," Julie said. "After a day out with Marti, he'll appreciate them."

"After a day out with Marti, he'll *need* them," Gideon said, picking up the carton.

NINE

THE Figline Valdarno of today is basically a small manufacturing center and Florence-area bedroom community, but some of it is centuries old, and Villa Antica was situated half in, half out of the old part. Half in, half out of the city, for that matter. The buildings of the one-time convent were just within the ancient city walls, with a hundred-foot section of the wall, including a romantic and evocative watchtower, providing the back border of its formal garden. Once upon a time, Gideon assumed, this beautiful, enclosed garden had been the nun's cloister. It had probably looked much the same then, six hundred years ago, as it did now, with four paths, bordered by well-pruned boxwoods, that intersected at its center, making four symmetrical triangles of lawn, lush and closely mowed. At the center, where the pathways met, there was an old stone fountain, now lichen-encrusted and still. Set along the outer edges of the lawns were clay olive oil jugs planted with shrubs. Lined up along the back wall was a row of cypress trees spaced a few feet apart. It was this beautiful garden that Gideon had most looked forward to seeing again, a lovely, tranquil space equally conducive to quiet contemplation or—even better—free-floating woolgathering.

But the greater part of the winery's property extended well beyond this enclave, on the other side of the wall. Go through a truck-sized passage that had been cut through the wall's five-foot-thick, buttressed base, and you were at the foot of row upon row of trellised vineyards that marched in gracefully arching ranks up and over and around the nearby low hills. If he remembered correctly, there were something like four hundred acres of them: mostly Sangiovese, merlot, and cabernet, but a couple of smaller areas of whites as well.

The villa building itself consisted of a large central section and two attached smaller wings that enclosed the two sides of the garden. The three wings were connected by a long, porticoed terrace that ran along the back of the central building and constituted the garden's front border. The central building now held the winery. The north wing contained the kitchen, the laundry, and the onetime refectory, which was essentially unchanged and still used for formal tastings and occasional dinners, mostly for members of the wine club that Linda had started. The larger south wing, once the sisters' living quarters, was now the Cubbiddus' residence. What had originally been thirty-five airless and austere cubicles were now five spacious, splendid apartments for the family and two smaller but almost equally handsome guest suites, all with canopied platform beds; twelve-foot ceilings; eighteenth-century furniture; nameless, noseless Roman busts on marble pedestals; and age-darkened old oil paintings. The Laus were being put up in one of the guest suites, the Olivers in Cesare's old apartment, as before.

Gideon and Julie had arrived a little after five, two hours before the reception, and with John having not yet shown up, they were on their own, and they spent the time wandering over the property on both sides of the city wall. Linda had said that nothing had changed, but something had, and in their opinion, Villa Antica was the poorer for it.

Despite Pietro's two decades on the mainland, the old patriarch had never felt himself to be in anything but an alien culture. To ease his longing for home, he'd created a little piece of rural Barbagia right there in the heart of worldly, trendy Tuscany. The last time they'd been here, there had been a fire pit and a kiln-shaped clay oven wedged into the niche created where a buttress jutted out from the wall. The goat or lamb or hare that had been served every day at lunch had spent the preceding morning roasting there. And just out-side the wall through a second passageway, this one human-size, had been a muddy, wire-fence enclosure that held six or seven primitive wooden pens. In them had been the living lambs and goats, along with chickens, rabbits, pigs, and even a couple of full-grown, small dairy cattle.

It was Pietro Cubbiddu's homesick approximation of the Sardin-ian *fattoria* in which he'd grown up; a primitive family homestead, basic but self-sustaining. But Franco was neither a sentimentalist nor a lover of old Sardinia. The pens, like the oven, were no longer to be seen. In their place were a couple of hundred square yards of asphalt that served as a private parking area for the family and an overflow lot to use when the one in front of the villa was filled by wine-tasting visitors.

To Gideon the animals, the primitive oven, the rich farmyard stink, had all been wonderful; hands-on connections to a past not very long gone but never to return, at least not to Tuscany, and he missed finding them there. A year ago, Villa Antica had been a one of a kind, like no other winery they'd ever seen. Now there were probably ten others right there in the valley that might easily be confused with it. Gideon wondered if the same was true of its wines.

They'd walked back to the winery wing of the villa to look around there as well. The old tasting room had changed quite a bit too. For one thing, it wasn't there any more. In Pietro's day, it had been in one of the old chapels, a cramped little windowless place that had a claptrap trestle table as its counter—a slab of old plywood nailed to some sawhorses—with a few bottles set out for that day's tasting. Five or six stools. No room for tables. If there were any decorative touches, Gideon couldn't remember what they might have been. But whatever else it was, the place hadn't been bogus funky, it was *genuinely* funky, a very different thing. *Sans pretensions*, as the French would say; nothing if not nondescript.

Under Franco, however, the chapel had been converted to a storeroom for equipment replacement parts. The new tasting room, sunlit and spacious, was housed where the old choir had been. A couple of the old stained-glass windows were still in place, but otherwise it had been completely—and expensively—redone. It was all clean lines, pale walls of flawless, satiny birchwood, and abstract copper sculptures. The slick, faux-marble tasting counter was thirty feet long, and behind it was a softly backlit, twelve-level wine rack that ran its full length. There were eight or ten small, round tables, and every one of them had people sitting at it, sipping wine and wearing astute, judicious wine-evaluation faces.

"Wow, it's beautiful," Julie had breathed. "And obviously, it's doing very well."

There was no arguing with that, but Gideon hadn't been happy with it all the same. "I suppose so, but it doesn't feel . . . I don't know, *real*."

"Feels real to me."

"You know what I mean," he'd grumbled. "It's too smooth, too *gleaming*. I don't feel as if I'm in a winery."

"Well, where else would you be?" She'd waved a hand at the counter, the bottles, the people drinking.

"Frankly, it feels more like I'm in some yuppie bar in Rome. On the Via del Corso, maybe."

Julie laughed. "And where would you prefer to be, in some dank, dark cellar? Maybe somewhere that looks like a setting for 'The Cask of Amontillado'?"

Gideon had thought about that for a moment. "Well . . . yeah," he'd said.

JULIE decided to go to their apartment and put her feet up for a while, but Gideon was still in the mood for wandering. He went down a set of stone steps to the barrel room, off-limits to the public except on organized tours, which were given only a peek at it from one end. He was hopeful that Franco wouldn't have worked his heavy-handed, modish wizardry there, and he was right. The barrel room—the old crypt—was beautiful; just as it had been in Pietro's day. Running the full length of the church above, well over a hundred feet, it was stone-walled, windowless, and dimly lit by dangling, unshaded bulbs. Four long rows of oak barrels ran almost from one end of the room to the other, the barrels set on their sides on adze-cut wooden trestles. The place looked the way an ancient wine cellar should: dank, spooky, moldy, and cobwebby. And it smelled terrific, a wine-lover's idea of paradise. It had been one of Pietro's favorite places in the villa, Gideon remembered, and at the far end a beat-up, wine-stained table and a few rickety chairs in the corner had served as a sort of family tasting room, where father and sons would meet to sample and judge the progress of their products.

To his surprise, it was in use. When he heard the drone of echoing voices coming from that direction, he looked down the corridor between the two right-hand rows of barrels, and there were Nico and Franco and some others he couldn't make out, gathered at the old table. On the table he could see several open bottles of wine. Franco, facing in his direction, spotted him right away.

"Well, well, can that be the famous Skeleton Detective himself?" he called in English, peering down the long aisle, one hand across his forehead as if to shield his eyes from the near nonexistent light. "Come join us." He used the hand to wave Gideon over. "We are in grave need of an educated palate and an unbiased mind, but we'll settle for you instead."

Franco Cubbiddu could sometimes demonstrate a dry wit, but he didn't do "jocular" very well and was wise enough not to try it too often. A year older than Luca, he had an obvious familial resemblance to his earthy, outgoing younger brother, but he was an attenuated Luca, long and thin, with sharper features—his nose, his eyebrows, his mouth were all straight lines—and an air altogether more arid and contained. Still, as Gideon approached, Franco tried a smile—his smiles were painful to watch, seeming to overstretch dry lips that weren't meant for the job. Then an easy wave, indicating the one empty chair. That single, magisterial gesture made it crystal clear that he was the man in charge now that Pietro was gone. This, of course, had been expected by everyone who knew them. In the Barbagia, primogeniture ruled, and in his heart of hearts, Pietro had never stopped being a Barbagian. Of course he would leave the winery in Franco's charge (unless he'd decided to sell it, of course, which he hadn't lived to do).

In the two remaining chairs were Luca, Nico, and a large, portly man in his late fifties with a self-satisfied, jowly face and a natural "don't-you-try-to-pull-anything-with-me" expression on it. This was Severo Quadrelli, not a Cubbiddu relative in the technical sense of the term, but one of the family in every other. It took him a moment to place Gideon, but when he did, he nodded soberly at him without getting up. In his tightly knotted dark tie, his three-piece suit of herringbone tweed (much too heavy for a Tuscan September, Gideon would have thought), and his thumbs hooked in the armholes of his waistcoat, he looked more like an actor playing a successful lawyer—a 1930s lawyer—than a real one. His hair, elegantly graying at the temples, was neatly parted an inch to the left of the center line. And he was the first man Gideon had met in decades who wore a vest-pocket watch on a chain. A pair of pince-nez on a string would have provided the perfect finish to the image, but maybe it was too outré, even for Quadrelli. Instead, he'd opted for the nearest thing in eyewear: a pair of round spectacles with steel rims that were so thin they were almost invisible.

He'd been Pietro's oldest friend, an upcoming young Florentine attorney when they'd met a quarter of a century ago. At that time, being fresh off the ferry from Sardinia, Pietro was trying to buy the decrepit old convent/winery that was to become Villa Antica. Quadrelli had been representing the absentee owner, a signor Cocozza, but he'd been an honest broker. When the scurrilous Cocozza tried to put over a fast one on the trusting greenhorn (Pietro, accustomed to handshakes, not contracts, had no lawyer of his own), Quadrelli had refused to go along. That had gotten him fired, and in righteous indignation he'd switched sides to energetically represent Pietro's interests with no more than a promise of payment sometime in the future.

The promise had been fulfilled within two years. They'd become fast friends, and Severo had come to serve as Pietro's trusted counselor, formal and informal, not only in legal matters, but in all things mainland-Italian. In time Villa Antica had prospered to the extent that Severo had given up his position with a Florence firm and taken a generous yearly retainer to concentrate solely on the winery and the Cubbiddu family as their attorney and financial manager. Julie and Gideon had met him on their visit of the previous year. At that time he had just been coaxed by Pietro into finally moving into one of the guest apartments in the villa's residential wing, living among the Cubbiddus and taking his meals with them. One of the family, indeed.

"Ah, Linda, she tell me you come," he said in his mellow, authoritative bass. "Is good to see you again. Welcome, welcome here."

Interestingly, while it was Severo who had reputedly convinced Pietro that fluency in English was a must for the sons, he himself, a cosmopolitan and well-educated man, sounded like a fresh-off-the-boat Italian in an old vaudeville skit. *Leenda, she tell-a me you come-a. . . .*

Not for the first time, Gideon wondered if his own Italian might not be quite as smooth as he imagined.

"Thank you, signor Quadrelli," he answered. "It's good to be here, and I'm glad to see you again." He spoke in English. To a self-regarding and somewhat pompous man like Severo, doing otherwise would have been perceived as a slur on his linguistic abilities.

There was a bit of friendly chatting, and then Franco, showing himself to be a busy man with many responsibilities, rapped on the table to bring them back to business. On the table were two partially emptied bottles of red wine and one full one, uncorked, along with a dishwasher rack half full of stemmed, ballooned wineglasses, a pile of cloth napkins, a pitcher of water, a basket of broken-up bread sticks, and a metal bowl with a little spat-out wine in the bottom. Eight used wineglasses stood in a clump a little away from the other things.

Franco now spoke in Italian. "*Nico, si prega di versare il vino.*" He gestured at the full bottle, making a pouring motion.

As Nico poured portions into each glass, Luca caught his arm to get a look at the label. "The 2010 Sangiovese grosso? What are we tasting this one for?"

Nico answered. "I'm off to the Wine Retailers Expo in Basel in a few days, and I need to know what to tell them about it. Will we be releasing it this year or not? Should I bring a couple of cases with me, or shouldn't I?"

"I can give you the answer right now," Luca responded. "No. It'll need another year at least. The tannin will still be too high. It'll be rough."

"You're wrong, Luca," Franco said. "I tasted it myself this morning. In my opinion it's ready."

Luca raised an eyebrow. "So what are you asking us for?"

"Because I am sincerely interested in your opinions."

"Fine, I just gave it. Not ready."

"I suggest you taste it first, Luca. You're forgetting something. This was the first of our wines to undergo maceration and extraction by means of the new rotary fermenter."

Gideon was pleased to see he could follow the conversation with ease. As he'd learned, technical terms were often practically interchangeable (*macerazione, estrazione, rotofermenter*).

Luca shook his head. "Rotary fermenter. God."

Except for a downturn of his mouth, Franco ignored the comment. "To begin, perhaps we should all have a little bread to clear our palates." It was hard for Gideon to tell whether it was a suggestion or an order, but they all followed it, including him. He plucked a breadstick from the basket, chewed away, and swallowed. They looked to Franco for further commands. Franco obliged.

"Nico, you begin. And if you're not going to be serious, then just stay out of it."

"Franco, there's no need to offend me. All right, let's see what we have here." He lifted his glass and went through as thorough a tasting routine as Gideon had ever seen. The glass was slowly rotated a couple of feet in front of his eyes, and then raised higher to study the wine's clarity and color against an overhead bulb. "Ah." He lowered the glass, swirled the wine, and stuck his nose as far into the glass as it would go. This was followed by an appreciative nod: so far, so good. At last, his lips were parted to admit half an ounce or so of the Sangiovese. The wine was held in his mouth while air was noisily and wetly slurped through it, then rolled around, from cheek to cheek, Finally, the metal bowl was lifted to his mouth and the wine spat into it. He gazed into the middle distance, down the long racks of barrels, sucking in his cheeks, then expanding them, then sucking them in again.

"This wine," he began, "it's—"

"Serious," Franco warned again, but Gideon could tell that Nico had a performance in mind, probably for his, Gideon's, benefit.

". . . it's elegant and yet . . . rustic . . . subtle yet . . . assertive . . ."

Franco sighed. "I should have known better," he mumbled to the walls.

". . . a big-hearted wine with overtones of leather and tobacco . . ." He was barreling along now, waving the glass around as he spoke. ". . . on a matrix of mushroom and meat—no, eggplant. But eggplant layered with—yes, cinnamon!"

They had all surely heard this kind of tomfoolery from him before, but their responses were very different. Severo sighed and looked the other way, but Luca was practically doubled over with laughter. Like old Pietro, he was easily amused, and when he was, he responded with gusto.

Not Franco. "I *said* that's enough," he said with more force. And to Gideon, with a stiff smile: "Why do I never learn?" Then he turned to Luca. "Luca?"

"No, seriously," Nico said, laughing, "it's all right, Franco, it's fine. I think I should take some with me. In fact, I would say that its eloquence is matched only by the subtlety of its—"

Franco waved him down with a disgusted gesture. "Just shut up, Nico."

Nico shrugged and poured himself a little more. "It's really hard not being appreciated."

"Luca?" Franco said again.

Like the others, Luca had already tried the wine, but now he poured a little more, took a piece of bread, dipped it into the glass, tossed the saturated chunk into his mouth, and slowly—very slowly—masticated.

Franco shook his long, bony head. "How you can tell what the wine tastes like with your mouth full of food . . ."

"I can do it because I'm not that interested in what it tastes like *without* food, Franco. For me—"

"Yes, Luca, yes, Luca," Franco said, making it clear that he'd heard from Luca on this subject more times than he cared to. "Can we just have your opinion on the wine, please."

Luca shrugged. "Not as bad as I expected."

"Would you mind trying to restrain your enthusiasm?" Franco said dryly.

"No, I mean just what I said. It's not a bad wine. You're right, it's not as tannic as I expected. It's even, in its way, a fairly good wine. But I'll be sorry to see it come out under our label, this year or any other year."

"I don't agree," said Severo. "What's wrong with it? I thought it was fine."

"Fine? Maybe, but also impossible to tell from a hundred other Sangioveses. If I put two glasses in front of you, could you tell the difference between this and a reserve from Carrucci? Or Castello Rugate?"

"Hmm," rumbled Quadrelli. "Well, now, I'd have to—"

"It's those damned cement mixers. They—"

Franco's eyes rolled ceilingward. "Not the cement-mixer speech again. We're in the twenty-first century now, Luca, and we're not running a little neighborhood family cantina. I have to worry about things you never have to think about: profits and losses and expenses. Efficiency. Effectiveness. Like it or not, those 'cement mixers' make it possible to produce our wines on a predictable, consistent schedule instead of waiting around twiddling our thumbs while nature takes its course—slow this year, quick next year. Those devices you hate so much have allowed us to speed up our production by thirty percent, do you realize that? *Thirty percent!* I wonder if you really understand—"

Luca put his glass on he table and made a grumpy display of shoving it as far away from him as it could go. "Fine, fine, you do what you want, signor *padrone*, you're the boss, only . . . ah, Franco, I would have thought if there was one thing *babbo* taught us, it was to trust nature to take its course, to help the fruit become what's in its essential character to be, not to hurry into a false maturity before its time."

"You're scaring me, Luca," Nico said. "You're really starting to sound like *babbo*. Are you channeling him or something?"

"And for his time, *babbo* was right," Franco said, "but he was from another century—the nineteenth, really, even more than the twentieth. I would think you'd understand that, Luca. With the proper application of modern scientific principles, we can force the grapes to—"

That brought an incredulous laugh from Luca. "Force the grape! How do we *force* the grape to do what it doesn't want to do?"

"We could always try using techniques of enhanced interrogation," Nico said, pouring himself a little more of the wine.

"Now, Luca," Severo put in, sounding like a chuckly, wise old owl of an uncle. "When Franco says 'force,' he doesn't mean literally—"

"I don't need you to interpret what I mean, signor lawyer," Franco snapped, upon which Severo's jaws clamped shut so hard that his teeth clacked and his jowls jiggled. His neck shrank into his shoulders (very owl-like, but no longer very avuncular) and he stared fixedly at the table, his ears slowly reddening. Apparently, thought Gideon, he wasn't quite so much one of the family after all, not quite so much the trusted and respected consigliere he'd been under Pietro's rule. And he still hadn't gotten used to the new state of affairs.

"I most certainly do mean 'force' in its literal sense," Franco went on. "With today's methods we can get *more* from the grape than it started with. Cross-flow filtraters, rotary—"

Luca made a disgusted motion. "Look, Franco, why are we wasting our time with this anyway? You know we're going to release it— you already said you liked it—so what are we even discussing it for? Just go ahead. It's your show now, isn't it?"

Gideon was getting uncomfortable. The atmosphere in the Cubbiddu household was another thing that wasn't quite the same as it had been in Pietro's day either. Oh, he'd seen a couple of wine and winemaking arguments among the family that were louder and livelier than this one, but the chill in the air, the edginess—that was something new.

"I'll let that pass, Luca," Franco said in his flattest monotone. "And now I'd be interested in hearing from our American colleague. Gideon, what do you think of the wine?"

"Ah. Well—"

He was saved by Luca, who exploded out of his chair and into English. "Jesus Christ, it's after seven! The reception! They're waiting for us out on the terrace! Franco, let's go!

"Hey, don't worry about it," Nico said. "Linda and Maria have everything in hand, and the caterers have already set everything up. Your people are very happy, believe me. They've got good wine, they've got good food, life is good. I don't think they're feeling too neglected."

But Luca and Franco were already halfway to the staircase, and Quadrelli got up too, more slowly. "I believe I'll drop in on that myself."

That left Nico and Gideon at the table. Nico was looking at him, an inquisitive smile on his face. He wasn't drunk, but he was happily buzzed.

Gideon waited for him to say something. "What?" he finally asked.

"Oh, I was just waiting to hear what you were going to say. What do you think of the wine?"

Gideon picked up his glass. "Ah. Well—"

"Yeah, I already heard that part."

"Okay, then." He sipped, swallowed, nodded, put the glass down, and authoritatively considered the aftertaste. "Mm . . . in my opinion, I would say it's . . . elegant yet rustic . . . leather . . . tobacco . . . eggplant under a layer of . . . of . . ."

"Cinnamon," Nico said.

"Well, no, I was thinking dorrigo pepper and viburnum bark. And maybe a tinge of kokam seed."

Nico laughed appreciatively and took a taste from his glass, then reached for the bottle. "Hey, we've got time; here, have another shot with me." He upended the bottle over Gideon's glass. Nothing came out. "Oops, sorry about that. Now how do you figure that happened?" He seemed honestly puzzled.

T E N

GIDEON had been told that eighteen people had signed up for the class, the maximum that Luca would accept. All of them seemed to be at the reception. Most of them were women; all were American. In the slanting evening sun, the porticoed stone terrace that fronted the garden was beautiful. The old marble columns were a buttery gold. Two buffet tables lined up along the wall of the main building held hors d'oeuvres and bottles of Villa Antica wine. Behind them, two tuxedoed young men smiled and expertly filled plates and glasses for the attendees. Another waiter circulated with a tray that held wine and appetizers. Most of the attendees were sitting in twos and threes at round tables that appeared to have been taken from the tasting room, happily shoveling in bruschetta, anchovies, and miniature tortellini, and washing them down with generous swallows of the 2005 Villa Antica Carmignano Riserva and one of their rare whites, a 2009 trebbiano. From the noise level of the conversation and laughter, it was clear that the festivities had gotten going well before the official seven o'clock opening time. And as Nico had surmised, nobody seemed to be the least upset about the late start of formalities.

Julie, Marti, and John were already there, speaking with a six-foot-tall, formidable-looking woman, who, unlike just about everybody else, already seemed bored. While she spoke, her eyes continued to cast about, as if hoping to find someone more interesting to talk to. Gideon was waved over and introduced.

His name produced a modest flicker of interest. "You know, I think I've heard of you. Aren't you the Bone Doctor?" She had the kind of voice that goes with a lorgnette, fluty and imperious.

"Skeleton Detective," the always-helpful John corrected.

"Yes. So what is it that a Skeleton Doctor does exactly, anyway?"

"Skeleton Detective," said John.

"Whatever."

This unpromising exchange went on for another minute or so and was then cut short by Franco's taking his place behind a lectern at one end of the terrace and managing to look both dignified and in a hurry at the same time. People quickly found seats. Gideon took the chance of risking Franco's disapproval by going to get a glass of the trebbiano before he squeezed in beside Julie, John, Marti, and Linda at one of the larger tables. He was the last person to sit, and Franco impatiently, pointedly waited until he was settled.

"I'm Franco Cubbiddu," he announced, "the president and CEO of Villa Antica Winery, and I want to welcome you to our facilities and wish you a very pleasant and productive week. Thank you. Luca?" He turned on his heel and headed back into the winery.

"Short and sweet," Marti said.

Linda laughed. "Franco might have a fault or two, but long-windedness isn't one of them."

Luca was now up at the lectern. "I won't take much of your time," he said. "You're here tonight to enjoy a little camaraderie and a few good wines. Tomorrow morning is when we get serious. For those of you who are staying not in Figline but in Florence, the easiest way to get here is to take the train from the Santa Maria Novella station. There is an 8:02 train that will put you in Figline at 8:37. A five-minute walk will bring you here with time enough for a cup of coffee and a brioche before we get started at nine. You'll find the rest of the logistical details in your packets and I'll answer any questions tomorrow. For now I would like to very briefly summarize the philosophy of *Vino e Cucina*."

He took a deep breath and surveyed the crowd, smiling and relaxed. He looked happy.

"This is a guy who likes having an audience," Gideon murmured to Julie.

That produced an elbow nudge and a smile. "Takes one to know one."

"First, the *vino* part. Have you ever wondered why Italian wines are so good with food? Because that's what they're made for, to go with food, to be enjoyed, and not merely *with* a meal, but as an essential *part* of it. It isn't made for people to spit into a bowl. It's made for them to *drink*, and to drink with food, with a meal. Wine is like bread or pasta. Without it a meal is not complete." He was growing more animated and enthusiastic. His opening sentences might have been prepared, Gideon thought, but now he was speaking spontaneously, straight from the heart. This was a continuation of the argument he'd been having with Franco, Gideon understood. Without Franco's presence Luca was a lot better at it: less heat, more light.

"And it's like anything we love to eat. Would you chew up prosciutto or *ossobuco* and spit it out? Of course not."

People were politely nodding their agreement, and there was some scattered clapping.

"And the *cucina* part? It's simple. You will not learn how to prepare nouvelle cuisine this week. In good Italian cooking, there is no such thing as *cucina nuova*. When it comes to preparing food, being trendy or innovative is not something we aim for. If a recipe has survived for four generations, handed down from mother to daughter, we figure it must be pretty good, so why would we want to change it? Our goal isn't to improve or build on grandma's dishes, it's to come as close as we can to *reproducing* them—but with the advantages of today's modern kitchen equipment and market goods. In fact—"

He stopped suddenly, straightened up from leaning over the lectern, and his low, husky laugh rolled out over the terrace. "In fact, I see my wife letting me know that it's time for me to sit down. Well, you'll hear more than enough from me in the next few days."

He had brought a glass of Sangiovese with him to the lectern, and now he raised it in toast to his audience—"*Buon appetito, mi amici!*"

DINNERS at the winery were part of the *Vino e Cucina* package on most nights, so when the reception wound down, Luca, Linda, Julie, and Marti went off to the refectory with the others, leaving John and Gideon on their own. Luca had provided them with a few suggested Figline restaurants, but none of them hit the right note with John.

"You know what I'd really like?"

"Yeah, but I don't think you're going to find a Big Mac in Figline Valdarno. Some Chicken McNuggets, maybe."

"Ho, ho."

"One of those giant Florence beefsteaks?"

"Nah, let's wait till we're in Florence for that." Both of them having had a few glasses of wine, they'd ruled out driving to the city. "But how about a pizza? I bet we can find one of those in Figline."

A perusal of the phone book turned up Ristorante Pizzeria Mari e Monti a few blocks from Villa Antica, and they walked there in a light, not unpleasant drizzle. It turned out to be a cozy little place with arched brick entryways, rough-stuccoed walls, warm lighting, and a big, ceramic wood-burning oven. Even with his tenuous hold on Italian, John had no trouble with the menu, quickly finding the pizza that struck the deepest chord in his essential being.

"*Pizza carnivora*," he announced. "*Mamma mia!*"

Gideon ordered *frutti di mare*, the seafood pizza. He asked about local beers, and the waiter recommended Birrificio Artigianale pale ale. "Is most same like bitter," he said, apparently thinking they were British. Gideon said fine, and John went along with him.

The beers came quickly, and while they worked at them, Gideon explained what Linda had told him at the wine festival about Cesare, the little-known stepson.

"Whoa," John said. "You're saying you think this guy killed the two of them?"

"No, I'm nowhere near there. Not yet, anyway. All I'm saying is that Rocco said that one reason they were so sure that Pietro did it was that everything pointed to him and nothing at all pointed to anybody else. They didn't have any other viable suspects. Any suspects at all. Well, wouldn't you say Cesare would be a viable suspect? Pietro was about to cut him out of his will."

"So why would he kill Nola? Christ, she was his *mother*, wasn't she?"

"And you never heard of anybody killing his mother before."

"Well, okay, that's a point. But *why* would he kill her?"

"That I don't know."

"What about the fact that it was Pietro's gun?"

"John, I still don't like it that that gun just happened to stay with him while he was falling two hundred feet and bouncing off rocks all the way."

"So you're still on about that."

"Yes, I am. It just doesn't sit right. You know that suicides generally don't hang on to the gun. A lot more likely for it to get flung five or six feet away than to stay in his hand."

"Well, actually, you got me thinking about that, and I came up with a perfectly good reason it didn't happen this time."

"Which is?"

"Cadaveric spasm," John announced brightly, referring to the rare bodily reaction in which a kind of rigor mortis sets in instantly (rather than several hours later), locking the muscles into whatever position they were in at the moment of death. In that case, if a gun had been grasped in one's hand to shoot oneself, it would conceivably continue to be gripped so rigidly that it would be hard to pry or jar it out of the death clasp. "It happens," he added when he saw Gideon's dubious expression.

"That's so, it happens, and I suppose it also happens a gun can get stuck in a jacket in such a way that any fingerprints that might be on it are still going to be there a year later—not that I've ever seen it personally, of course."

"Well, no, me neither," John agreed. "But it *could* happen, right?"

"Sure, but what would you say the odds are of both things happening together? Cadaveric spasm, and then the leather-jacket thing."

"Not great," admitted John. He held up his beer bottle. "Hey, you know, this isn't bad. Hoppy, malty. Citrusy, is that a word?" Of the two of them, John was the beer authority.

The waiter came back with their pizzas. John looked at his with a sigh. "I'm in hog heaven." The pizza was thick with prosciutto, ham, pepperoni, and mortadella. And a few chunks of artichoke for the health-minded. Gideon's looked terrific too, a plain marinara sauce, no cheese, covered with mussels and clams in their shells, shrimp, and crabmeat.

"Well," Gideon said, cutting into his, "maybe it'll all become clearer tomorrow."

"Boy," John said, "will you look at all this bacon?"

"It's prosciutto."

"You call it prosciutto, I call it bacon," John sang happily. "Let's call the whole thing off."

ELEVEN

IN the morning, Gideon and John had to get started for Florence before the attendees' buffet breakfast had been laid out, but they found the kitchen, begged some caffe latte from Maria, and took them out to the garden to drink, which they did, John wrapped in moody silence. "Okay, I think I'm probably capable of walking now," he said after he'd gone back for and drunk his second giant cupful, but with a dirty look at Gideon. He still hadn't forgiven him. "Only don't expect me to talk."

Considering that it was a workday, they thought they'd be better off avoiding the morning traffic into Florence, so they walked to the Figline train station to catch the 7:11 on its way from Rome to Florence, which showed up in Figline bang on time. Except for the signs in Italian, it might have been a morning commuter train in any American city: reasonably clean, rows of seats all facing the same direction (as opposed to European-style separate compartments), serious, suited businessmen reading *Il Corriere Fiorentino* or *Milano Finanza*, fashionably dressed young women applying the final touches to their hair or makeup, and a few sulky, slouching teenagers coming in for a day in the city and up to no good.

John ordered an espresso in a plastic cup from a vendor who worked his way up the aisle, and it seemed to finally do the trick. "Okay, you can talk to me now."

But by then they were already pulling into Florence's Santa Maria Novella train station exactly at 7:39, as scheduled, and all Gideon said was, "I guess Mussolini really did get the trains to run on time."

"Yeah, sure, except when they have a strike," a man behind him muttered in good American English. "But no sweat, that's only once or twice a week or so. Have a nice day."

As Rocco had told them, it took about ten minutes to get to Borgo Ognissanti, a narrow street of somber, gray, two-and-three story palazzos that cut diagonally through the city. *Carabinieri* headquarters was in one of these, a few doors down from the equally gray and somber façade of the thirteenth-century All Saints Church, which had given the street its name. They walked by the headquarters building twice before spotting the inconspicuous CARABINIERI COMANDO PROVINCIALE plaque beside the tall, double-doored entry. Like most of the entrances to these old palazzos, it was big enough to admit a good-sized coach, and it opened not into the interior of the building but into a courtyard. A couple of steps into the courtyard there was a roofed corridor, in which a uniformed young *carabiniere* sat behind a counter and in front of a switchboard.

He looked up with a smile. "Signori?"

When Gideon told him they were there to see *Tenente* Gardella, he said a few words into a telephone and a minute later a heavy, studded wooden door creaked open a few feet away, and out popped

Rocco, resplendent in a smart, tailored uniform of dark blue, with epaulets, medals, ribbons, and collar tabs on the jacket and crisp red stripes running down the sides of the trousers.

"Whoa, look at you," John said. "You're beautiful. Jeez, I wish they dressed us like that in the Bureau."

"Believe me, you don't," Rocco said. "So come on up." Moving at a trot, he led them up two flights of stone steps and into his office, the kind of office that any mid-level cop anywhere in the world might have. Not an office, per se, but a twelve-by-twelve space enclosed by three fabric-covered, shoulder-high partitions, the open side facing out into a bullpen area of desks for the less lofty. Rocco's office had no ornaments of any kind, and the furniture—a two-drawer file cabinet, a desk, a desk chair, and two visitors' chairs—was all stainless steel and vinyl. The only books were a few procedural manuals and volumes of legal code that leaned crookedly between a pair of inexpensive metal bookends on top of the file cabinet.

Rocco sat behind his desk and motioned John and Gideon into the visitors' chairs. "Got it right here," he said, poking through the clutter on his desktop. "Somewhere. Ah. Here. I was able to get away with making a couple of copies. You can't take them with you, though."

He pushed copies of Pietro's autopsy report across the desk, leaned back, and waited.

John glanced only briefly at his before tossing it back down with a snort. "This isn't gonna mean too much to me, Rocco. Wouldn't mean much to me even if it were in English. Can I get a cup of coffee somewhere in here while the doc does his shtick?"

"Yeah, sure, I'll take you. I could use one myself. What about you, Gid?"

"Um . . . no." Already, he was absorbed.

"We'll be back in a minute."

They were out the door and halfway through the bullpen before Gideon even nodded. "Take your time," he mumbled, or at least he meant to.

Autopsies of skeletal remains that are performed by forensic anthropologists are generally detailed and lengthy. When done by pathologists, however, they tend to be on the sketchy side, to put it mildly. It isn't that that pathologists are by nature less thorough or observant than anthropologists; it's a matter of where their interests and education lie, and the less soft tissue and fewer organs that are present, the less interested they are, and the less informed. Naturally enough, it works the other way around as well. Give Gideon a kidney or a liver or a lung to report on, and he wouldn't have much to say.

This particular report, having been performed by a *medico* named Bosco, consisted of only a page and a half. He hadn't even bothered to record all of the bones that were found, only the ones that had suffered damage, and even there, the trauma were merely listed in the most general way and not described at all. ("Multiple fractures of the left scapula, the left humerus, etc.") It certainly supported Rocco's statement that Pietro was as every bit as "busted up" as Nola, but it was nowhere near the detail Gideon would have liked. Dr. Bosco had, however, extended himself when it came to the presumptive cause of death. An oval, beveled hole, a ballistic entrance wound, had been found in the left temporal bone. On the opposite side of the skull, another larger *difetto*—the equivalent bland, undisturbing term *defect* would have been used in English—had been left where size-able parts of the right temporal, sphenoid, and parietal bones had been blown away. Pretty much the entire right half of the cranium was gone. Bosco's conclusion, like Rocco's—and Gideon's—was that Pietro had been shot, left to right, behind the eyes and almost straight across the head . . . a typical left-hander's suicide by handgun, as Rocco had pointed out.

In addition to the left scapula and humerus, the other postcranial traumas were fractures of seven of the twelve ribs (sides and rib-numbers not specified), the bones of the left arm and forearm—radius and ulna—the sacrum, eight of the twelve thoracic vertebrae, and four of the five lumbars.

"Huh," Gideon muttered to himself. "Almost totally axial. Except for the left shoulder and arm, the appendicular skeleton is undamaged."

"Come again?" said Rocco. He and John had returned without Gideon's noticing and were in their chairs sipping black coffee from tiny, espresso-sized cardboard cups.

"I was just remarking that the axial skeleton is all broken up, but the appendicular skeleton is hardly touched. Just the one arm."

"We *heard* you, Doc," John said. "We just don't know what you're talking about."

"Oh, right, sorry. Axial skeleton, the bones that form the central axis of the body."

"The spine," Rocco said.

"Yes, the vertebral column. Plus the skull and the ribs. The center pole of the body, more or less. Eighty bones in all."

"And the appendicular skeleton, those are, like, the appendages?" By way of illustration, John waved his arms around.

"Right, arms, legs, collarbones, scapulas. And the pelvis. The things that kind of hang off the central axis."

"Uh-huh. And?" John made a *go-ahead* motion.

"And what?" Gideon said.

"Aren't you now going to tell us how many bones the appendicular skeleton has?"

"No. Well, all right. The usual count is a hundred and twenty-six, if you insist."

"Thank you, I feel better. More complete, you know what I mean?"

Gideon spotted a third tiny cup of coffee on the desk. "Hey, is that for me?"

"Yup," Rocco said. "You said you didn't want it, but we figured you'd take it if we brought it."

"I'll take it if you don't want it," John said.

"No, thank you, I can deal with it." He downed the three ounces in a couple of swallows that lit him up. He shuddered pleasurably. "Thank you. Now *I* feel more complete. Okay. Now, you remember how Nola had all those broken bones in her legs, but hardly any above the waist, other than some vertebrae, and none at all in her arms?"

"Sort of," John said. "Which proved she was conscious when she fell, right? Because she landed on her feet."

" 'Proved' is maybe putting it a little strongly, but yes, that's right. But Pietro, you see, is almost the exact opposite: no broken bones at all below the hips, and—with the exception of the left arm and shoulder—no fractures to his appendicular skeleton."

"So he *didn't* land on his feet?"

"Correct. He landed flat on his back; well, apparently partly on his left side, it looks like. That would have been when the arm was broken. But legs, feet . . . all undamaged."

"Meaning he was probably *not* conscious when he fell." This from Rocco after a moment's processing.

"Correct."

"O . . . kay," John said thoughtfully. "So what does that tell us?

"Not much, I'm afraid, when you come down to it. It's interesting, but it doesn't really change anything; it just confirms what we thought before—that Pietro, unlike Nola, was dead before he fell. But we already knew that because the skull fragments found on site showed that he blew half his head off up at the top." He sighed.

"Well, what did you expect to find?"

"Who knows? I guess I was hoping for something a little more definitive, something that might lead in a constructive direction as to what really happened up there. I just cannot buy the idea of his climbing down the cliff to shoot her after *her* fall, and then huffing all the way back up to the top to kill himself. The more I think about it, the less sense it makes. You said that yourself, Rocco, and it's true."

They sat mulling this over for a little while, and then Gideon abruptly shook his head. "Nope, it's too weird. I tell you what, Rocco: I don't think Pietro killed her at all. I think you've got a double murder here."

"But that wouldn't explain—" Rocco began.

"There's a lot it doesn't explain," said Gideon. "But it *does* give us a credible answer to the question of why Pietro would have shot her down at the bottom and then climbed up to the top to shoot himself."

"The answer being that he didn't, is that what you mean?"

"Exactly. Someone else killed them both."

John nodded. "Seems like a possibility to me."

They both looked at Rocco. His response came only after taking in and letting out two long breaths. "Well, it doesn't to me. I mean, yeah, I guess it's possible but, let me tell you, you don't start a reinvestigation because something's *possible*. You need a lot more than that. Like a little evidence, for instance? You need someplace to start."

"Would a few plausible suspects help?"

"Depends on what you mean by 'plausible.'" But he didn't look optimistic.

Gideon told him about the once-imminent sale to Humboldt-Schlager and what it would have meant to the Cubbiddu sons, and about Cesare and how Pietro had been on the verge of cutting him out of his will. Rocco listened, but it didn't make him any more receptive. "I appreciate all your help with this, I really do, and—who knows, maybe there's something to it. But I'm sorry, it's just not enough to get this thing reopened."

John agreed with him. "If it was my case, I'd have to say the same, Doc. Just because some other guy *might* have some possible motive . . . that's not grounds for committing your resources to a formal investigation. But," and he slowly shook his head, "*something's* sure screwy about the way it stands now."

"Nobody's arguing with you there," Rocco said.

"All right, let me introduce another possibility," said Gideon. "Another possible scenario."

Rocco lifted and eyebrow. "Could I stop you?"

"Not a chance," John said.

"Well, I was thinking about the vendetta angle," Gideon said. "Both families were upset with the two of them for getting married. Maybe this was the result. And then it was covered up to look like a suicide."

"They were married twenty-five years ago," Rocco said. "Why wait till now?"

"Maybe they didn't know where they were," John suggested.

"Nah. Look, I wondered about that myself at first, but that's not the way vendettas work. They don't cover up their assassinations. They *want* people to know who did it and why. And in Barbagia—I looked into this, see?—the standard finish is to shotgun the victims in the face, so the family can't even have the satisfaction of saying good-bye to them in an open casket."

"Nice people," John said. "Salt of the earth."

"Anyway," Rocco said, stifling a yawn, "it's all worth thinking about, but it's not enough to go on. Regardless of how weird the situation was—Pietro shooting her *after* she fell, then climbing back up to shoot himself—it's still where the evidence points. Mostly."

"Well, we tried," Gideon said. "Look, Rocco, I really think the family has a right to know what I've come up with, even if it doesn't add up to anything solid. It just doesn't feel right to keep it from them. I mean, living there, seeing them every day—I feel like some kind of sneak. And who knows? Maybe when they hear about it they'll come up with something more."

"I wouldn't count on that, but okay, sure. I wouldn't have any right to stop you anyway. And if they do come up with anything use-ful, let me know, will you? I'm keeping an open mind here. I just need more."

"KIND of a waste of time, wasn't it?" Gideon said on their walk back toward the station.

"You're telling me," John grumbled. "And for that you got me up in the middle of the night."

"John, I really don't think six thirty qualifies as the middle of the night. I understand some people regularly get up at that time."

"Yeah, but not on purpose. I should *still* be sleeping. This really messes up my twenty-four-hour biological clock, you know?"

"Gosh, pal, I'm really sorry. How can I ever make it up to you?"

John stopped and looked up and down the street. "Well, you could buy me a breakfast *panini* in that bar over there. That'd be a start." But as they headed toward the café-bar, he stopped again, looking worried. "Or should I have said *panino*? I mean, God forbid I should get it wrong."

"Tell you what," Gideon said. "How about if I buy you two of them? That will make the grammatical niceties moot."

TWELVE

"**THIS** is ridiculous," Franco Cubbiddu said with an impatient gesture at the clock, the only infringement on the pristine perfection of the walnut-paneled walls other than the thermostat and the light switches. "Who the hell does he think he is? I'll give him exactly two more minutes, and if he's not here by then, this meeting is concluded."

"Let's not be too hasty," Severo Quadrelli said. "I think it would behoove us to hear what he has to say."

Franco tapped his watch. "Two minutes."

The eldest Cubbiddu was not having one of his better days. Things had started going wrong at breakfast. When he'd come down for his latte, brioches, and fruit—a time usually given to quiet reflection—he'd found the refectory full of jabbering, cackling attendees of *Vino e Cucina* (about which he'd completely forgotten). He'd made a quick job of it, but even so he hadn't been able to avoid a slew of inane questions: What wine would he recommend to go with chili?

Why didn't Villa Antica produce any fruit-flavored wines? Had he heard about the new method (scientifically proven!) of aging wines by means of a "magnetic flux path" that produced the same results in thirty minutes that would otherwise require laying down the wine for years?

On escaping he'd told Maria that from then on, until the conference was over, he would take his breakfast in his apartment. But as far as today was concerned, the damage had been done: his morning was ruined. And then an hour later had come a stupid dispute with Amerigo, his dim-witted cellar master, who was refusing to let his workers use the brand-new, phenomenally expensive, ozone-based sanitizing system because he'd heard somewhere that the ozone would get in the air and give them all cancer. Ordinarily, Franco would never have heard about it because dealing with this kind of problem was Luca's job, but Luca was busy with his damned cooking school, and Franco had wasted half an hour of his own time setting Amerigo straight, or rather convincing him that if he didn't stop arguing and start following orders, he'd be out of a job.

It was all too much to put up with. Never again would Villa Antica host *Vino e Cucina*, that was certain. If Luca wanted to put it on again next year, he would have to find someplace else.

And then, to top it all off, into his office a couple of hours ago had walked Cesare, twitching and jittery and looking even more like hell than the last time Franco had seen him, when he had appeared, unwelcome and uninvited, at Pietro's memorial service. He had something of importance to say to the brothers Cubbiddu, he said now, and they would be well advised to assemble at two o'clock in the small conference room to hear it. Oh, and it might be a good idea for them to have *il consigliere*—fat, old Quadrelli—there as well. Thank you.

That had been it. No explanation of the reason, no inquiry as to whether the time was convenient or whether the conference room would be free. Just be there.

So here they were, gathered around their glossy new conference table in their new, mesh-backed, seven-hundred-euro Aeron chairs, watching the clock's minute hand slowly stutter its way toward 2:06.

"If he doesn't show up pretty soon, I'm out of here too," Luca said. "Afternoon break is over at two thirty. I have to be back with my class."

At 2:10 Cesare finally shuffled in accompanied by a gray-haired, square-built woman well into her seventies carrying a worn, old-fashioned, brown briefcase with straps, and dressed in a blue velour tracksuit and bulky, clacking Birkenstock sabots. No socks. On Cesare's face was a smug, self-satisfied look, a cat-that-was-about-to-eat-the-canary expresssion that raised alarm bells in Franco and Luca. What was their little turd of a stepbrother up to now?

Even Nico, who was the closest thing Cesare had to an ally, didn't like the looks of it. He didn't like Cesare's looks either. The previous weekend he had driven to Florence for the sole purpose of having a heart-to-heart with Cesare, toward the end of getting him to sign up for (yet another) drug rehab program before he was too far gone altogether. Nico had offered to cover all expenses. Cesare had said he'd think about it, but from appearances, it didn't look as if he intended to take the advice. He was stoned. Nico's heart sank to look at him.

"Hoo-hoo, what do you know, the whole family's here," Cesare said. "I'm flattered."

"You asked us to be here," Franco told him coldly.

"No, I asked *you* to be here, Franco." He said it like a man who was enjoying a good joke.

"No, you asked—"

Luca began gathering himself to rise. "Good, if I'm not needed—"

The woman with Cesare interrupted. "You gentlemen are the family? The brothers? I think it might be better if you remained." She had a surprisingly resonant voice, straight from the chest and almost as deep as Quadrelli's basso.

Quadrelli now donned his mantle as Protector of the Clan. "I don't believe we know this lady?" he said to Cesare with rising inflection.

"This is my lawyer, signora Ornella Batelli."

The three brothers exchanged glances. A lawyer? Now what?

"Please sit down," Franco said, gesturing at the two empty chairs. He was coldly polite. "I'm Franco Cubbiddu, signora, and these are my brothers, Nico and Luca. That gentleman is *our* attorney, signor Severo Quadrelli. What can we do for you?"

Cesare answered. "I'm suing you," he said breathlessly. "That's right, I'm suing the shit out of you. Ha. Ha-ha."

Another shared, wary glance between the brothers. This was not going to go well.

"Now take it easy, bro," Nico said with his easygoing smile. "Let's not get carried away here."

"Screw you," Cesare said. "Bro."

"Oh, man, Cesare," Nico said with a genuinely sad shake of his head. There had been a time when he had loved Cesare more than he'd loved anyone else in the family other than Pietro. They had played together when no one else would play with them, they'd had their first taste of wine together, they'd created make-believe castles and fought make-believe battles in the vineyard with wooden stakes for swords for hours at a time. Time and time again, Nico, as the older boy, if

154

only by a few months, had taken his stepbrother's side against his own blood family. Cesare had responded by looking worshipfully up to him as his role model, his protector, and his one real friend among the Cubbiddus. Whatever Nico wore, or said, or did, Cesare had aped it.

Even now, despite the many changes in Cesare—the growing recklessness, the frightening free-fall into drug-addled stupidity and selfishness, and all the misery that went along with it—Nico still loved him, still had hopes, despite everything, that he could save him from himself and, against all odds, bring him back into the embrace of the family.

Not that he wasn't sympathetic to Franco's and Luca's feelings. It was certainly true that the kid wasn't the most agreeable person in the world. But he'd had a tough time of it. Not only was he the stepbrother—the son of the hated stepmother—but he'd wound up with the short end of the genetic stick when Pietro and Nola had joined families—a skinny, undersized little troll skulking among handsome, confident giants—and he'd never managed to fit in, although God knows he'd tried hard enough (which was part of the problem).

"Come on, Cesare, don't be like that," he said. "What kind of crap is this about suing us? Why don't you just tell us what's on your mind, and we can take it from there? You know, get it out on the table and talk it out."

"No, you don't get it, Nico. There's no *us*, there's only *him*. I'm suing Franco."

"Well, whatever it is," Nico said soothingly, "I'm sure we can work it out without involving all these lawyers. No offense, signora."

Cesare wasn't buying it. "Oh yes? Ha-ha. I'd like to see you work your way out of this. No, no, no, no, we're not talking anything out—"

When he began to blink and cough, Franco cut in flintily. "You're damn right we're not talking anything out. You've been treated far more fairly by my father and by this family than you deserve, and you know it. There's nothing to work out," he finished with a warning glance at Nico, who had looked as if he were about to speak.

"I quite agree," signora Batelli said. "There is nothing to work out. Let us be clear. We are not here to negotiate with you or to make demands. We are here, as a courtesy, to inform you of a civil action we are about to pursue."

The brothers' uneasiness increased. Despite the woman's age, there was an air of resolute immovability about her. Built along the lines of a washer-dryer combination, she brought to mind the alarming images of Bulgarian lady shot-putters from the 1950s, an impression the voice and the tracksuit did nothing to lessen.

Severo's eyebrows shot up. "A civil action?"

"My client intends to bring suit against Franco Cubbiddu in the amount of four million euros."

"*What!*" Franco demanded with a shriek of not-quite-hysterical laughter. "Are you out of your mind?"

Luca shook his head and addressed the fluorescent-lit ceiling. "I don't believe this."

Severo contributed a magisterial frown and a low, warning rumble: "See here . . ."

Nico just leaned over and banged his head on the table. "Aww, Cesare. You gotta be kidding me."

None of it discomposed the signora. "We intend to claim this amount as recompense for damages suffered by my client as a result of the murder of his mother, Nola Baccaredda Cubbiddu, by signor Cubbiddu—your father, gentlemen—in September of last year."

"Our *father*!" Franco exclaimed. "He's dead and gone. What are you suing me for?"

"As I'm sure signor Quadrelli will explain to you," said signora Batelli patiently, "in such cases, under Italian law, it is permissible to file against the estate and the heirs. We will be filing against you as the primary heir." She smiled at him. Nothing personal, of course.

"Now hold on right there," Severo said. "Just you hold on one minute. I have to tell you right now that what you're demanding is preposterous. No judge in his right mind would even consider such an outrageous sum as recompense for emotional damages suffered—"

Signora Batelli's forefinger rose. "Permit me, signor Quadrelli. We are speaking about emotional damages *and* monetary damages—"

"Monetary damages!"

Nico chimed in as well. "I honestly don't see how you were damaged, Cesare. Not in that way . . . monetarily? You got a lot of money from *babbo's* will, buddy—the same as I did, same as Luca did. I mean, you have to admit—"

"You don't see how? You don't see how?" The whispery drumming of Cesare's feet on the carpet, audible since he'd sat down, picked up speed. And now the new bumping of his knees against the underside of the table set it to thrumming. The kid himself was practically thrumming. "I'll tell you how. I'll tell you how." But he was racked with a ferocious, phlegmy bout of coughing. "I'll . . . I'll tell . . ."

He rummaged frustratedly through his pockets. "Shit—"

"I have it, Cesare," signora Batelli said, reaching into her briefcase for a small bottle of an Italian cough medicine.

Cesare snatched it from her hand almost before she'd gotten it all the way out, took a couple of gulps straight from the bottle, and flinched at the taste but seemed to find some relief. Nico, concerned, had gone to the phone and asked for some water to be brought. When it arrived, Cesare downed some, recovered himself a little more, and started to talk again, but was once more convulsed, this time spraying a grimacing Franco with water, cough medicine, and who knew what else. Cesare did some more pocket-plumbing and came up with a handkerchief that had obviously seen earlier use, with which he wetly, lengthily blew his nose. Not only Franco, but Luca, Nico, Quadrelli, and even signora Batelli all shifted their chairs a little further away from him.

"Perhaps it would be best if I continued, Cesare," signora Batelli said soothingly, upon which Cesare, lifted his hand in acquiescence. "You see, gentlemen, my client will contend—and I don't see how it can be denied—that the murder of his mother deprives him of an inheritance that is rightfully his."

"*What* inheritance?" Quadrelli demanded. "All of the Cubbiddus' property was held in her husband's name. All she owned in her own name were a few Baccaredda heirlooms . . . which I have made sure have gone to Cesare, as is only right."

Cesare, his coughing under control, if only barely, broke in. "He killed my mother, and he profited from it! I thought that was against the law in this country!"

"How did he profit from it?" Luca asked angrily. "He's *dead*."

"Well, yes, technically—"

A snort from Luca. "What the hell is 'technically' dead?"

"I mean . . ." He didn't quite cough, but another fit was clearly on its way if he continued. He gestured to signora Batelli, who took over.

"What my client means, of course, is that his *estate* profited by Nola's death, which, in a legal sense, can be interpreted as the same thing. And Franco Cubbiddu was the primary beneficiary of that estate."

"Now, signora." Severo was practically oozing condescension. "As an experienced attorney I'm sure you know perfectly well that, while it is true that our laws prohibit a murderer's profiting from his crime, that prohibition applies to the contents of the *victim's* will, not the murderer's, so you see, the issue is moot."

"Severo," Franco snapped, "will you kindly stop calling our father a murderer?"

"What would you call him?" Cesare snarled.

"Please, gentlemen," said Quadrelli, "I am speaking in general terms. Let me continue—"

But signora Batelli was running out of patience. "You do not understand me, signore. We are not challenging signor Cubbiddu's will. We are bringing a wrongful death suit—"

"A wrongful—"

"—to recover damages for the loss by my client of his mother's love, affection, companionship, and emotional support, as well as the financial and economic support that would have eventually ensued had she not been so tragically murdered."

"Please, signora," Severo said more severely, "do not play these semantic games with me. You know perfectly well that that your client has no standing from which to bring suit. The codes involved are entirely clear on this. If you are unfamiliar with them, I would be happy to provide you with the relevant citations."

Signora Batelli, now openly irritated by Quadrelli's manner, stood abruptly and shoveled papers into her attaché case. "As I've said, gentlemen, we're not here to argue. We came to tell you what to expect, and we have told you. Signor Quadrelli, you'll hear more formally from my office very shortly." A crisp nod. *"Arrivederla, signori.* Come, Cesare."

Cesare, tottering and blinking, already unsure of what had just transpired, followed her.

"You did well, Severo," Franco said once their visitors had left, although he didn't look so sure about it.

Severo accepted the praise with a sober nod.

"What you said is true, isn't it, Severo?" Luca asked. "He can't really do that, can he? Sue us? The little turd?"

Severo responded with a grave, sympathetic smile, kind and kingly. "I'm afraid he most certainly can, my boy."

THIRTEEN

IT had been overcast in Florence, but a fine, crisp day all the same, so John and Gideon, having been cooped up at the conference for most of the past week, had simply wandered the city for a few hours after their meeting with Rocco, not going into any museums or churches or palazzos but basking in the fresh air, the architecture, and the chic bustle.

Lunch had been at one of a string of funkily quaint old sidewalk eateries on Borgo San Lorenzo, the narrow, cobblestoned alley, now a pedestrian walkway, that served primarily to lead tourists to the Medici Chapel and the Laurentian Library. This particular place featured an outdoor menu held up by a four-foot-high plywood figure that looked like one of the Mario Brothers in a chef's hat. Mario's stubby, white-gloved, four-fingered hand pointed directly to a boldly lettered message at the top: *The Biggest, Most Delicious, Most Authentic* Bistecca alla Fiorentina *(Beefsteak Florence Style) in the City. One full kilo (2.5 pounds), only €21.*

"Now that's what I've been looking for," John said, stopping in front of it. "The real thing. What do you say?"

"Well, I tell you, John, I'm not sure that the restaurant that serves the most authentic Italian food in Florence would have a sign out front that was in English, not Italian. Or serve lunch at a quarter-to-twelve, for that matter."

"Yeah, but two-and-half *pounds*."

There was no arguing with that, Gideon knew, so they took a table at the railing and John ordered his *bistecca* rare. "Raro," he said. "Peenk."

"*Al sangue*," the waiter said, nodding approvingly. Like Bruno the previous evening, he kissed his fingertips. "Ah, a very wonderful choice, signore. You will enjoy."

Gideon was less hungry and ordered a simple *ravioli burro e salvia*, ravioli with butter and sage. About this choice the waiter was less enthusiastic, merely shrugging and writing on his pad. But then, the *bistecca* was the most expensive item on the menu; the ravioli, meant to serve as a starter, not as a main dish, was only €7. John ordered a glass of cabernet, Gideon one of pinot grigio. On these, the waiter was noncommittal.

The steak, when it came, was as advertised: truly enormous, a two-inch-thick slab of porterhouse so big that it hung over the sides of the plate, and bloody enough to please the most dedicated of flesh-eaters. By the time Gideon, who was not a particularly fast eater, had finished his pasta, John was only halfway into his steak, but there was little doubt that he meant to see the job through. Gideon settled back comfortably to watch, ordering a plate of assorted cheeses to go with his remaining wine.

"Say, John, are you sure you don't want a couple of pounds of fries to go with that?"

John just grinned and chewed away, jaws grinding and neck tendons popping. "Let me finish this first. Then we'll see."

It took him another forty minutes to reach his limit, at which point he regretfully but contentedly set down his knife and fork.

When their waiter brought coffee and cleared their plates, he looked at the tiny amount of meat that John had left and shook his head wonderingly. "Only Americans can eat so much. And Germans."

"Was that a compliment or an insult?" John asked Gideon afterward.

"John, I honestly don't know."

AS one would expect, John took a long time over his coffee, so it was two thirty by the time they got back to Figline and the villa. There was a tour bus at the front of the building—*Degustazioni di Vino, Visite Guidate* it said on the side—and the occupants, two dozen or so rather beat-looking older people, were slowly descending the steps and moving toward the entrance, so John and Gideon went around to the back and entered through the opening in the section of the old city wall that served as the back wall of the garden.

At the other end of the garden were two people seated at a table on the terrace: a placid, sturdy-looking older woman in Birkenstocks and a young man who was anything but placid. The woman sat there stolidly. The young man was agitatedly gesturing and talking angrily away despite a near-continuous, shuddering cough. The closer Gideon and John came, the more obvious his agitation was.

"Guy's on something," John said.

"Sure is. He's practically vibrating."

As they neared, a particularly violent bout of coughing shut down the young man's ranting, and he reached for a purple, hourglass-shaped bottle on the table. Gideon recognized it as Giorniquilla, an evil-tasting Italian cough medicine that he'd tried when he'd had a cold during an earlier visit to Italy and had found to be about as effective as American cough medicines were, which is to say not very.

The young man tipped the bottle to his mouth and took an alarmingly long swig.

"What do you want to bet that isn't cough medicine?" John whispered—they were getting close to hearing range. "I don't think it's booze either. This guy isn't drunk, he's totally stoned. Wired. Baked. Probably got it mixed with something—coke, that'd be my guess."

"I don't know. Seems to have stopped his cough."

They had to pass within a few feet of the table to get into the villa, and they nodded at the couple. The woman responded with an abstracted nod, the young man, no longer coughing but seemingly trying to head off another spell of it, stared blankly at them, hand pressed flat to his chest, not registering anything.

"Did you see the guy's eyes?" John asked as they entered the villa.

Gideon nodded. "Pupils twice their normal size, whites of his eyes—what there was of them—more red than white."

"Stoned," John said again.

In the hallway they ran into Luca heading from the winery building to the north wing, where *Vino e Cucina* was being held in the great kitchen. Head down, he was shaking his head and mumbling to himself.

"Luca?" Gideon said. "What's wrong?"

Luca stopped, startled, so buried in his thoughts that he hadn't been aware of them. "Ah, it's that miserable, sneaky, two-faced . . . it's Cesare, goddamn him."

"What'd he do?" John asked.

"He's suing us, can you believe it? Suing Franco, anyway, which means we could lose the damn winery." He jerked his head and grumbled a little more to himself. "He walks in out of nowhere with his lawyer, and calmly informs us he's going to sue us. Well, not so calmly, I guess."

"What's he suing you about?" Gideon asked.

"Ah, who knows? I didn't understand it all, but I think *he* thinks that he was going to inherit all this money from his mother, which *she* would have inherited from *babbo*, except that he killed her first—which *I* still don't buy, by the way—and therefore deprived him of it . . . I don't know, something like that, they lost me there. I have to go, I'm already late."

Gideon grabbed his arm. "Wait, hold on a second, Luca, there's something you need to know."

Luca paused.

"Luca . . . I'm not so sure your father *did* kill Nola. Some of the evidence seems to suggest—"

"What?" Luca was staring at him. "How do *you* know? When did you get involved? What's going on, Gideon? What—" He shook his head. "No, dammit, I have to go. Look, Franco and Nico are still in the small conference room; you know where it is. Severo too. If you've really got something, go and tell them, will you? I'll find out about it later."

"Wait just one more second," Gideon said. He pointed through one of the windows that lined the corridor. "Is that him out there?" The two were still sitting at the table, and the young man was tipping the bottle to his mouth again.

Luca looked and growled. "Yeah, that's him, the little . . . Gotta go." And off he hurried.

In the conference room, Severo, Franco, and Nico were huddled over the table immersed in whispered conversation. The door was open, but John knocked on it anyway.

Franco turned, looking displeased. "*Si?*" It was not an invitation.

"Franco," Gideon said, "we were just talking to Luca—"

"Gideon, could this possibly wait? We've got something important going here and—"

"Luca told us about Cesare's suit, Franco. I thought you'd want to know that I've been looking at some of the evidence, and in my opinion there's some doubt—serious doubt—about whether Nola was actually killed by your father." He spoke in English, wanting to make sure that he wasn't misunderstood.

The three men, Severo, Franco, and Luca, all stared uncomprehendingly at the newcomers. Severo was the first to surface. He gestured at the empty chairs. "Come, come in. Ah, perhaps you would . . ."

Franco cut him off. "I don't understand," he said to them as they sat. "What are you saying?"

"He's saying," John said, "that some pretty strange things have come up that make us think that maybe your father wasn't the murderer after all, that maybe somebody else killed him *and* your stepmother."

"I knew it!" Nico exclaimed, coming half out of his seat, hands flat on the table. "Didn't I tell you? Oh, Gideon, that'd be great, that'd be so—" He clapped a hand to his forehead. "Jeez, did I just say what I think I said? I didn't mean—"

"We know what you mean," Franco said, "and I assure you we all feel exactly the same way. If it can be shown that *babbo* did not kill her, then Cesare has no case whatever. Gideon, what—?"

Nico interrupted, showing a rare flash of anger. "No, that's what *you* would have meant, Franco, that's not what I meant. I meant that for me the fact that *babbo's* dead is bad enough, but the idea that he was a murderer—that was almost too damn much too to bear." Tears glistened at the rims of his eyes. "But if it turns out that it wasn't that way at all, that he didn't kill anybody—including himself—that would throw a whole new . . . ah, the hell with it, it's too much to take in," he finished weakly. He fell back in his chair, and covered his eyes with his hand.

It was a surprise to Gideon, an unmistakably real display of emotion from Nico, who was usually so lazily affable.

"Are you finished, Nico?" Franco asked coldly. When Nico responded with no more than a listless wave, he turned to Gideon and John. "Now, what is this all about?" He glanced up at the doorway, where Luca had shown up a little out of breath. "What are you doing here? How are your faithful disciples getting along without their guru?"

"I changed the schedule. They're taking the winery tour now instead of tomorrow. Linda's showing them around. I told her to make it last." He took the one remaining chair, next to Quadrelli. "So. What's going on? Gideon said—"

"Gideon said that *babbo* didn't kill anybody. We're waiting for the explanation."

"No," Gideon said, "let's get that straight before we go any further. I didn't say that your father didn't kill anybody, and I'm not saying it now. What I said was that some questions have arisen that tend to confuse—"

"No," said Nico, "you said that you had some serious doubt that—"

"No, you said more than that." Luca said. "You said that you didn't think *babbo*—"

"No," Luca said, "what he said—"

"Well, whatever the hell I said," Gideon declared, rather too loudly, "do you want to hear the rest of it or don't you?" He was annoyed with the whole bunch of them. Here he'd devoted hours of his time to looking into the case, he'd gone out of his way to be careful of their feelings, and now he had something to tell them that could turn out to be of tremendous emotional and financial benefit to them, and what were they doing? They were sitting around like a high school English class, parsing his damn sentences for him.

The tension was cut by Maria's entrance with a tray of espressos and biscuits and a stern look that said, *Drink. Now, before it gets cold.* Everybody obediently downed their coffee, and an atmosphere of calm, reasonably good fellowship was restored.

The explanation took a long time. To start with, Gideon had to explain his involvement in the case by way of the forensic seminar, and to (not very successfully) justify his keeping it from them until now. Then there was the matter of making it clear how the accepted murder-suicide scenario was muddied by his conclusions that Nola had been shot *after* the fall had already killed her, and that Pietro would have had to clamber back up the cliff afterward to shoot himself.

"No, no," Quadrelli said excitedly. "Climb up the cliff? Pietro was not a climber of cliffs. Why would he do such a thing? No, no."

"That's the question, Severo," Gideon told him. "It's one of the things that makes the whole scenario suspect."

And of course there were questions to be answered about how it was possible to tell such things from skeletons, and about how confident he was in his findings. But it was clear that he'd made an impression.

"So what happens now?" Nico asked. "Do the *Carabinieri* get back to work on it?"

"They're thinking about it."

"Well, do they have any suspects?"

"Nobody serious, as far as I know." *Just you three and Cesare, to start with. And maybe an unknown lover.*

"Gideon," Franco said, "we very much appreciate all that you've done. If there's any way we can thank you . . . a fee—"

Gideon held up his hands. "I didn't do anything. I'm just glad I was able to help a little. I wish I could do more."

"Well, actually, I have a thought, Gideon," Luca said. "You got some pretty amazing clues just from looking at *babbo's* autopsy report. Would there be anything more to learn if you examined his actual remains? I know I'd certainly be willing to authorize an exhumation."

Franco wasted no time correcting him. "I believe that such authorization would have to come from me, Luca. That's correct, isn't it, Severo?"

Before Severo could answer Luca bowed his head Indian style, fingers steepled at his forehead. "I crave forgiveness, elder brother."

Franco smiled skeletally.

It had taken until now for Gideon to process what they were

talking about. "Wait a minute, do you mean your father's remains are still there? He wasn't cremated?"

Franco stared at him. "Where'd you get that idea?"

"I . . . I'm not sure . . ."

"That's what Rocco thought," John said. "He mentioned it in class."

"Well, he was wrong," Nico said. "Jesus, *babbo*'d never let us get away with *cremating* him. Are you kidding me?" He made the wrist-wobbling gesture that Italians use where Americans might say, "No way."

"But Nola was, wasn't she?" Gideon asked. "The mortician, Cippollini, said it was set for yesterday."

Franco's mouth turned down. "That's Cesare's doing. She would have preferred otherwise, I'm sure, but it wasn't up to us."

"Well, *could* I see your father's remains? Would you object? Would you be willing to authorize it, Franco?"

Franco didn't look happy about it. "I don't like to do it, to disturb his bones."

"Get real, Franco," Luca said. "We're trying to clear his name here. I don't think he'd mind having his bones poked at if it would help."

"Well, what exactly would you be looking for, Gideon?" Franco was unconvinced.

"I don't really know. It's impossible to say. Anything I can find that might be pertinent."

Franco shook his head. "I really don't . . ."

"Oh, Franco, for Christ's sake—" Luca began.

"Yes, yes, but you know, these things take time. I'm not sure it can be arranged before you leave, Gideon."

"It will take no time at all," Quadrelli said, joining in on the pressure on Franco. "Pietro is no' buried, they no' need picks and shovels. They are in a vault in the crypt. To turn a key and open the door is all that is necessary. I will call signor Cippollini myself."

Franco reluctantly gave in. "You would treat them with respect, Gideon?"

"Of course."

"Very well. Call signor Cippollini, Severo. Tell him he has my permission."

"If you could do that right now, I'd appreciate it," Gideon said. "As Franco said, we'll only be here another couple of days."

Quadrelli promptly hauled out his phone. He spoke in rapid Italian, nodding at Gideon and making a circle with his thumb and forefinger at one point to indicate it was a go. He hung up, pleased with himself.

"Ten o'clock tomorrow morning. He will have the remains ready for you. But he makes a request. He says please not to bring this time the entire police force with you."

FOURTEEN

WITH no memorial service under way at Onoranze Funebri Cippollini, Gideon and John were not required to go around to the back door this time. Signor Cippollini, wearing what seemed to be the same tightly fitting black suit and pretty much the same hassled demeanor, distractedly ushered them in through the front entrance, took them through the church-like chapel with its faux stained-glass Gothic windows, and into the strangely cheery, brightly colored workroom. On a flatbed, wheeled table lay something quite different from Nola's child-size cardboard box. Pietro's casket was the full-size item and made for the long haul, rather than for a single incendiary appearance. Constructed of ebony or something like it, it was elegantly traditional in style, with ornate brass handles and carrying rods, an arched, carved lid, and, on the side, a plastic-coated black-and-white studio photograph of Pietro as a young man, along with his name—*Pietro Vittorio Teodoro Guglielmo Cubbiddu*—and dates—*1953–2011*—incised in flowing gilt script. It all was clean and gleaming, as if it had gotten a coat of furniture oil that morning, which it probably had.

Cippollini himself unlocked and opened the coffin's upper panel—the lid was in two parts, Dutch-door style, as if in preparation for an open-casket display—which Gideon very much doubted had taken place. The broken, gaping, lichen-blackened skull was nothing the mourners would have cared to look at, but it was reverently placed, face up, at the center of an immaculate, satin pillow. The rest of the bones were neatly hidden beneath a padded white coverlet, equally spotless. Cippollini stood admiringly before his creation for a few seconds, then opened the lower lid as well, and, with a bullfighter's flourish, removed the coverlet to reveal the earthly remains of Pietro Vittorio Teodoro Guglielmo Cubbiddu in their totality.

Their condition came as something of a surprise. Dr. Bosco's report had listed the trauma, all right, but when he'd written "multiple fractures," Gideon had taken him to mean that the skeleton as a whole had suffered many breaks, not that each named bone was broken into separate *pieces*. But unlike Nola's bones, which were cracked and splintered but mostly in one piece, these were *shattered*. The most cursory of glances showed him three pieces of the left scapula alone.

That got him thinking. *Why the difference? Two bodies undergoing exactly the same terrible fall and impacting on the very same rocky scree—why should the injuries to their bones look so different? Could they be the results of "taphonomic" changes—natural postmortem changes that had occurred as a result of lying out in the open for almost an entire year? No, they'd lain right up against each other and endured exactly the same weather conditions and animal depredations for exactly the same length of time.* He could come up with only one answer, but it seemed too bizarre to . . . He tucked the question away for later, when he had time for solitary cogitation.

Despite his trade, it was clear that Mr. Cippollini had little knowledge of skeletal anatomy. Either that, or his penchant for symmetry outweighed his care for anatomical precision. The bones of the legs and pelvis, which were among the few that were unbroken, were in place (although he'd gotten the left and right tibias and fibulas confused), but just about everything from the hips up was arranged strictly for show. "Matching" pieces of scapula and ribs were placed on either side with no regard for what had gone where in the living body. The "spinal column" consisted of vertebrae, whole and in chunks, that tapered beautifully down from skull to pelvis—in complete defiance of nature's way. At their bottom, between the hipbones, was the broken sacrum, misarranged, but at least in the right general area.

Cippollini was quite proud of the totality of his efforts and even more of the quality of the coffin. Gideon couldn't follow it all, but he understood enough to learn that the exterior wood *was* ebony, the interior wood was mahogany, the soft interior fabric was arranged and sewn in a French-fold design, and the mattress was his own patented invention, the Eternal Rest Adaptable Couch.

"Well, next time I need a coffin I'll sure know where to come," John said, but of course he said it in English and with a smile, so Cippollini happily nodded along with him. Encouraged, he began to get into the finer points of the wood molding, but Gideon politely told him that they were pressed for time and needed to get on with it.

"Once again, for the sake of decency, I have cleaned the bones," Cippollini told him. "Would you like me to take them out of the casket for you?"

"No, thank you."

"If you let me know when you're done, I will put them back."

"I can do that for you," Gideon said.

"No, signore, I want to be positive that they are in their natural order, as close as possible to the way God made them."

"Well, then, you better let him do it," John said to Gideon. "You might not get 'em right."

When Cippollini left, they stood looking at the remains. Gideon found the whole thing creepy, and not only because of the misplaced bones. He'd looked at his share of newly exhumed burials, and many of them had been skeletonized, but always before: the coffin fabric on which they lay had been gray and mottled with age, and stained with the effluents of decomposing tissue. It was anything but pretty, but it was as it should be. But Pietro's bones lay on brilliantly white bedding—French folded, no less—and while it made things less nasty (as did the pre-cleaning), it just didn't seem right. It was as if he were looking at a wax museum exhibit or a dubious reliquary purportedly containing the toe bones of an obscure saint, and not at what was left of a once-living human being

"Well, let's get them laid out on the table," he said. "Forget about the order for now. We'll just—hey, wait a minute . . ." He was doing a double take at the bone he'd just picked up; the third rib on the right-hand side. "Damn, now that's really funny. . . ."

"Well, that didn't take you long," John said casually, transferring a hip bone to the zinc work table. "So, what'd you find?"

Gideon gave him the rib. "Anything about it catch your eye? Any difference from what we found with Nola?"

"Not really. It's kind of chewed up."

"Bingo. It's *very* chewed up. Animals have been all over it. All those scratches and these conical indentations—gnaw marks, mostly from canid teeth."

"Okay, if you say so, but what's the big deal? Nola's bones were plenty chewed up too. Why wouldn't they be? There'd be plenty of forest critters up there. Ferrets, weasels, wolves—"

"John, would you do me a favor, please? Get Rocco on the phone?"

He took Rocco's card out of his wallet and handed it over. While John made the call, Gideon did a quick examination of the rest of the skeleton. He was puzzled by the absence of cranial fragments, which Rocco said had been recovered from the top of the cliff and along the route the bodies had taken down it, but then under the pillow he found a red velvet sack tied with a golden cord, like some top-of-the-line old cognac, except for the tape label, which read *Frammenti di calotta cranica*—skull fragments. He began to untie the cord but was interrupted by John's proffering the telephone.

"Got him. Here he is."

"Thanks, John. Rocco? Hi. Listen, you told me they were both—"

"Who were both?"

"Nola and Pietro, of course."

"What do you mean, *of course*? What do you think, I'm a TV detective or something? I only work one case at a time? Hell, I'm not working *that* case at all, remember? That case is over and done. And I'm sitting here looking at a goddamn desk full of—"

"Not having such a good morning, huh?"

Rocco laughed, and Gideon heard some rustling that suggested he was settling back in his chair. "Sorry. Okay, I told you they were both what?"

"Both wearing leather jackets."

"Umm . . . yeah, they were. Matching ones. Good ones. From Forzieri. I wish I could afford one."

"What kind of condition were they in, the jackets?"

"Condition? They were fine."

"Not torn up at all?"

"No. I mean, they didn't look like anything you'd want to slip into, but no, no holes, no rips. Their pants had some holes in 'em. Not too surprising, after all that time outside. But the jackets, they were good, thick leather; they held up. I mean, there might have been some pinprick or crack that I missed somewhere or other, but—"

"They must have been wearing shirts or something under the jackets. What about them?"

"Uh, that I don't know. I don't really think anybody paid attention. Everything was pretty ratty and moldy and all. They just cut the clothes off them for the autopsy, and as far as I knew they just threw them away. Is that bad?"

"Rocco, could you possibly get away for a while? We're down here in Figline, at your cousin's funeral home, and we're looking at Pietro's remains."

"You're looking at his *ashes*?"

"No, his bones."

"But I thought he was—"

"Well, he wasn't. He's lying here right in front of me."

"Huh. I thought . . . I guess I just assumed . . . So you're asking me to come there? Right now?"

"I am, yes. I think I'm onto something."

"Gid, how important is this? Because I got a lot of stuff that needs doing, and Captain Conforti is breathing down my neck."

"It's important. I think."

A hesitation, a sigh, and then: "Half an hour. Ciao."

"What's up?" John asked. "What's so special about this rib? Why *shouldn't* it be chewed up?"

"John, it's not that I want to keep you in suspense—"

"No, of course not. Why would I think that?"

"—but Rocco's on his way, and I want to get my act together before he gets here, so give me a few minutes, okay?"

"Sure. Far be it from me to interrupt the Skeleton Detective when he's communing with a skeleton." He pulled up a stool and leaned over to watch, his elbows on the table.

"And no offense, but maybe you could give me a little breathing room?"

"Jeez, talk about prima donnas. Okay, I can take a hint. There was a café up the block. How about I go away and come back in a little while with a couple of cappuccinos?"

"Good, great, thank you. I'll have a latte, though. Give me ten minutes. Make that twenty," he yelled as John went through the door.

Left alone, Gideon went back to his examination of the bones, most of which were still in the casket. Opening the velvet sack that held the cranial fragments, he separated one that was actually a curved chunk of scapula, spread the rest out on the table, and fitted some of them together. They represented much of the right half of the cranium, and they held no surprises. Entrance wound in the left temple, much larger exit wound in the right temple, exactly as described in the autopsy report.

Overall, the postcranial trauma were also as reported: fractures of most of the ribs on the left side, the left scapula and left arm bones, the sacrum, and many of the thoracic and lumbar vertebrae.

But while Dr. Bosco had done an accurate enough job of listing them, that was where he'd stopped. No detailed descriptions, no analyses, no conclusions derived from them. But for Gideon, when it came to bones, the devil lay in the details, and ten minutes spent examining them and comparing them in his mind to Nola's injuries made him even more certain he was onto something.

His excitement building, he took a break to refresh his thinking. Going out to the rear parking lot, he put two one-euro coins into the vending machine for a nougat candy bar, sat down on one of the nearby benches, leaned against the wall, and—slowly, thoughtfully chewing—gazed eastward across the valley to the gentle, green foothills of the Apennines and the pretty little puffballs of clouds that clustered around their tops.

"Whew," he said aloud. "It's going to take me a while to get my head around *this*."

HE was finishing the candy bar when he heard the front door to the workroom open and close. "I'm out in back, John," he called, and a second later, out came John with Rocco trailing a couple of steps behind. "Hey, Doc, look who I found loitering on the street out there."

"Hey, Gid," Rocco said. Again, he was in his splendid, tailored uniform, billed cap and all.

John handed Gideon a typically capacious bowl-shaped cup, kept one for himself, and sat down on the other bench. Rocco, with an espresso cup of his own, sat beside him. "I ran into him right outside the café," John said. "Lucky for us. They don't do takeaway, but when the generalissimo here walked in, they decided to make an exception. Anyway, don't let me forget, we gotta bring the cups back."

Rocco looked harried. "So, what have you got?" he asked, with an unsaid *This better be good* in its wake.

Gideon smiled and reached for his latte. "It's going to knock your socks off. Let's go inside."

FIFTEEN

"TO start with," he said, "take a look at the bones of the torso and the arms as a whole. Anything strike you?"

Rocco tossed his cap onto a chair and studied the bones for a minute, hands clasped behind him. "Well, as far as fracturing goes—"

"We'll get to the fracture patterns in a minute, but for now, does anything else catch your eye?"

"Not really, no. What else is there?"

John sent the same message, along with a shrug. "What are we supposed to be looking for?"

"Compare them in your mind to what Nola's upper body looked like," Gideon suggested. "How are these different? Anything pop out at you?"

Rocco began to shake his head no, but suddenly stopped. "These have been chewed on!"

Gideon nodded. "Exactly."

"So?" John said. "Nola's were chewed on too."

"Not the ribs, not the arms," Rocco exclaimed, his interest growing. "But *these*, they're all . . . but how the hell could that be?"

"That," said Gideon, "is the question."

"*What* is the question?" John demanded. "How could *what* be?"

Rocco answered. "He was wearing a leather jacket, John. They both were. Down to the waist, with long sleeves. Good, thick jackets. And there weren't any holes or tears in them. So naturally, the animals couldn't get their teeth into Nola's upper body. But they did plenty of chewing on this one, on Pietro's. So . . . how come? That's the question."

"Well, what's the answer? If his jacket wasn't torn, how could the animals get to the bones under it?"

"Indeed," said Gideon with a more or less inscrutable smile. "And the answer is: they didn't." Fun time again for the hardworking anthropologist.

"They didn't . . . ?" Rocco echoed, brows knit.

" 'Splain yourself, Lucy," John growled.

"There weren't any holes in the jacket because he wasn't wearing it at the time."

The other two stared at him. Rocco spoke. "What did you say?"

"I said there weren't any—"

"We heard what you said. Are you telling us the jacket was put on him *later*—after he was dead? *After* the bugs and animals got to him? I'm sorry, Gid, but—"

"That's what I'm telling you, Rocco."

They waited for him to explain while he waited for what he'd said so far to sink in. "Consider. In Nola's case, although her skull and lower body were gnawed, and her hands were gone, nothing that would have been covered by her jacket was touched by animals. Not so with Pietro. Logical explanation: Nola was wearing the jacket from the beginning; Pietro wasn't—and it didn't go on him until some time after he was killed—time enough for the animals to get in there and chew him up the way they did."

"Which would be how long?" Rocco asked. "Are we talking hours? Days?"

"In this particular case, I'd say weeks."

"Weeks!" Rocco shouted. The creases on his forehead got deeper. "Christ, it's not enough that Nola was shot after she was dead, but now you're saying someone changed Pietro's clothes *weeks* after *he* was dead? Why? What for?"

"Hey, I'm just an anthropologist. I don't deal with the *why*s. *Why*s are your problem, *Tenente*."

"Yeah, but . . . "Rocco scowled. "Aw, this is nuts, Gid."

John was laughing. "Good old Skeleton Detective. Does it every time." He sipped some of his cappuccino and licked foam from his lips. "Okay, guys, let's think this through. To start with, we've established *where* he was killed—the top of the cliff. We know that because that's where you found the skull fragments, Rocco."

"Yeah, there and some more of them along the way down the cliff wall, so we know . . . well, unless somebody scattered them there to make us think—"

"No-o," Gideon said, "there's such a thing as *too* weird, and that's what that is. I think we can safely assume that that the top of the cliff is where he was shot."

"All right, scratch that idea," Rocco said. "So, now what's our scenario? We're up at the top of the cliff. Nola's already been pushed off—"

"How do we know that again?" John asked.

"Because she was found up against this big rock, and he was found up against *her*, so she had to have gone first."

"Oh, right—but hang on, how do we know someone didn't arrange the bodies that way later? Or do you figure that's too weird too?"

The three of them agreed that, while it might be weird, it was by no means *too* weird. It was something to be considered.

"Well, whatever," Rocco said. "Thanks to you, at least we know that he *was* killed up there—"

"No, you said that. I didn't say that," said Gideon.

"The hell you didn't."

"Yeah, you did, Doc," John said. "You said—"

"I said that he was *shot* up there."

"And we can't say for sure that a .32 slug that blows away half his head didn't kill him?" John said, his voice rising. He was starting to wave his arms around, the way he did when he got excited. Then, suddenly, he sagged. "Oh no, what are you telling us? He was shot after he was already dead too? Like Nola? I think I saw this movie before. Come on, man, you gotta be kidding us."

"Almost like Nola, but not quite," Gideon said. "You're forgetting. Nola was alive when she fell, and shot only afterwards . . . down at the bottom. Pietro was shot—not killed, because he was already dead—but *shot*—up at the top. *Before* he fell."

"I'm starting to get a neck ache here," Rocco said warningly. "Every time we think we figured out what you're saying, you shake your head and say, 'No, that's not what I said.'" He turned abruptly to John. "Is he always like this?"

Gideon was all innocence. "Hey, I just figured it was better to explain things step by step. You know, build a foundation to establish that the underlying premises are valid before attempting to demonstrate that the ensuing deductions necessarily follow from them." He smiled sweetly.

"Oh yeah," John said airily to Rocco, "this is exactly what he's always like." And to Gideon: "Okay, Doc, don't you think you've boggled the minds of us poor dumb coppers long enough? I mean, I know it's one of your few pleasures, but how about just getting to the point of it and stop beating around the bush? We're getting lost here."

Rocco agreed. "Yeah, screw the underlying premises. How about just coming out and telling us what your ensuing deductions are?"

"Right," John chipped in. "Get to the part that knocks our socks off."

Gideon flopped into a chair, suddenly tired. "All right, here's the punch line: Pietro Cubbiddu didn't kill his wife. Or himself."

"Well, you were kind of thinking along those lines before, weren't you?" John said.

"Yes, but now there isn't any 'along those lines.'" He looked at Rocco. "I *know* that Pietro Cubbiddu didn't kill his wife. He couldn't have. There's no longer any doubt about it. I think you're going to want to reopen the case, Rocco."

Rocco wasn't pleased. He went back into his scowl. "And you 'know' this how?"

Gideon sighed. "You people are so untrustful. I know it because, at the time Nola was killed, Pietro was already dead. *Long* dead."

"Long dead," John repeated. "What does that mean? Hours, days . . . ?"

Gideon shook his head. "What I said before: weeks."

"Weeks!" Rocco shouted. Now he was confused as well as unhappy. "How the hell can that be?" He was close to being angry as well. "How do you *know* that? What, from these stupid gnaw marks?"

Gideon drank down the rest of his latte before answering. "No, not from the gnaw marks. From the fracture patterns of the bones."

"The fracture patterns of the . . ." Rocco dropped heavily into the chair beside Gideon and appealed to John. "He's wearing me out. What the hell is he talking about now, do you know?"

John hunched his shoulders. "I don't have a clue." He looked at Gideon. "Doc?"

"The fracture patterning," Gideon said. "That's one of those underlying premises I was referring to."

"Well, on second thought, maybe you ought to go back to establishing them, after all."

"I would, John, but if I recall correctly, this gentleman from the *Carabinieri* advised—with some considerable heat, I might add— that I screw them." The shot of caffeine in his system was already perking him up.

Rocco closed his eyes. "I'm gonna kill him," he muttered, but he was laughing. John had already been laughing for a while, and now Gideon joined in too. "Okay," he said, slapping his thighs and getting up, "come on, I'll show you what I'm talking about."

When the three of them stood over the bones, Gideon said, "We have a really strange situation here."

"No kidding," John said.

"No, this is one I've never run into before. Or anything close. All right, first a little general background on bones."

"The underlying premises," Rocco said, nodding.

"The underlying premises of the underlying premises," Gideon corrected, and went on before they could comment.

"Living bone," he explained, "is a very different thing than dead bone. The first is infused with fluid and grease and covered with moist tissue, something like a bark-covered branch on a living tree. The second is dried out, like a dead twig that's been on the ground for a long time. The result is that they tend to fracture in different ways. For example, when a fresh bone—a living leg bone, say—is subjected to extreme pressure, it doesn't just break: it bends. It's actually flexible to some extent. So it's more resistant to breaking, and when it does break, there's a good chance it will splinter but stay in one piece, like a living branch—which is why that kind of break is called a green-stick fracture. But dead bone—like the dead twig—is no longer flexible. Try to bend it, and it just snaps into two pieces. Or three or four or five."

"Like these," John said, surveying the shattered bones on the table. "Clean breaks, almost all of them. But with Nola, a lot of them were those . . . what was it, green-twig fractures."

"Green-stick," Gideon said. "Right. Conclusion: unlike Nola, who was alive—whose bones were still moist, living tissue when she went off that cliff—"

"Alive and *conscious*," Rocco added.

"—Pietro was already dead. And not only dead, but *thoroughly* dead. Long enough for his bones to start to dry out."

"But what about these?" John asked, indicating a couple of ribs that had clear green-stick fractures, and two similar ones in the sacrum.

"Well, that's why I said 'long enough for his bones to *start* to dry out.' It doesn't happen all at once. And as to which ones dry first and which don't, there are a million variables. In the case of these green-stick ones—the sacrum, the eleventh and twelfth ribs—they're all in the body's core, the area most thickly covered with fat and muscle and other tissue—clothing too—so they'd stay moist longer and be protected from drying. The other bones would dry out faster. So the same fall could very well have produced dry-stick fractures in some of the bones and green-stick fractures in others. Which is exactly what I think happened."

"Hey, Doc, let me ask you something else," John said. "When you say he had to have been dead long enough for the bones to start drying out, how long would that be?

Gideon sighed. "Maybe one of you ought to write this down. What we're talking about here are *weeks*."

Rocco's expression was pained. "Oh, please . . ."

"Weeks," repeated Gideon. "Look, he left home for his cabin on, what was it, September first, right?"

Rocco nodded.

"Okay, so we know he was definitely alive then. And we're assuming that the two of them got thrown off the cliff a month later, on October 1, when she came to pick him up."

"It's a pretty safe assumption," Rocco said. "She left her aunt's that morning, but she didn't show up—neither of them showed up—at Villa Antica that afternoon."

Gideon nodded. "Well, I tell you, how long it takes for human bone to dry out is extremely variable. It depends on temperature, humidity, the health of the victim, what he was wearing—"

"Here we go again," said John.

"No," Gideon said firmly. "Here we do *not* go again. I will say—and I'm willing to go on the record with this—that Pietro Cubbiddu had to have been dead a minimum of two weeks, and most likely more, when he was shot and his body thrown off that cliff. And my guess—which I'm *not* quite willing to go on the record with—is that it had to have been closer to four weeks than to two. In other words, not very long after he arrived at the cabin, sometime in that first week or so of September."

"Which would have made it kind of hard for him to kill Nola in October," John observed with a baffled frown.

No one said anything for a few seconds, and then Rocco asked: "So exactly what the hell do we think *did* happen?"

"Don't look at me," John said with a shake of his head. "I'm more lost than I was before he started."

"I don't have an answer to that either," said Gideon, "but it does seem to me there are some pretty interesting threads you can pull out of the circumstances as we now understand them, Rocco. However it worked—and whatever was behind it—the killer had to be there waiting when Nola arrived, to make it look as if Pietro killed her."

"Which means he had to know *when* she was coming," John said. "The exact day she'd show up at the cabin. Which must mean we're not talking about a whole hell of a lot of people. I mean, how many people would know something like that?"

Rocco was nodding along with him. "Right. And then who would even know where the cabin was? The family kept that to themselves. Pietro insisted on being left alone up there. Even *they* weren't welcome during that one month. He kept a cell phone for emergencies, and that was all the contact he wanted with the outside world. So . . . I think maybe—*if* we reopened the case—we'd be looking at the family itself and any really close confidantes. That would be the place to start, anyway."

"So that would include . . . ?" Gideon asked.

"The sons, of course—Franco, Luca, Nico . . . and Cesare, naturally . . . and Luca's wife, Linda, I guess. And the lawyer, Quadrelli; he's in on everything." He'd been counting the names on his fingers as he said them, and he was on the first finger of the second hand. "Six in all. And probably some of the employees. But not a whole lot of people, at least to start with. It's doable. You got any tips for me?"

That was Gideon's cue to tell him about Cesare, and about the aborted Humboldt-Schlager deal. He half expected Rocco to flare up again, but he was uncharacteristically grateful instead. "You guys have been a huge help. I want to thank you. It's obvious we screwed up the first time around, and you opened up my eyes."

"I appreciate that. And if there's any other way I can help, just ask," Gideon said.

"Me too," John said. "Count me in."

Rocco smiled. "Yeah? What are the two of you doing right now?"

"Not a lot," John said hopefully. He'd been getting a little bored with life in Figline.

"Good. Let's drive back up to Florence. I'm gonna have to get my boss to agree to it, and I don't think I can do it without you guys there to help me explain. Captain Conforti's a tough nut to crack. He's a very smart guy, don't get me wrong, but he's also a bureaucrat, and he hates it when things aren't nice and neat. He also doesn't like it when you tell him he got something wrong."

"Who does?" said Gideon.

SIXTEEN

BUT Captain Conforti proved to be a surprisingly easy nut to crack. After an unpromising start, twenty minutes was all it took. He'd made no secret of being displeased when they entered his office, which was much like Rocco's in its unadorned functionality but three times the size and with solid walls, a real door, and two tall windows looking out on the street. The first thing he did was to glare silently at Rocco until Rocco figured out what he was driving at and responded with a jaunty, casual salute that didn't do much to ease things. The second thing, once introductions had been made, was to declare that only twice in his career had he been party to reopening a closed case, and both times the results had been legal and political disasters. And the third was to ask Rocco just what it was that was supposed to be so different about this particular case that would make him even consider doing it again.

"What's different, captain, is that this gentleman"—he gestured at Gideon—"showed up on the scene and didn't waste any time tell-ing us everything we got wrong."

"Which was everything," John said with an amiable smile.

"Just about," Rocco agreed, as Conforti's expression darkened more with every word.

But almost as soon as Rocco turned things over to Gideon, things improved. Conforti, a steely, distinguished, gray-haired man in his fifties, self-assured to the point of intimidation, proved to be an excellent and intelligent listener. Since the captain had little En-glish and they were speaking in Italian, Rocco furnished the correct terms when Gideon couldn't come up with them. John sat, silent and patient, his Italian nowhere near up to following the conversation. Conforti's few interruptions consisted of brief, piercing questions. There was no argument on his part, no further defensiveness.

"You're right," he said as Gideon finished. "Given what you've found, the findings we arrived at earlier are not supportable. I will see the public prosecutor this afternoon. Damn it." The prospect had done nothing to improve his mood.

"I'll be glad to refer you to the relevant forensic literature, if you think it would help," Gideon said.

Conforti produced his first thin smile. "We have heard of you, Professor Oliver, even here in Tuscany. The word of the Skeleton Detective"—*il detective delle ossa*—"is all the support I need."

Modestly, Gideon dipped his chin.

"You will lead the reopened investigation, of course, *Tenente*."

"Thank you, sir. With your permission, I'll take *Maresciallo* Martignetti as my second."

"Approved."

"I believe one of the first things I'd like to do is inform the Cubbiddus that we are reopening the case and begin our interrogations. If you don't object, I'd like to do that this afternoon."

Conforti nodded, then stood up. The others immediately followed suit. The conference was over. There was a round of handshaking. "I have a suggestion for the second thing you might do," the captain said to Rocco as all four men moved toward the door.

"What would that be?"

The corners of Conforti's mouth turned down—there were better ways to respond to the "suggestion" of a senior officer—but he went on without comment. "I would send a few people up to the cliff top tomorrow morning, see if they can find the bullet, the one that shot signor Cubbiddu. It would be nice to have that, don't you think? The one that was never found."

"Sure, but we already went over the area pretty thoroughly, captain. Checked every tree trunk for fifty meters around, scoured the ground—"

"But you didn't *dig* in the ground, *Tenente*. I suggest you scrape the soil down a few centimeters, say three or four. Not for fifty meters around, but perhaps for two meters surrounding the area where the skull fragments were found. It shouldn't take long."

Rocco looked uncertain "Ah . . . dig?"

"Dig, *Tenente*," said Conforti with the smallest of sighs. He went on with a slow, grinding show of patience. "We now know that signor Cubbiddu was already dead when shot, no? Therefore don't you think it is reasonable to assume that he, like signora Cubbiddu, might also have been lying down at the time, with his head against the ground?"

"Mm, I don't think so. If he had been, wouldn't the ground have shored up his skull and prevented the bullet from exiting—as with signora Cubbiddu?" He looked to Gideon for support.

"Not necessarily in his case, Rocco," Gideon said. "The captain's making a good point. Remember, his skull would have been more dried out than hers, and much more likely to break and let the bullet out, regardless of what it was up against—as opposed to hers, which more readily 'dented'—the reverse depressed fracture."

"That is exactly correct," said Conforti with the sort of approval one might give to a clever student, as if Gideon were reciting something he'd just learned from him, instead of the other way around. "So wouldn't the most likely path of the bullet be straight down into the soil . . . rather than into the trunk of some nearby tree?"

"That might be a good idea, Captain. I hadn't thought of that. I'll send a couple of men up there first thing in the morning. Anything else on your mind?"

Another sigh from Conforti, this one louder and longer. "No, *Tenente*," he said with a long-suffering smile, "that is all." After one more round of handshaking at the door, the door was closed behind them.

"WELL, you're right," Gideon said as they trotted down the stone stairway, their clacking footsteps echoing off the old walls. "He's a smart guy. I don't know why that didn't occur to me."

"You mean about digging in the ground for the bullet? You mean you hadn't thought of that?" Rocco mimed surprise. "Hell, I thought of it a long time ago. I was just making the old guy feel like he was being helpful."

Gideon looked at him from under a raised eyebrow.

"I wonder what you guys are talking about," John said. "The last thing I understood was *buongiorno*."

"We'll fill you in on the way," Gideon said. "We're heading back to the villa."

"All of us?" John asked, meaning *Rocco too?*

"All of us," Rocco said. "I'm driving you. You're going to be seeing a lot of me over the next few days."

They were halfway down the steps when they heard someone hurrying after them. They looked back to see Captain Conforti, brandishing something in his hand. "Here," he said, speaking English now, a little out of breath. "For you. I forget. Is a gift for to remember us." And he happily handed John and Gideon each a blue-and-red (the *Carabinieri* colors) plastic ballpoint pen with *www.carabinieri.it* on the clip and *112*, Italy's version of the 911 emergency number, on the barrel. "Please."

Gideon appreciated the gesture. "Thank you very much, Captain."

"*Muchas grazie, mon capitán,*" said John grandly.

SEVENTEEN

IF Rocco was right about there being a surplus of bureaucratic red tape in the *Carabinieri*, it certainly didn't show in the way they handled the reopening of the Cubbiddu case. On the drive down to Figline, no more than fifteen minutes after they'd left Conforti's office, Rocco got a call from Cosima, the captain's secretary, telling him that the new investigation had been provisionally approved. Did the lieutenant want her to call Villa Antica and inform them that he would like them to make themselves available for a meeting shortly; at, say, two o'clock? Would he like her to contact *Maresciallo* Martignetti to tell him to be there as well?

The answers were yes and yes, so that when they arrived a few minutes before two, having stopped for *panini* at a dreary roadside café, the Cubbiddus were already waiting for them in the frescoed sitting room (decorated with faux eighteenth-century depictions of the villa and its rolling green vineyards—which hadn't been planted until the twentieth) of Franco's suite. They sat, singly and in pairs, on slender, elegant, flute-legged Louis XVI armchairs and settees. They all knew the meeting concerned Pietro and Nola, but none of them had any idea of what to expect, including Martignetti, who was in a corner, a little away from the others, with a pad and pen at the ready on his lap. Franco and Nico shared a settee, as did Luca and Linda. The Cubbiddu's lawyer, Severo Quadrelli, was twiddling his thumbs, prudently seated in the only chair really suited to his heft: a so-called tub chair, a wide, substantial object built along the lines of a half barrel set atop short, thick legs. A sort of chair version of the man himself.

Antonio Martignetti was seated against a wall and partially hidden by an ornate, eighteenth-century ceramic heating stove. During the drive, Rocco had told them that Martignetti was a trusted associate, among whose many virtues were fluency in English and skill at shorthand. Rocco went directly to him and squatted on his haunches to confer briefly. Then he stepped out to the middle of the tapestry-carpeted floor and greeted the rest. He was friendly enough—he knew them all—but got quickly down to business.

"Dr. Oliver will carry the main part of this, so to make it easier for him, we'll do it in English. Is that a problem for anyone?"

Quadrelli lifted a hand. "Well . . ."

"If there is difficulty at any time, signor Quadrelli, simply say so, and we'll translate. Is that satisfactory?"

It was, and Rocco continued. "Let me come right to the point. Your meddlesome pal there"—he pointed at Gideon—"has convinced us that we had it all wrong. It didn't happen the way we thought it did." He waited a few seconds for dramatic effect. "Your father didn't kill anyone, and certainly not your stepmother. We are therefore reopening the investigation into their deaths."

"Great!" Luca said.

Nico pumped his fist. "Right on."

Franco said nothing but looked pleased.

"This is terrific news, Rocco," Nico said. "But what changed your mind? Is it what Gideon told us about yesterday—that *babbo* would have had to climb back up the cliff, and you didn't think—"

"No, there's more to it than that now. Gid, would you take it from here, please? Tell them what you found."

He went to lean against a wall to make room for Gideon at the center (and to observe the people in attendance), but Gideon spoke from his chair, giving them a fairly thorough description of what his examination of Pietro's remains that morning had added to the picture he'd drawn for them the day before: mainly that Pietro, having preceded Nola in death by several weeks, could hardly be guilty of her murder. There were questions, of course, and he answered them as factually as he could but refrained from getting into anything deeper than necessary, which Rocco had earlier asked him to do. Predictably, this satisfied no one.

The last question came from Luca. "Okay, one thing I don't quite get—"

"Only one?" Nico said. "You're way ahead of me."

Me too, Gideon thought.

"Okay, so what was it that *killed* him?" Luca continued. "You said—I *think* you said—he was shot and thrown off the cliff weeks after he was dead, but what killed him in the first place? Did you find any, what do you call them, the causes of death on the bones?"

"Not so far, no," Gideon answered, and explained a little more about the green-stick fractures and how they might or might not be perimortem. "But John and I will be heading back over to the funeral home to see if we can't find something more definitive."

"Oh, you mean I'm invited along?" John asked. "That's great, it's been hours since anybody told me to shut up or get the hell out of their face."

Quadrelli, who had been growing restless, got to his feet. "If you will excuse me, lieutenant, I must make a telephone call."

"Right now, this minute?" Rocco's eyebrows went up. "Who to?"

Severo hadn't expected to be impeded. He was flustered. "To . . . signora Batelli."

"The lawyer?" Rocco, of course, had already heard about signora Batelli and Cesare's suit from Gideon.

"Yes, I want to call her, the lawyer, to inform her of what I have just heard." He had retreated to Italian. "I hope to put a stop to a pointless and unpleasant proceeding. I am sure she'll see that their suit is no longer tenable."

"Very well, signor Quadrelli," Rocco said. "But please make yourself available to us over the weekend. We'll want to speak with you again."

"With me? Why?"

"With everyone. We'll want to interview you all. If any of you have problems with that, I need to know now. Anything we should be aware of?"

"I'll be here, I'll be here," Quadrelli said, and scuttled off.

"How long are these interviews going to take?" Luca asked. "I have this class I'm doing all day long Saturday."

"Not long," Rocco said, switching the conversation back to English. "A half hour should do it, I'd guess. An hour at most. We'll try to accommodate your schedules as much as possible, and we do appreciate your patience. Well, thanks, everybody. I think we can wrap up for today. Anybody have any questions?"

"I sure do," Luca said. "Who do you think did kill them? Do you have any leads? Do you have a motive? *Why* would anyone kill them?"

"Give us a chance to get going, Luca," Rocco said, smiling. "We haven't even—"

"*Faida*," Franco murmured darkly. "The marriage."

"That's always possible," Rocco said. "We'll be looking into that angle."

"Oh, but do you really, honestly think that was it, Franco?" Linda asked skeptically. It was her first contribution of the afternoon. "It was so long ago."

"There's no statute of limitation on *faida*, Linda, no sell-by date. It never ends. Now think about it. Someone might have wanted to kill *babbo* for one reason or another. That's certainly possible. And, conceivably, someone might have wanted to kill Nola, although I can't think of any reason why. But can you come up with any possible reason, other than the old vendetta, that someone might want to kill *both* of them?" He shook his head. "No, you cannot. They have a very long memory in Barbagia."

Nico snorted. "Give us a break, Franco. "This is 2011, not 1911."

"Well, then why? Who?"

Rocco waited a few seconds to see if anybody would respond. When no one did, he said: "As long as you've raised the question, though, Franco, let's give it a little thought. Who do you think might have killed your father?"

"I just told you. The families back in Barbagia—"

"No, I'm not asking you who might have killed them both, just your father."

"Just my father?" Franco seemed confused by the question. "I have no idea. Why ask me?"

"Because you said you did have an idea."

"No, I explicitly said I didn't have any idea. Other than *faida*."

"No, you said you had no idea who might have killed *Nola*."

"No—"

From his chair near the wall, Martignetti interrupted, reading from his shorthand notes. " 'Someone might have wanted to kill *babbo* for one reason or another. That's certainly possible. And, conceivably, someone might have wanted to kill Nola, although I can't think of any reason why.' "

" 'Certainly possible,' " said Rocco. "It seems to me that suggests—"

"It was just a figure of speech, for God's sake. Oh, I suppose I might have been thinking of various feuds *babbo* had over the years. With other vintners, distributors, some of our own people . . . He could be a difficult man to get along with."

"I see," Rocco said, unimpressed.

"I can give you some names, if you want, although, really, I doubt—"

"Let's be honest for once in our lives," Nico said. "If you're looking for people with motives, Lieutenant, you're sitting in a room full of them."

"What the hell are you talking about?" Franco exclaimed angrily "Us? We had motives to kill *babbo*? That's a hell of a thing to say. I can't believe—"

"Whoa, calm down, buddy," Nico said, putting a placating hand on Franco's shoulders as if to keep him from exploding off the settee they shared. "I'm not saying anybody here killed him, God forbid. I'm just saying the motive was there. It *was*, Franco. He's gonna find that out anyway, and I just figured we might as well tell him about it now."

"*What* motive? Are you crazy? I don't—"

"Humboldt-Schlager," Nico said quietly, which shut Franco down in mid-sentence.

"Humboldt-Schlager," Luca said musingly. "Yeah, the kid's got a point, Franco."

"I think," Rocco said pleasantly, "it would be really nice if somebody told me what you're talking about."

Gideon and John shared a mildly amused glance. Rocco had said it in all innocence, just as if Gideon hadn't told him all about the Humboldt-Schlager affair not even three hours earlier.

"Go ahead, kid," Luca said to Nico. "You started this."

"Okay. In a nutshell, Humboldt-Schlager—you know, the brewing company—wanted to buy the winery, and *babbo* was gonna sell it."

Franco had his arms folded. "We don't know that for a fact."

"Yeah, we do," Nico said. "Get real, Franco. Of course he was; it was written all over him. Am I right, Luca?"

"You're right, Nico."

Franco shrugged.

"And none of you wanted him to do it?" Rocco asked.

The three brothers looked at each other for a second before Franco replied. "We did not. We felt the terms were inimical to the interests of the family."

Luca hooted with laughter. "Translation: they were gonna boot us out on our asses. The minute the contract was signed."

"And Linda, how did you feel about it?"

"I felt the way Luca did."

"I see," Rocco said. "Okay, guys, telling me about it was the right thing to do. We'll be following up with you on this."

"May I point out that Nola was also murdered?" Franco said. "And Nola had nothing to do with it, so how is it relevant?"

But Rocco was tiring. He'd had enough. "I think we can wrap this up for now. Thank you all for your cooperation. Franco, I'm gonna want to confer with the *maresciallo* here for a minute. Okay if we just stay here?"

"Actually, I think the small conference room might be better suited, Lieutenant. You remember where it is?"

"Sure, fine, whatever," Rocco said, annoyed. "Any chance of having some coffee sent over there for us? I'm flagging."

"That might be problematic. I'm afraid Maria is tied up in the refectory kitchen with Luca's—"

"I'll take care of it, Franco, don't sweat it," Linda said, getting up, and then under her breath: "Sheesh."

As people filed thoughtfully out, Luca caught Gideon and John. "Tonight the group is on its own for dinner. How about you and the girls join Linda and me for something special? I want to take you to the best restaurant in Tuscany."

"You're too late," John said. "We already found it. I had *pizza carnivora. Fantastico, tremendoso!*"

Luca responded with a hearty, appreciative laugh. "I think maybe we're talking about different places. Eight thirty okay? We'll be driving to Arezzo."

EIGHTEEN

IN the conference room, Rocco leaned back in one of the pearl-gray Aeron conference chairs with his feet up on another. He sat with his hands clasped behind his neck, a Marlboro between his lips. Across the table Martignetti jotted notes in his pad.

"You think there's anything to this Cesare angle?" the lieutenant asked, blowing smoke toward the matte white panels of the fluorescent-lit ceiling. "You think he could have killed them both? On account of the will?"

"I'd say he's our best bet right now. Better than the beer company angle."

"You think he'd kill his own mother for a few thousand euros?"

"He's a cokehead, *Tenente*," Martignetti said, as if that was more than enough to explain things.

Which it was, in Rocco's opinion. "Yeah, you're right," he said sleepily. "Look, you come right through the Santa Croce district to get to work. Why don't you pick him up on your way in tomorrow morning and bring him in? I'm interested to meet the guy."

At which point Linda swept in with a tray on which were two espresso cups, a glass pot of coffee holding an additional three or four cups of coffee, and a plate of almond-orange biscotti.

"Linda, God bless you!" Rocco said. "I was just gonna fall asleep. You saved my life."

She set down the tray. "If Franco saw you with your feet up on one of his chairs like that, your life wouldn't be worth much, Lieutenant."

Rocco, leaving his feet on the chair, poured the coffee for himself and Martignetti. "But you won't tell him, will you, sweetheart?" He drank the entire cupful and sighed with pleasure. "The heart begins to beat again," he said. "The blood flows."

"Nothing in comparison to how it'd flow if he knew you were smoking in his conference room. But no, I won't tell."

"You're a wonderful woman, Linda," he said, but he ground the butt out on the heavy paper doily on the tray. "Wait, before you go," he said as she turned to leave. "Do you think there's anything to that Humboldt-Schlager thing? Is that something we should be focusing on, in your opinion?"

"No. None of those guys killed Pietro, Lieutenant. They worshipped the man."

"Sometimes, disappointed worshippers can turn—" Martignetti began.

"They *loved* him too, *Maresciallo*. I know you two have to investigate every lead that turns up, but believe me, there's nothing in this world, no disappointment, no resentment, no argument—and there were plenty of those—that would have been capable of leading any of them to lay a hand on him. It would have been like laying a hand on God."

"How about on Nola?" Rocco asked.

"Well, now, that's a different question," Linda said, smiling. "But as Franco said, Nola had nothing to do with the Humboldt thing, so—"

"She had no say in it at all? It wasn't a joint decision?"

Now she laughed outright, a husky, pleasing chuckle. "That, Lieutenant, was not a term in common usage around here in Pietro's time." She paused, then added in an undertone: "Not so common now, either."

"Franco runs a one-man operation too?" Rocco asked. "Like his old man?"

"Very much like his old man, although he'd hate to hear anybody say it. Is there anything else you need, Lieutenant? I have to get back to the course. I'm demonstrating this afternoon, and my *torta di riso* is coming out of the oven in five minutes."

"Go in peace," Rocco said, and raised his cup to her in heartfelt appreciation. "And thanks!"

On her way out, she very nearly collided with Severo Quadrelli, who was striding buoyantly down the hall. "Linda, Linda," he greeted her. "Lovely girl."

Linda looked at him curiously. "Hi, Severo."

Martignetti, facing the open doorway of the conference room, called out to him. "Hallo? Signor Quadrelli? Could we see you again for a moment, please?" He spoke in Italian.

Quadrelli stopped and came to the doorway. "Yes, what is it?"

"We realized there are a few more things we need to ask you about. Come in, please. Sit down."

"Will this take very long? I have quite a number of things—"

"Please," Rocco said. "Sit."

"Very well, very well." The chairs were a bit narrow for him, but he waggled his bulk into one of them with a sigh, smiling forbearance. "Now, then, what can I do for you?"

"Your call to Cesare's attorney went well?" Rocco asked. "You seem pleased."

"Very pleased, yes. She very politely thanked me for the information. She was quite subdued, as I would have been in her place. I'd venture to say that's the last we've heard of signora Batelli. How could it be otherwise? This suit of theirs is founded on grievances suffered as a result of signora Cubbiddu's "wrongful death" at the hands of signor Cubbiddu. Now we learn that he was not among the living at the time of her unfortunate death, so how can he have been responsible? *Causa finita est.*"

"I'm happy that we've been of service. The suit was against signor Cubbiddu's estate?"

"Against Franco."

Rocco frowned. "I understood that all three sons were beneficiaries of his will."

"Yes, that's so. But Luca and Nico—*and* Cesare, may I point out—received stipends, extremely generous stipends. Franco, naturally, was bequeathed the great bulk of the physical estate, including the winery and this property."

" 'Naturally' because he was the oldest son?" said Martignetti.

Quadrelli correctly sensed an implied criticism and drew himself up a little. Into the armholes of his vest went his thumbs. "It is thanks to the institution of primogeniture, *Maresciallo*, that many historic and culturally precious properties have been kept from dissolution.

Could Villa Antica have remained as it was, had it been divided among the four young men? Especially with Cesare having a quarter interest?"

"True, but it is also thanks to primogeniture—" began Martignetti, but Rocco quickly cut in. Tonino was the second oldest of seven children in the family of a wealthy publisher who also subscribed to primogeniture, and he, like his siblings, had wound up out on the street when the eldest brother inherited. Tonino was a good-humored man, but primogeniture was his bête noire, and Rocco had learned it was best not to let him get started.

"You served as the executor of signor Cubbiddu's estate, is that correct, signor Quadrelli?" Rocco asked.

"Yes, quite correct, quite correct," Quadrelli agreed, feathers only slightly ruffled.

"And what about the time during which the two of them were missing? The time before they were found? You acted as . . . I don't remember what it's called."

"It's called 'conservator.' Yes, I was appointed conservator. By the courts."

"Right, conservator. Which means you oversaw the accounts and handled finances in general, both the Cubbiddu family accounts and the Villa Antica accounts. You saw that debts were paid and so on, do we have that right?"

"Yes, quite right, quite right. And I requested and received a judgment permitting me to make disbursements in accord with his will."

"Good," Rocco said pleasantly, although the lawyer was getting under his skin with his jovial, patronizing condescension. You could practically hear a benevolent "my boy" tacked on at the end of his responses. "We'd like to have copies of those accounts, if you don't mind. Tonino, maybe you could go with signor Quadrelli to his office—"

"The accounts? But you already have them. I gave them to you—to *Maresciallo* Martignetti, actually—at the time of the disappearance, don't you remember, *Maresciallo*? But if you need duplicates, I'll be more than happy to provide them. Anything at all I can do to help." *My boy.*

"No," Martignetti said, "those were the accounts up until the time the two of them disappeared. What we'd like to see now are the accounts for the time just afterward; say, October through November of last year."

"I don't understand. Pietro was already deceased by then, no? What possible relevance could his—his *postmortem* finances, so to speak—what possible relevance could they have to your investigation?"

"Well, it's just that we have to cover every possible source of information," Rocco said.

Quadrelli coughed gently and cleared his throat. "You're welcome to them, of course, but I must admit to a certain hesitance. The privacy of the entire family is involved, you see, and I consider myself the custodian of . . . not that any of them have anything to hide . . . but you see, a natural, ah, prudence constrains, ah . . ."

A barely perceptible look passed between the two *carabinieri*. Over the years, Rocco Gardella and Antonio Martignetti had developed a highly productive interview routine when the situation called for it. Not bad cop vs. good cop so much as dumb cop vs. smart cop; or maybe friendly, easygoing, what-you-see-is-what-you-get cop (think Columbo) vs. streetwise, don't-mess-with-me cop (Kojak in a smaller, quicker, better-looking version). Martignetti was the nice guy, Rocco was the dangerous one.

The roles came naturally to them: wearing a leather bomber jacket, Rocco would pass more easily as a hood than as a cop. But when he was a cop, everything about him practically said out loud that he knew you were lying, and if you weren't lying you were covering something up, and if you weren't covering something up you were, at the very least, fudging the facts. And you'd better shape up if you knew what was good for you. Martignetti, five years older and ten years longer in police work, took a more tolerant view of human nature, and his kindly, world-weary mug and intelligent, blue-gray eyes told you he was more happy than your average police officer to take you at your word and less eager to toss you in the clink if you inadvertenly said something you hadn't meant at all. At least until contrary evidence came along.

The glance between the two was accompanied by the barest of nods from Rocco, a signal that he was jumping into character. "If there's nothing to hide," he said crisply while Quadrelli was still hemming and hawing, "then there's no problem. Let's go get them now."

"Yes, but you see, it's not as easy as that. As I've tried to explain, it's, ah, my job to protect the welfare and privacy of the Cubbiddu family—"

"You just told us there wasn't anything to hide. Am I right, *Maresciallo?*"

Martignetti looked at his notes. "'Not that any of them have anything to hide,'" he read.

Quadrelli twisted his neck as if his collar were too tight and the fluorescent panels caught the gleam of sweat on the curve of his forehead. "And there *isn't* anything to hide. All the same, I feel it's incumbent on me to ask that you provide a warrant—"

"Didn't you just say we were welcome to them? *Maresciallo*, didn't—"

"Yes, yes, yes, that's what I said, but on second thought—"

"You didn't ask for a warrant before, when you gave us the earlier records. Why is this different?"

Quadrelli appealed to Martignetti. "*Maresciallo*, I really . . ." His tone and manner were somewhere between entreaty and indignation, but closer to the first: *Why am I being harassed in this manner?* But Martignetti merely smiled pleasantly, while Rocco continued to fix him with a cold stare.

Quadrelli rose, lifting his double chin and tugging down the bottom of his vest. There was a massive gold-banded Rolex on his wrist. "I have nothing more to say. Those accounts have been entrusted to my guardianship. I do not feel I can surrender them to you without the safeguard of a judicial warrant demanding them. Gentlemen."

"If that's the way you want it, fine," Rocco said, biting off the words. "We'll be back here with one first thing tomorrow morning." *Talk about wishful thinking.*

"You know, signore," Martignetti said slowly, as Quadrelli turned to go, "it's really up to you. We'll do it the way you want, but if we could get the accounts today with your cooperation, which we'd very much appreciate, it'd save us a lot of paperwork."

Quadrelli remained standing, silent and glowering, but a muscle under his right eye twitched. He brushed at it with his hand, as if it had been caused by a flying insect.

"And between us," Martignetti continued with his friendly smile, "I'd sure do it that way if it was me. Why in the world would you want to call attention to yourself and irritate an overworked magistrate, when the result would be no different—either way, you relinquish the accounts. That makes sense to me. Doesn't it make sense to you?"

"Are you threatening me, *Maresciallo*?"

"Absolutely not," Martignetti said earnestly. "Look, signore, all I'm trying to do is to make things go as smoothly as possible for everybody concerned. But it's your choice."

"We've wasted enough time here," Rocco abruptly announced. "Let's go. We'll file for a warrant as soon as we—"

Quadrelli sighed. His fat-padded shoulders sagged. "If you come with me, *Maresciallo*, I will turn them over to you. I will want a receipt."

"Absolutely," Rocco said.

Ten minutes later, Martignetti was back with two thick folders. "Well done, Tonino," Rocco said. "So what did you think of that whole routine of his?"

Martignetti stroked his chin and pondered. "After due consideration," he said, "I think he just might have something to hide."

Rocco smiled. "Well, enough for today. You can start digging into that paperwork tomorrow morning." He got up and took a long, luxurious stretch. "What would you say to a Cinzano before we head back?"

"I'd say, lead me to it."

NINETEEN

JULIE peered doubtfully up at the time-eaten marble street plaque affixed to the corner of an old building. "Via del Bicchieraia," she read aloud. "This is it."

"Nah, can't be," John said.

The other two in their party, Marti Lau and Gideon, had to agree with him. More alley than street, barely two car widths wide, lacking sidewalks, and bordered by moldering eighteenth-century, three-story apartment houses faced with peeling stucco that showed their rubble-stone construction, Via del Bicchieraia didn't look like a street that housed the best restaurant in Tuscany.

It was only two blocks long, overshadowed at one end by the stark "tower of a hundred holes," the grim, thirteenth-century Romanesque bell tower of the Church of Santa Maria della Pieve, so called because of the eight forbidding stories of mullioned windows that encircled it. At the other end it was closed off by an old apartment building on a cross street. With the looming tower and the leaning buildings, it was doubtful if the sun ever made it all the way to the street itself.

"Well, he said it was here," Gideon said. "Number twenty-three. Let's have a look."

They had to watch their step because there was no sidewalk; the irregular, stone-block pavement was uneven; and they had to negotiate around cars that were parked along the sides, jammed up against the walls of the buildings. When a small panel truck came down the street, they had to hurry to get around a parked car and flatten themselves against a wall.

"If two cars come along from opposite directions, it's every man for himself," John muttered.

But they were lucky, making it without incident to number twenty-three, the address Luca had given them. It was a storefront, its two windows partially covered by warped, gray shutters that surely hadn't been repainted in this century, and maybe not in the last. No menu outside—not even a chalkboard—no stickers indicating acceptable credit cards, nothing but a couple of barely legible words painted in fading green directly on the stone lintel above the door: La Cucina di Nonna Natalia. Grandma Natalia's Kitchen.

"This is it, all right," Marti said.

"Well, he did say it wasn't very impressive," Gideon said.

"He got that right," said John.

"Or very welcoming," Julie said. "Do you think maybe it'd be better to wait for them?" She glanced up the street for Luca and Linda, who were parking the winery van in an underground lot a few blocks away. "They should only be another minute."

At that moment, though, two automobiles did turn onto the street from opposite ends, and that decided them. Something had to give. Gideon pulled the door open—predictably, the hinges squealed—and in they went.

The aromas were wonderful; homey and warm, but with something subtle about them that was hard to pin down. The restaurant itself was less wonderful, a narrow room, only two tables wide, with an aisle down the middle. The walls held a single row of shelving on which bottles of red wine were sporadically displayed, the flooring was of much-worn tiles of cheap, wood-veneered plywood, and the tablecloths (which were white linen or cotton in almost every eating place in Italy) were red-and-white-checked plastic, the kind you found in cheap Italian chains in America. The diners, mostly older people, didn't seem to be bothered by their shabby surroundings. They were eating happily and with gusto. Even for an Italian restaurant, the noise level was high. There was lots of laughter and the frequent clinking of glasses.

"You know, I like this place," Gideon announced. "It's, I don't know . . ."

"Real?" said Julie, laughing.

"That's it."

An overweight woman came heavily forward to greet them. Other than wearing a scowl instead of a smile, she was an Italian version of Aunt Jemima: a white kitchen towel was wrapped bandanna-like around her head, and a white, stained apron covered a shapeless red-and-white-checked housedress that matched the tablecloths.

"You came here to eat?" she somewhat suspiciously asked in Italian.

"No, to buy car," Marti said, but only to herself.

"Yes, please, signora," said Gideon, the designated Italian-speaker.

"*Americani?*"

"Yes."

"Not many Americans like this food."

"We'd like very much to try it."

"Dinner costs fifty euros. Including wine and mineral water." It was delivered more like a warning than an information bulletin.

"That's fine," Gideon said.

"*Bueno*," said John. "*Bene, bene.*"

She appeared to be of two minds about whether or not to let them come in any farther, but finally she nodded with a sigh. "All right, follow me."

"There'll be six of us altogether," Gideon told her. "Our friends are on the way."

This was met with a shrug. She led them through an archway to a smaller, extremely plain room that held only two tables, both unoccupied, and began to shove them together. Gideon and John jumped to assist, receiving no thanks for their efforts. "She's not exactly thrilled to see us, is she?" Julie whispered to Gideon. "I'm getting a little uncomfortable."

"How long until your friends come?" the woman asked.

"They'll be here any minute."

She grunted and moved off.

"Perhaps we could have some wine while we wait?" Gideon called.

Another nod.

"White wine for me," said Marti, who had enough Italian to manage that much.

"No white wine. Only red. You want white wine, you have to go someplace else. Plenty of other restaurants in Arezzo."

Marti didn't understand it all, but Gideon did. He was ready to go find one of the other restaurants, but he didn't want to disappoint Luca. But his tone was sharp: "Please bring us menus to look at while we wait. The special menus."

"No menus."

"No menus? How will we know what to order?"

It appeared that Gideon wasn't the only one who was annoyed. Clearly, the woman had had it with them, and her voice went up a few decibels. "Hey. You go to the symphony, to the opera?"

"What? Yes." But he stared at her, wondering if he'd misunderstood.

She stared fiercely back at him. "And when you go to the symphony, do you tell the conductor what to play?"

"I . . ."

"No, you trust that he knows what he is doing. You put yourself in his hands."

"Signora—"

But whatever he was about to say was cut off by a burst of booming, full-throated laughter—only Luca laughed like that—from the archway. The woman looked up and, like some kind of quick-change magic trick, her scowl was replaced by a lovely if crooked-toothed smile that completely altered her personality and would have lit up the room on its own. "Luca!" she cried joyfully. She pointed at Gideon and then shook the finger at Luca. "You put them up to this, you scoundrel!" She was laughing almost as hard as he was, and her bare upper arms jiggled like Jell-O.

"Indeed I did, Amalia," Luca said.

Indeed he had, Gideon thought. "And make sure to ask for the special menus," he'd told them earnestly an hour earlier. "It will show them that you know what you're doing, that you're not just a bunch of dumb tourists who wandered in by mistake."

It took a few seconds to explain to the others what had been going on, by which time everybody was laughing and was friends with everybody else. Amalia actually squeezed Gideon's shoulder affectionately, a friendship offering. "I bring wine now," she said in English.

"You have to stop doing that, Luca," Linda said as they sat down. "One of these days, she's going to dump a pot of *pasta e fagioli* on your head."

"Yeah, thanks a whole lot, Luca," John grumped.

Luca was still chuckling. "I can't help it. I love to hear her do her symphony speech." He went into an Italian-accent falsetto. "'Do you tell the conductor what to play?'" A little more laughter, and then he sobered. "That lady, Amalia Vezzoni, is the finest cook I know, the finest in Tuscany. She's my, what do you call it, my role model. In fact . . . well . . ."

"Oh, go ahead and tell them," Linda said. "Why not?"

"Sure, why not? Well, the fact is, Amalia's getting older now, and her husband, who used to work with her, died last year. So we've been talking about buying into this place, working with her— and learning from her—for a while, and then, when she's ready to call it quits, buying the whole thing from her. Time for me to get out of Villa Antica, anyway. It's not the same with Franco in the driver's seat, and anyhow, it's really food I'm excited about now, not wine-making. What do you think?"

Gideon couldn't help glancing around the place. "Um—"

His expression gave him away. "Yeah, we know," Linda said.

"It's a little tacky. Amalia's kind of let the place go. We plan on putting some money into making some improvements."

"But not too many," Luca said. "We don't want a fancy place, that's not the point." He leveled a forefinger at Linda. "And nothing changes at all in the kitchen."

"Well, maybe some of those old cast-iron pots, the ones with holes in them?" Linda suggested.

"They can be repaired. No, the kitchen is beautiful, it's like my grandmother's, just five times as big. The sign out front will have to change, though. It's going to be *La Cucina di Nonna Gina*." With that happy thought, he settled back, smiling.

Amalia returned with a waiter and with two bottles of wine, six glasses, and a couple of baskets of crusty bread. Proudly, she held up one of the bottles for Luca to examine.

"Oho, Brunello di Montalcino," he read. "From Mastrojanni. Wonderful. Is this what everybody's getting tonight, or just us?"

"Shh, better not to ask," Amalia whispered.

The waiter didn't bother to offer him the cork to sniff or a dollop of wine to sip, but simply filled all six glasses, confident they'd be acceptable.

And they were. Luca raised his glass in salute after tasting.

"They wanted white wine," Amalia told him, obviously an in-joke, but an indulgent one, like a story one parent tells to another about their child's escapades that day. Luca smiled in response.

"So what's wrong with white wine?" a pouting Marti wondered. "We've been to some first-rate restaurants in Florence and had no trouble getting a pretty damn good local pinot grigio, or a Soave, or—"

"Well, yes," Luca answered, "it's true you can get some 'pretty damn good' whites here, but Tuscany's *red* wines are matchless. Its whites . . . can be matched. And Amalia, like me, is a perfectionist. As you'll see shortly." He dunked a crust of bread in his glass, popped the sopping chunk into his mouth, and rolled his eyes with contentment. "Ahh. So. Well. Gideon. You said you were going back to the funeral home to look at the bones again. . . ."

"Which we did." He and John had spent two frustrating and ultimately unproductive hours with the remains. They'd filled their wives in, but not Luca and Linda.

"And did you come up with anything?" Linda asked. "Do you know what killed him? Any ideas at all?"

Gideon was surprised that they wanted to talk about it at dinner, but if they were game, he was game. Linda and Luca were technically suspects, but, perhaps unwisely, he had excluded them from his own list of possibles. "Not really, Linda. There are those green-stick fractures I was telling you about, but I'm guessing they probably came from the fall. Or put it this way: I have no reason to think they didn't; they're perfectly consistent with a fall from a height."

What he didn't tell them—why confuse things even more than they already were?—was that the fact that they were consistent with fall-type injuries didn't mean they were *inconsistent* with ballistic-type injuries. When bullets hit long bones, or flat bones, or ribs, they didn't necessarily make the nice, round, internally beveled holes that they made in the skull, and which were instantly recognizable as entrance wounds. Instead, they often just broke or shattered the bones, so they looked no different than bones that had taken some other kind of blunt-trauma hit . . . such as a fall. And Pietro's remains had plenty of those.

"Nothing else, huh?" Luca asked. "No clues at all?"

"Afraid not, but look, you have to remember, there are all kinds of ways to kill someone without leaving any marks on the skeleton."

"That's true," Linda agreed. "Poison, suffocation—"

"Well, yes, but even knives and guns. It's not all that rare for a knife or even a slug to penetrate the heart without touching a rib or the sternum or the scapula or anything bony. So not finding anything doesn't prove that there wasn't anything."

"But Gideon, I was thinking," Julie said slowly, "if you didn't find anything, doesn't that mean it's possible there *wasn't* anything? That nobody killed him? That he just died from, I don't know, a stroke, a heart attack. Anything. People die."

"Well, yes, of course it's possible, but if he died of natural causes, why shoot him a month later?"

"Why shoot him a month later if he died of *unnatural* causes?"

"And why kill Nola?" John asked her.

"And why throw them off the cliff?" Marti asked.

"Heck, I don't know. Don't jump all over me. I'm just thinking out loud. I don't see that the experts"—an eyebrow-raised glance at John and Gideon—"are doing any better. In fact, for all we know, maybe killing Nola was the whole point of it, and making it look as if Pietro did it was a way of covering it up so—"

"If that's what it was about," Gideon said, "then I'd have to say it sure was convenient for the killer that he just happened to have Pietro's dead body lying around just waiting for him. Talk about lucky heart attacks." He began to laugh, but then caught a glimpse of Luca's face. "Luca, I'm sorry. I keep forgetting. It's your father we're talking about. I shouldn't be—"

Luca waved him silent. "Forget it. Time to change the subject anyway. Here comes our dinner. Get ready for the best that Italy has to offer."

But Gideon found the five-course meal disappointing. There weren't many Italian dishes that he actively disliked, but this meal had them all, starting with *ribollita*, the bread-thickened bean-and-cabbage affair that was somewhere between soup and stew, that you could eat equally well with a fork or a spoon. Then came a *taglierini* and truffle dish about which he had no complaints, but the main course of *ossobuco*—veal shanks braised in wine with tomatoes, carrots, and onions—was his least favorite Italian dish of all.

The others all seemed to love everything that was put in front of them (Marti passed on the *ossobuco*, of course, having two lip-smacking bowls of the *ribollita* instead), and after a while Gideon realized what his problem was, and why he'd never liked these particular foods. Nonna Natalia's cooking reminded him too much of his own Polish-Austrian great aunt's productions. The *ribollita* was blood-brother to her gluey cabbage and barley soup, and the *ossobuco* was close kin to her dreaded *schmorbraten*—rump roast simmered on the range top—and simmered, and then simmered some more, until the gray meat literally slid off the bone and fell apart into shreds. It was from *Tante* Frieda's pot roast that he'd learned first-hand that muscle was constituted of long, separable, stringy fibers.

Even the dessert was straight out of *Tante's* kitchen: bread pudding. But here he had to admit that Nonna Natalia's *budino di pane,* had *Tante* Frieda's *ofenschlupfer* beat by a mile. Frieda made up for overcooking everything she cooked on the range by under-baking everything she did in the oven. Her "famous" bread pudding was a crustless, sodden, overly sweet lump of dough, edible because it had cinnamon and raisins in it, but nothing to look forward to. Nonna Natalia's *budino* was another thing altogether, brown and crunchy on top, delicate as a fine soufflé inside, only slightly sweetened, and filled with perfectly cooked apples, figs, and pears; as warming to the soul as it was to the body as it glided down his throat. Eating it was enough to make him forgive Nonna Natalia for her *ossobuco*, and he happily spooned up a second helping from the family-style bowl it had come in, as did most of the others.

Only as they finished their desserts, pushed back from the table a little, and turned to their espressos, biscotti, and glasses of Vin Santo, did the talk return from food and wine to the events of the day.

Luca loosened his belt a notch or two, shoved his chair back from the table, and patted his belly. "Well. I suppose, except for Linda, none of you guys have heard the latest development from the Cesare branch of the family."

"We know about the wrongful death suit, if that's what you mean," Marti said.

"No, that was hours ago, ancient history. This is a weird new twist."

"This sounds bad," Gideon said.

"It's not good. You remember when Severo went out to call his attorney? He couldn't wait to tell her she might as well forget about suing us, because, what do you know, *babbo* couldn't have killed Nola, being dead himself at the time?"

Gideon nodded. "Sure."

"Well, it worked. She listened to what he had to say, she took an hour to think it over, and she did it. She dropped the suit."

"And this is not good, why?" John asked.

"Because, instead of suing Franco for four million or whatever it was, now she's challenging the entire will. She wants it declared invalid."

"On what grounds?" Marti asked.

Luca waited while Amalia returned with the bottle to refill the glasses of those who wanted more Vin Santo. Only Gideon declined: too sweet for his taste. He considered asking if there was any brandy, but decided it was safer to let it pass.

"So, what you think?" a smiling Amalia asked in English when she'd finished pouring and setting the bottle down on the table for their continuing use. "Pretty good dinner, no?"

Everyone, Gideon included, agreed that it had been superb, even better than they'd expected. Only when she departed, broadly smiling, did Luca come back to Marti's question.

"On what grounds? On the grounds that, since Pietro died before Nola—*weeks* before her, according to the brilliant, world-famous Skeleton Detective . . ."

Gideon sighed. "Gee, why do I have this feeling that I'm about to get blamed for something?"

". . . that, since Nola outlived Pietro, everything should technically have gone to her when he died."

"Wait a second," Gideon said. "I thought his will left pretty much everything to Franco—the winery and all—with you and Nico and Cesare getting monthly stipends for a few years. Is that not right? Or did he leave something to Nola too?"

Luca poured some more wine for Linda and for himself, and passed the bottle to John. "No, that's not right, not quite. The two of them had—I forget what it's called in English—they had the same will—"

"A joint will?" Marti suggested.

"That's it, yeah. Consisting of one paragraph. Three sentences. Exactly a hundred and fifteen words; I counted them once."

"Pretty short for a will disposing of an estate like that," said John.

"No kidding. And they didn't even have that until Severo practically forced them into it, kicking and screaming."

The Cubbiddus, it seemed, like many of their brethren in Barbagia at that time, didn't believe in written wills. When a man died, his possessions passed to his eldest son, and that was that. Attorneys? Probate? The courts? No need for them, not in those mountain villages. Everyone knew the way it worked, and no one would think of contesting it when it happened. For one thing, nobody had anything worth fighting over, but even more important was the fear of what they called *malocchio*, the evil eye that was always on the lookout for you to make some slip, leave some opening that would let the spirits of misfortune and calamity into your life. And one way to do that, sure to bring laughter to those malevolent entities, was to "make plans" for your own death or that of someone you loved, or to talk about it, or even to think about it. So . . . no wills. And the authorities couldn't be bothered with doing anything about it, not if it took going into those primitive, bandit-ridden mountain villages.

Luca paused, remembering. "I know this sounds like something from the Middle Ages, but, you know, I was born there, and I lived there, in Nuragugme—population forty-two, including us—until I was fifteen and *babbo* got married and moved us all here. Believe me, that's the way it was, and that's the way the two of them were. And the way they stayed. You'd think a guy with so much on the ball, all that business sense, couldn't possibly be that superstitious—"

"No, I wouldn't think that at all," said Gideon. "Smart people can be pretty dumb when they venture outside of their own ball-parks."

Luca smiled. "Yeah, you're right about that. Anyway, for years they refused to consider having wills at all. It drove Severo nuts, and then finally—this was, like, no more than five years ago—"

"Four years," Linda said. "They did it just after I got here."

"Four years ago," said Luca, "he finally convinced them things were different here, and if they didn't have a will, there'd be hell to pay when they died. I think they agreed to sign the thing just to make him stop talking about dying."

"Well, what *did* it say, Luca?" Julie asked.

"It didn't leave everything to Franco; they left everything to each other."

"Each other?" John said. "So how did Franco wind up with the winery?"

"Here's the way it worked: The first sentence says that they leave everything to each other. The second one says something like 'If my spouse should predecease me, then I leave everything to my beloved son Franco,' with those stipends to the others."

"To Franco? Nothing about Cesare? I'm surprised Nola would have gone along with that," Gideon said. "I only met her a few times, but she struck me as being pretty strong-minded. I'd have thought she'd have fought for more than that for him."

"She probably did," Luca said. "I wouldn't be surprised. You're right about her being strong-minded, and she sure as hell didn't hesitate to speak her mind."

"I'll say," Linda said with a chuckly laugh. "If you think it was tough being her stepson, you should've tried being her daughter-in-law."

"Yeah, but when it came to final decisions, she was just as old-school as he was. It's the husband, the *papà*, who decides, and he does it on his own. He doesn't take a vote."

"That's true," Linda said, "and there's something else. I don't know about you, Luca, but I'm not really positive that Nola understood what was in that will. For one thing, she never did learn to read that well. For another—and Severo told me this—she seemed to think that if she didn't look at it when she signed it, it might get around that evil eye she was worried about. So she kept her eyes closed. Severo had to guide her hand to the right place."

"Hadn't heard that," Luca said. "Sounds right, though."

"What did the third sentence say?" Gideon said.

Luca had to think for a moment. "Oh, yeah, that was the short one. It names Severo as executor. That's it."

"I don't get it," Marti said. "If I understand you right, it says that Franco gets it all, whoever predeceases whoever, right? So what's Cesare's grievance? What's the lawyer expect to get for him?"

"That I can't tell you. I'm already confused enough. Maybe she's going to say Nola could have fought to change the will, if she'd lived. Severo thinks it's just that she wants to get it hauled into court. Once that happens, all bets are off."

"Just like in the States," Marti said.

"Not only that," said Linda, "but the way things work here, once the lawyers really get their teeth into it, it'll be tied up for, like, the next ten years, and everything around here would be in limbo."

"Just like in the States," Marti said again, and hoisted her glass in toast. "Here's to Shakespeare's finest quote—"

"*Henry VI!*" someone said

And then, amidst general laughter spontaneous enough to turn heads: "The first thing we do, let's kill all the lawyers."

TWENTY

THE following morning Gideon was on his own. Julie and Marti were learning how to make *zabaglione*, and John had turned down his invitation to join him at the Museo Galileo, formerly the Museo di Storia della Scienze, in Florence. Having the morning to himself suited him fine. The museum, which he also had pretty much to himself, was housed in yet another gorgeous sixteenth-century palazzo (yawn) on the Arno. The building directly abutted the Uffizi, but while the line to enter that celebrated museum already wound around the corner at nine thirty in the morning, getting into the Galileo was simply a matter of walking through the human-size entry cut into the great wooden portal and paying one's eight euros at the desk.

Once having paid, he paused in the anteroom to call Rocco and suggest lunch if the *tenente* was available. Rocco was all for it and recommended a little mom-and-pop place he liked on Via della Condotta, a block or so from the Piazza Signoria. "Good food, and we can be in and out in half an hour."

Gideon wasn't ordinarily a quick eater, but after last night's three-hour marathon, "in and out in half an hour" sounded wonderful, and they agreed to meet at one.

"There are a couple of quick things I should probably tell you now, though," Gideon said. "I don't really know how important they are. Do you know about the will Pietro and Nola had? What was in it, I mean?"

"It might be in the file somewhere, or maybe Martignetti knows about it, but, no, I don't think I'm familiar with it. So tell me. But make it short."

Gideon explained about what he'd heard at Nonna Natalia the previous night. He could hear Rocco's pen or pencil scratching away intermittently.

"Oh, and the situation with Cesare's suit has changed since you heard about it too. Now he's contesting the entire will. Says it's invalid because Pietro was killed first."

"That doesn't make sense to me. Same will, what's the difference?"

"I know. Severo thinks his lawyer just figures if you open up a can of worms, something good's bound to come out of it."

"Out of a can of worms?"

"Bad metaphor."

"Hold on," Rocco said. "I got a call coming in from Martignetti."

The call must have been on a different telephone because Gideon heard what was said, or rather the start of what was said.

"*Si, Tonino, che si dice?*"

Martignetti's reply was audible, if only barely. "*Houston, abbiamo un problema.*"

A few seconds later, Rocco jumped back on the line with Gideon: "I think I better hang up, Gid. See you at one—no, make it one thirty. Leave your cell phone on in case I can't make it at all." He clicked off, leaving Gideon to wonder what was up. If the *problema* had anything to do with the Cubbiddus, though, he expected he'd hear about it at lunch.

The museum was a bigger place than he'd expected, with more rooms, and as far as he knew there were no more than half a dozen visitors in it. It was a shame, he thought, that science drew so paltry an audience, but it certainly made museum-going a lot more pleasant than those folks had it in the next building over. He was able to wander at his leisure and pause as long as he wished at the objects that caught his interest. Of which there were many: evocative, sepia-colored antique maps, huge sixteenth-century globes made to adorn royal apartments, fabulous golden armillary spheres that had tracked the heavens five hundred years ago. There were six-foot-long wooden astronomical telescopes, an ingenious sixteenth century calculator, frightening old surgical instruments, and even an eighteenth-century "mechanical paradox" in which a cylinder placed at the bottom of a set of rails rolled quite indubitably upward when released.

And of course there was a room devoted to Galileo Galilei, which Gideon saved for last, like dessert, and in which he wandered, blissfully absorbed, for almost an hour. There were prisms that the great man had used in his experiments with light, his magnetic lodestones, his precious, wood-and-leather *occhialino* (little eye) that future generations would call a microscope.

There was even a skeletal remnant for the anthropologist in him: in a transparent, egg-shaped reliquary filigreed with gold resided the gracefully extended middle finger of Galileo's right hand, pointing straight up.

—————

THREE blocks from where Gideon stood pondering the implications of that upraised middle finger (a last message from beyond the grave to the Inquisition that had so hounded and persecuted him in his last years?) lay the rest of the scientist's remains. Housed in a suitably grand marble tomb in the Basilica of Santa Croce, they had rested for almost three hundred years alongside those of Michelangelo, Machiavelli, and Leonardo Bruni.

In front of the basilica was the usual broad piazza, at the far end of which, perhaps three hundred feet from the great façade, Rocco Gardella stood before the window of a top-floor apartment, his back to the famous scene. The building in which he stood was yet another restored old palazzo, distinctly upscale, with rental prices to match, but this particular apartment was anything but. The place was squalid, fetid. There were microwave trays and bowls of congealing food from more than one meal—more than five or six meals—on the kitchen counter, on the stove, in the sink. Some of them had been there so long mold was growing on them. There were blackened banana peels, shriveled brown apple cores, cups of caffe latte in which the milk had curdled halfway to yogurt. Emptied, unrinsed cans of soup, beans, and stewed fruit filled the sink. Candy wrappers everywhere. Discarded clothing, mostly socks and underwear, lay in tangled clumps and piles on the floors of all three rooms, and the bathroom as well. The whole place stank of rotting food, dirty laundry, and mildewed towels. Rocco, thinking about rats, had moved with care in looking into dark corners or closets when he'd first arrived, but if there were rats around, they'd scurried into the walls by now.

His attention was fixed on a bed containing yet another set of mortal remains. This one was curled on its side among twisted, grungy sheets, dressed in a shirt and trousers, and still wearing shoes. Bent over the body was the *medico legale*, doing what they do at such scenes: pressing eyeballs, raising limbs and letting them drop, sniffing at the dead, wide-open mouth. With them in the apartment were a photographer, along with two crime-scene officers busily plying their forceps, plastic envelopes, and mysterious lights, sprays, and powders. *Maresciallo* Antonio Martignetti was also there, wandering around and poking into drawers and closets.

Ordinarily, the death of a known addict under circumstances that practically screamed *overdose* wouldn't be getting the level of scrutiny that this one was, but when the addict himself happened to be a suspect, or at the very least a potential material witness, in a double murder currently under investigation, a different level of effort was called for. And this particular corpse, the former Cesare Baccarreda Cubbiddu had fit that description to a *T*.

Happily (from Rocco's point of view), Captain Conforti hadn't felt that it was necessary to bring in the public prosecutor yet, so there was no officious Migliorini clone to deal with. It was also fortunate, he thought, that the *medico legale* who had been assigned was the one he found easiest to work with, the round, smiling, and Buddha-like Dr. Melio Bosco, the seventy-six-year-old physician who had been on the scene in the Casentinese when the Cubbiddus' skeletons had been found.

Bosco had been at it for twenty minutes, and when he straightened up he did it with a groan. "My lumbar spine's getting too old for this, Rocco," he said, kneading his back with the fingers of both hands. "I need to find a new line of work, something easy. Look into applying to the *Carabinieri*, maybe. What do you think?"

"I don't know, Melio, it *is* awfully easy work. Wouldn't be challenging enough for you. So, how long has he been dead?"

Bosco stripped off his gloves, tossed them into his bag, and steepled his fingers before his chest. "I would say that it was somewhere between six and twelve hours ago—thirteen to be on the safe side—that this gentleman embarked on his passage across the Styx with that ferryman of ghosts, grave Charon at his oar."

"Dante?"

"Euripides."

"See, that's what I mean. You're too smart for the *Carabinieri*. Six to thirteen hours. So that'd be, uh, eight o'clock or so last night at the earliest, four o'clock this morning at the latest?"

"Say, you're pretty smart yourself."

"Anything to say on the . . . wait a minute . . . yeah, on the *cause* of death?"

"Heart failure, I would guess."

"Induced by a cocaine overdose?"

"Let's wait for the toxicology report on that, but the circumstances would seem to point us in that direction, wouldn't you agree?" He nodded toward the marble-topped nightstand beside the bed, with a number of items scattered across its surface: a nail clipper, a ring of keys, a bottle of cough medicine, a couple of ballpoints, some used, wadded tissues. And, more significantly, what was known in the trade as a snuff kit: a makeup-size mirror, a single-edge razor blade, a tiny spoon, a three-inch-long copper tube about the diameter of a drinking straw, and a little bottle with a bit of white sediment in it. Alongside them was the open case, made of expensive leather, that had held them neatly in their places with elastic loops and zippered pockets. It was called a snuff kit because, when advertised for sale, it was uniformly described as a set of accessories for those who took snuff. Advertisers with a sense of humor sometimes made a point of stating that it was never, ever, under any circumstances, to be used for inhaling illegal substances. Rocco had run across a lot of these in his time, but he had yet to run into one owned by an actual snuff-taker. In fact, he had yet to run into an actual snuff-taker.

"Yeah, I'd say so," Rocco said. "I don't suppose you'd have anything to say about whether it was accidental, or whether he had somebody helping him across that river?"

"Homicide, you mean? Why would you suspect that?"

"Melio, this guy was Pietro Cubbiddu's stepson; Nola's kid. We'd been wondering if he was somehow involved in their deaths. And then, he also happened to be suing the hell out of the Cubbiddus."

"*Was* he? Yes, I can see why you'd find this a bit suspicious."

"The only reason we're here right now is that Tonino came by to bring him in for questioning on the murders. And this is what he found."

"Oh my. Well, all I can tell you is that I've thus far found no signs of violence on the body, and nothing to suggest forced ingestion. But that doesn't mean we won't find something when we get him on the table and have a more thorough look. And when the laboratory tests are analyzed."

"When can you do the autopsy, Melio?"

"I'll do it today. I'll call you later with results and have the written report tomorrow; all part of the cheerful Bosco service, my boy. Oh, I can also tell you, for what it might be worth, that he appears to have died right there in his bed. Livor mortis is consistent with his not having been moved."

"In other words, you haven't found anything at all so far to indicate that we're looking at a homicide. A murder."

"Which doesn't mean one didn't occur, of course."

"Of course. What, Tonino?"

Martignetti had appeared at his side bearing two glossy booklets. "These were in a drawer in the kitchen."

Rocco looked at the cover of the top one: *Manuale ufficiale all'uso dell'Acro PC 1420.* He shrugged. "So? A computer manual."

"Right."

He glanced at the other one; an owner's manual for a printer. "And these are significant for some reason?"

"You've looked around the place, *Tenente.* You remember seeing a computer anywhere? Or a printer?"

"No, but maybe they're out in his car, or in another drawer somewhere, or—"

Martignetti flipped the computer manual open to the photo on the first page. "It's a desktop, not a notebook; it's not going to be in any drawer. The printer's full-size too. It's not there either. There's also no keyboard, no mouse, no cables, no nothing."

"Well, couldn't it be that—?"

"But there *is* an empty space on the desk in the other room that would just fit them. Just about the only empty surface in the whole room."

Rocco nodded slowly. "So you think somebody came in and took his computer, along with everything that goes with it, after he died, is that what you're getting at?"

"Or before," Martignetti said.

"Or during," said Bosco, and the three men looked at one another.

TWENTY-ONE

"HOW do you know they haven't been missing for weeks, or months?" Gideon asked.

Rocco shook his head. "Nah. Look, the whole place was covered in dust an inch thick. All except the desk, which was squeaky clean where the stuff had been. You could see the outlines—even the mouse—just like somebody drew them right on the wood."

"So what's your hypothesis? Why take them?"

"Obviously, to keep something on the computer from coming out."

"Okay, but why take the printer, the mouse?"

"Because if they'd left the printer and the mouse, we'd know right away they took the computer, wouldn't we?"

"We do know they took the computer."

"Yeah, but only because they forgot about—or didn't have time to look for—the manuals." He paused, holding up the spoon he'd been using to scoop up his beef stew. "Hey, what did I tell you: is the food here good, or what?"

They were having lunch at Il Cernacchino, an out-of-the-way eating place on an out-of-the way street a block from the Piazza Signoria, that fully lived up to Rocco's "mom and pop" description. ("Hole-in-the-wall" would have been equally apt.) No more than fifteen feet wide and twenty feet deep, Il Cernacchino had two levels, with a window-side eating bar and stools on the ground floor along with three small tables, and another five tables squeezed together in the minuscule loft above. Behind a cafeteria-type counter at the back of the ground floor were Mom and Pop in person, smilingly ladling out soups and stews, deftly whipping up *panini*, and looking as if there was nothing in the world they could possibly have been happier doing.

The *panino* that Gideon was in the process of demolishing was indeed mouth-wateringly good, although it had taken Rocco to overcome his initial reservations. *A hot chicken-liver panino?* But Rocco was right; the *panino con i fegatini* was wonderful, a five-napkin affair, dripping with olive oil, but well worth the risks to his shirt. They each had a glass of rough, anonymous red wine as well—*vino a bicchiere, €3,00*—that would probably have delighted old Pietro, but would never have made it on the lunch table of today's Villa Antica, not with Franco in charge. But for what they were eating, nothing could have suited better.

But Gideon chewed almost absentmindedly. The news about Cesare's death was still sinking in. "Rocco, does the family know yet? I'm heading back to the villa right after lunch. Would you like me to tell them?"

"No, Tonino will do it. He's on his way there now."

A few more slowly masticated mouthfuls, and then Gideon

asked, "Did the *medico* have any preliminary opinion? Accidental overdose? Suicide? Murder?"

"All he could say was there wasn't anything to indicate violence or that anyone forced the dope into him."

"Which doesn't mean they didn't happen."

"Which was what he said. What's your take, Gid?"

"Personally? I think he was murdered, one way or another. Whatever it was he had on his computer that made someone nervous, Cesare himself had to have known about it too. So they both had to go. I don't see that there's much doubt about it."

The spoon stopped on its way to Rocco's mouth. "I'm surprised. I mean, it's not that I don't think you're right—we're looking at murder here, I can feel it in my bones—but that's not exactly your style."

"What's that supposed to mean?"

"Well, hell, you haven't even seen the body. Where are all the qualifiers, the *tend to*s, the *in most case*s, the—"

"I'm not speaking as a scientist here, Rocco. I'm not giving an expert opinion; I'm just giving an opinion. I'm talking to you, not to the court."

"Fair enough, and I agree with you, but based on what, really?"

Gideon put the *panino* down and snatched another handful of napkins from the dispenser to wipe his fingers. "You've got a newly reopened murder investigation going into the deaths of two people. *One* day after the investigation starts—*two* days after the stepson brings a gazillion-dollar suit based on the murders—said stepson, who also happens to be your number-one suspect in the case—dies of an overdose. His computer and its contents are seen no more. It all has to be related, Rocco, and to suppose that his death was a mere inadvertence seems to be stretching coincidence to its limits. There must have been dozens of times in the past he could have died from an overdose—but he didn't. Kind of provocative, wouldn't you say, that it happens right now?"

"Well, maybe, but, you know, that suit throws a new angle into things. Maybe it's *not* all related. Even if it's a murder, it might not tie back to the old murders. Maybe it strictly has to do with the suit. A lot of people, that whole family, stand to lose a ton of money. Especially Franco. I'm not sure we're not confusing things by balling everything up into one package."

"I don't agree. There wouldn't be any suit if there hadn't been any murders, would there? No, it's all tied together."

"You think Cesare had something to do with the murders?"

"*Something*? I do, yes."

"I can't see why."

"Because of what we've been talking about. Because he's dead and his computer was stolen."

"Man, I'm trying to follow you here. Are you saying you think it was Cesare that killed them?"

"No, I'm just saying there's a connection. Maybe he knew who did kill them. Maybe he knew something that could incriminate the killer. Maybe he *did* kill them. Maybe it was something else. But one way or another, it's all tied together. They're too close together, especially in time."

"I don't know. Coincidences do happen, you know. If they didn't, we wouldn't have a word for them." He laughed, struck funny after the fact by what he'd said. "Hey, you know what Woody Allen said about time? 'Time is nature's way of keeping everything from happening at once.'"

Gideon smiled abstractedly, then murmured: "Within any set or set of sets, the probability that the components of a series of improbable events are unrelated is inversely correlated with the frequency of occurrence of such events."

Rocco just looked at him for a long, penetrating five seconds before he spoke. "No shit," he said.

Gideon burst out laughing. "I saw it written up that way in a journal once. It's an academic-speak translation of something an old professor of mine came up with, and I quote: 'When you got too much monkey business going on, too many unrelated things happening all over the place at the same time, to the same people, in the same context; buddy, you can bet your life there's something funny going on and they ain't so unrelated after all.'"

It didn't sound as good to his ears as it did when it had been said with Abe Goldstein's Yiddish accent, but he believed it wholeheartedly, and he had often put it to good use in his forensic work. He smiled, remembering his friend and mentor. "The Law of Interconnected Monkey Business, he called it."

"Yeah, well, okay, maybe there's something to that, but let's focus on just *one* event for a minute. Cesare. If someone did kill him by getting an overdose into him, I can't see how we're ever going to prove it, even to ourselves, can you?"

"Not really."

Rocco finished his stew, wiped his mouth, and sat contemplatively back with his wineglass. "You know, when you think about it, what do we really have in the whole damn case that's solid? Not a whole hell of a lot. We have exactly one definite murder that we're convinced of, and that's Nola's. But that's based on your theory about the way people *tend* to fall off cliffs, not on anything anybody would call hard evidence." He waited for an argument from Gideon, but got none.

"I agree with you, Rocco. Hard evidence it's not."

"And then there's Cesare. We just said ourselves he's kind of a gray area—maybe somebody killed him, maybe not. And the same goes for Pietro."

"Rocco, Pietro was shot and thrown off a cliff."

"Yeah, after he was dead. *Weeks* after, from what you said. That's weird, but it doesn't mean he was murdered in the first place."

"Well, why would somebody shoot him and throw him off a cliff later on if he hadn't been?"

"Why would someone shoot him and throw him off a cliff later on if he *had* been?"

Gideon laughed; Julie had said the same thing the previous night. "You've got a point there, Rocco. I sure don't have an answer. It's all pretty equivocal, isn't it?" He carefully downed the one remaining chunk of his *panino* and applied some more napkins to his fingers and his chin. As far as he could tell, his shirt had made it through unspotted.

Rocco, gazing mournfully out the arched window, sighed. "Was it really only last Tuesday—ah, how fondly I remember—that I had this nice, clear murder-suicide all tied up in a neat little package with not one loose string in sight. Well done, Gardella; case closed, on to the next one. And then *you* come on the scene, and suddenly it's totally screwed up. It's all fuzzy, nothing is clear-cut, everything is as equivocal as hell."

"I hear that a lot," Gideon said pleasantly. "I don't know why that is."

Rocco's answering grumble was unintelligible, but then he

yawned and laughed. "Oh, hey, I got some of the death-scene photos from today with me. Wanna have a look at 'em before I take off?" He was unwinding the string from the little buttons of a large-sized envelope, the kind used for internal office communications.

"Why would I not?" Gideon said, reaching out his hand. "The perfect ending to a perfect meal."

They were a dozen or so full-color shots, about five by eight. Sipping his wine, Gideon went quickly through them, moving each viewed picture to the rear of the pack as he finished with it. The body, the surroundings, looked both pathetic and squalid, as they somehow always did in crime-scene photos, even when no overt violence was involved. Maybe it was something about the cameras they used.

The last one was a slightly out-of-focus close-up of the night-stand, and on that one he paused. "I see the snuff kit," he said, "but what's the other stuff? Are those Kleenex?"

"Tissues, yeah. And some pens, a toenail clipper, key ring—"

"A bottle of some kind . . ." He peered at the photo. "Oh, it's cough medicine. Giorniquilla."

"You got good eyes. Can you actually read that?"

"No, but I saw him gulping it down it down the other day." He shrugged and handed the wad of photos back.

Rocco seemed disappointed. "That's it? You didn't see anything else?"

He laughed. "I didn't see *anything*, Rocco. You should be glad. I haven't screwed up one single thing. Well, nothing that wasn't already screwed up before."

Rocco was grinning as he rewound the string to close the folder. "Thank God for small favors."

WHEN Gideon arrived back at Villa Antica, he went to look for Nico and Franco (Luca was at his class) to express his condolences. He found them with Quadrelli in the rear of the garden in the shade of the cypresses at the base of the ancient wall, where they'd pulled together a few of the folding lawn chairs that were scattered about, and they half-heartedly welcomed him to join them.

"Only for a minute," he said, remaining standing.

They didn't seem to be in need of much in the way of consoling, but when they learned he'd just come from talking to Rocco, they made him sit down and pumped him with questions. Gideon answered them as well as he could, keeping to Rocco's suggestion that he be honest with them . . . but not to the extent of raising the possibility that he'd been murdered. He didn't, and neither did they.

"So terrible about the poor boy," said Quadrelli after Gideon ran out of information.

"Terrible," Franco agreed. "A wasted life. It could have been so different."

Their remarks notwithstanding, they both seemed distinctly undisturbed by the event, even complacent. It didn't surprise Gideon. Not only had no love been lost there, but with Cesare dead and gone, the suit that was hanging over their heads was dead and gone too. Who else was there to challenge the will? As far as they were concerned, there was no downside to Cesare's death; it was all upside.

These were ungenerous thoughts to have about these people, his friends, on whose freely given hospitality he was currently living. But there was no getting around it.

Only Nico, sitting there shaking his head, showed anything close to emotion. "I did my best to turn him around. I never stopped trying. It wasn't enough."

"We know you did," Franco said. "No one could have tried harder. But when it came to Cesare . . ." He finished with one of those says-it-all Italianate shrugs: *Even with the best of intentions not every problem can be solved; life is what it is; what can one do?; one can only try; it was bound from the beginning to end this way.*

Quadrelli nodded gravely "*Ad incunabulum*," he observed.

Gideon suspected he was trying for *ab incunabulis. From the cradle.* His Latin was as shaky as his English.

"The thing is, you know," Nico said, "he was just here, right in the conference room, talking to us, a couple of days ago. It's hard to believe he can be dead."

How many times had Gideon heard similar thoughts expressed? *But he was alive only yesterday; how can he be dead today?* As if death was a gradual phenomenon. It wasn't. *Half-dead* was a figure of speech, no more. Death itself—not the illness or infirmity that might precede it—was an instantaneous phenomenon. The light was on; the light went off. The brain was getting blood from the heart; the brain wasn't getting blood from the heart. The end.

"Talking to us," Franco said with a snort. "That was some talk."

"At least he was honest," Nico said, but with little conviction.

A little later, during the predinner wine and apéritif hour on the terrace, Gideon joined Julie, John, and Marti. There, over a glass of 2004 Villa Antica Cabernet he sat for half an hour for more questions, many hypotheses, and no answers.

TWENTY-TWO

THE following morning, the *Vino e Cucina* contingent departed early for a full-day tour of Tuscan wineries and food cooperatives that met Luca's exacting standards, with meals at two of his favorite restaurants and an overnight stay in Pisa. John and Gideon had been invited along, and John, more and more bored with life in Figline and with no developments expected in the case for the next day or two, had decided to go. Well, not quite *decided*. He'd flipped a coin: *Heads I go; tails I don't*, and it had come up heads.

Gideon had politely declined. He had no desire to encounter another *ossobuco* or anything like it. With plans for the day that were neither pressing nor particularly attractive—he had to read a dissertation submission from a PhD candidate in physical anthropology, on whose advisory committee he served—he made what was for him a rare decision and decided to sleep in. So after Julie left at seven thirty, he went back to their canopied bed, leaving the windows wide open for the fresh morning air and the lulling smells and sounds—browning leaves, twittering birds—of the Tuscan countryside in fall. They were more lulling than expected, so when his cell phone jogged him awake a little after nine, he just groaned, muttered, pulled the pillow over his head, and went back to sleep.

It was ten when he finally got up, the latest he'd slept in years, and he felt great; he was beginning to think that John might have a point about the benefits of dozing half the morning away, after all. Only after he'd showered and shaved, did he remember the phone call. But first things first. He went yawning to the door to retrieve the tray with the pot of coffee and canister of hot milk (cool by now) that waited outside for them every morning, took it into the sitting room— not quite as grand as Franco's, but grand enough, with its frescoed ceilings and tapestried walls—squeezed himself into an interesting but not overly comfortable settee that had been made from the prow end of a gondola, and checked his phone. The message was from Rocco, saying he'd already gotten the autopsy report and that if Gideon was interested he should return the call.

This prompted a few (but not too many) feelings of guilt. Here he'd been snoozing half the day away while the intrepid lieutenant was hot on the case. *Well, why not?* he asked himself. *Rocco's working; you're on vacation*, but it didn't help. With a sigh he poured himself a cup of espresso, which still had a little warmth to it, decided against the cold milk, and dialed the number.

"You already have the autopsy report? You guys are fast."

"You ain't heard nothing yet. The lab report just came through too."

"Wow, that's amazing," said Gideon, amazed in truth. "You only found the guy yesterday morning. What did you do, hold a gun to their heads?"

"Yeah, well, I guess Conforti leaned on them a little. Anyway, here's the upshot. It was a cocaine overdose, all right, which they say was—well, let me read you what it says in the lab report. 'Primary cause of death was acute cocaine intoxication with related factors contributing . . .' Blah blah . . . let me see. . . . Umm . . . the rest is more blah blah, a lot of zero-point-x-milligram stuff."

"What about the manner of death? Did they make a determination? Homicide? Suicide? Accidental . . . ?"

"Undetermined."

"So, can you can keep working on it?"

"Oh yeah. Like you said, one way or another, it's gotta tie in with everything else, so I'm just treating it like part of the Cubbiddus' murder investigation. And Conforti's cool with that."

Gideon poured himself a little more of the cold coffee. "Rocco, what was that about 'related factors contributing'? Did that get explained?"

"Yeah, it's all related to the coke. Wait a minute. . . . Yeah, here it is: 'While the blood cocaine levels found in the deceased are certainly within the potentially lethal range, they would in most cases not be fatal in themselves to an individual whose tolerance had been raised by habitual usage. In this instance, however, it is probable that the early-stage hypertensive cardiovascular disease and pulmonary emphysema'—I think that's what it says; I'm translating as I go here—'found in the deceased were contributing factors. These conditions are well-established concomitants of cocaine ingestion.' Does that tell you anything you didn't know before?"

"Nope."

"Me neither. Okay, stay in touch, buddy. If anything comes up at your end that might be important, you'll let me know?"

"Absolutely."

WHEN Gideon went to the high-ceilinged, flagstone-paved old refectory a few minutes later hunting for breakfast, he found it deserted but with plenty still on the buffet table from the *Vino e Cucina* send-off meal, a bigger, more varied one than usual. He helped himself from platters of cheese and ham sliced so thin you could see through them, and cut a couple of chunks from a loaf of cakey, flour-dusted Italian bread to go along with them.

The buffet also held an anachronistically modern, science-fiction self-service coffee machine with about twenty different buttons one could press for espresso, cappuccino, macchiato, and just about every adaptation of coffee ever invented. Having had enough coffee to last him for a while, he hit the button labeled *cioccolata calda* and watched as a sludgy but wonderful-smelling liquid flowed steaming into his cup like brown lava. Next to this apparatus was a similar but smaller machine (only twelve buttons), with TUTTAFRUTA on the front and pictures of various fruit juices. Gideon tried the buttons for pineapple juice and grapefruit juice while the chocolate was going into his cup but with no luck, and he settled for orange juice.

He took everything to a table beside a swung-open casement window that looked out on the garden, and ate, drank, and dreamed a few minutes away enjoyably. But after a time, after he'd gone back to the buffet table and returned with another hot chocolate and a slice of almond sponge cake, he began to replay his recent conversations with Rocco, especially the one at Il Cernacchino, where Rocco had told him about Cesare and shown him the crime photos.

And a little later he lifted his eyes, and softly said, "I wonder . . ."

HALF an hour later, having followed directions from Nico, whom he'd run into in a hallway, he had found a *farmacia* on the town's main street, which, as in half the towns in Italy, was Corso Vittorio Veneto. There he made two purchases, which he brought back unopened to Villa Antica. He got two glasses from the tasting room, went out to the back terrace with them, and sat down at one of the tables. He removed from the paper bag two half-liter bottles that held purple liquid. One them had *Giorniquilla* on a bright red background; this was the same cough medicine he'd seen Cesare guzzling. The other, identical except that its label was moss green, said *Dormiquilla*. He undid both screw caps and poured some from each into separate glasses. He sipped from one, then the other. Thought a minute. With his eyes closed, he switched the bottles themselves around enough times to turn it into a blind tasting. Sipped directly from the first bottle that came to hand, then from the other. Opened his eyes. Thought again.

He got on his cell phone to call Rocco, but got a secretary instead: The lieutenant was out of the office. Could she take a message?

"Would *Maresciallo* Martignetti be available? My name is Gideon Oliver."

Martignetti was available. "Hello, Dr. Oliver, what can I do for you?"

"Make it Gideon, will you? I was calling Rocco to suggest that he have the lab run another couple of tests. Can I leave it with you?"

"Let me get a pad. Okay, shoot."

"First, have them do an analysis on the cough medicine that was on Cesare's nightstand."

"Okey-doke."

"Second, and more important, I'm assuming that Cesare's toxi-cological screening didn't include testing for cocaethylene, would that be right?"

"I don't know. Far as I know, they did the usual routine screen-ing, the regular tox panel."

"Then they probably didn't include it," Gideon said. "They usu-ally don't in the States. So would you see if you can get them to test specifically for it?"

"For what again?"

"Cocaethylene."

"Co . . . You wouldn't happen to know how to say that in Ital-ian, would you?"

Gideon laughed. "Hell, I can barely say it in English, Tonino. But they'll know what I'm talking about. It'll be spelled something like c-o-c-a-e-t-h—"

"Gideon, hold on a minute, will you? The switchboard's trying to get me." He was back after a few seconds. "I'm sorry, there's another call coming in that I need to take. Is there anything else?"

"No, that's it. You'll let Rocco know? Sooner the better."

"I'll take care of it for you myself."

"You can do that?"

"Not really, but I'll sign Rocco's name to the requisition; no problem. Appreciate the help, Gideon."

"OKAY, Pino," Martignetti said in Italian once Gideon had dis-connected, "I'll take that call."

On the line, the *carabiniere* at the switchboard had told him, was a man who identified himself as Philario Tognetti, representing Scacco Matto Investigazioni—Checkmate Investigations.

The private-eye firm and the man were both familiar to Martignetti. Philario didn't "represent" Scocco Matto; he *was* Scocco Matto: a one-man operation a few blocks south of the Arno, in the Oltrarno District. Philario was an ex-*carabiniere*, an old friend, never close, but a friend. They had gotten to know each other as rookies attending the Cadet Training School in Rome in 1992. But Philario wasn't made for the work. He'd scraped through the academy by the skin of his teeth, then lasted only a year in the corps before resigning at the suggestion of superiors that he might be better suited to another line of work. There wasn't anything dishonorable or particularly bad in his record; he just wasn't up to the job. Mentally. Not to put too fine a point on it, his sewing machine, as the old saying went, was a little short of thread.

He'd started Scacco Matto after trying a few other things that hadn't worked out for him, and, as far as Martignetti knew, he'd made a go of it; he'd found his niche.

"Hey, Philario, thanks for calling back."

"So what can I do for the mighty *Carabinieri*? Are you in need of the services of a good private investigator? I can give you a special rate."

Martignetti produced the required chuckle. "Actually, I just need a little information from you. I've been working on the Cubbiddu case, Philario"—he sensed a sudden wariness on the other end of the line—"and your name has come up."

"In what way?"

"I got their financial records from their executor, and on them is a bill from you for twelve hundred euros that was received in

October of last year, not long after their deaths. All it says is 'for services rendered.' You want to tell me what that was for, please?"

"Ah . . . I'd like to help, but I don't think I can do that, Tonino. It's a matter of professional ethics. Whatever passed between signor Cubbiddu and me is privileged information. You know that."

"Of course. But Cubbiddu *was* your client?"

"Ah . . . yes."

"And can you tell me what he engaged you to do?"

"As I just said—"

"I wouldn't ask you to tell me what was said in confidence, but can't you at least give me an idea of the work you were doing for him? This is a murder investigation, Philario, a double murder investigation. Any help you can give us would be very much appreciated."

He expected more hedging, but Philario came through. "He suspected his wife of cheating on him. I was engaged to find out if this was true."

"And was it?"

"It was. It only took me two days to establish it."

"Did you get to tell Cubbiddu that before he died?"

"I did. Called him on September second—maybe the third. And that's it, Tonino, really. That's all I can tell you. I shouldn't have said that much."

"I only have one more question, Philario."

"Yes, and I know what it is. I cannot tell you the identity of the person, Tonino. That must remain between signor Cubbiddu and myself."

"Philario, I remind you again that your client is dead and it is his murder we are investigating. And his wife's as well. Surely you can see that a lover of signora Cubbiddu would be a person of interest. I appeal to you as a citizen and as a friend."

Rocco Gardella had just come into his cubicle and, seeing that Martignetti was on the phone, started to turn around, but Martignetti waved him to the chair. "One minute," he mouthed, holding up a single finger.

"Yes, certainly, I can see that," Philario was saying, "but I cannot . . . I'm sorry, we must end this conversation now."

Martignetti spoke quickly before he hung up. "I am not asking you to tell me anything that signor Cubbiddu told you in confidence. I am only asking what you told *him*." Was there a difference when it came to privileged information? Martignetti doubted it. But he did know that splitting hairs was not one of Philario's strengths. He heard a sigh at the other end and held his own breath.

"Oh, all right. If I were to give you this information, Tonino—could my name be kept out of it?"

Martignetti couldn't help punching the air, a little gesture of triumph. Good old Philario, still the same guy, still not the brightest crayon in the box.

"Absolutely." He meant it too.

"Very well. His name is Severo Quadrelli. Would you like me to spell that for you?"

"SOMETHING interesting?" Rocco asked when the call had ended.

"I'll say." He told Rocco what he'd just heard.

Rocco was as surprised as Martignetti. "What do you know: Quadrelli. Well, at least now we know why he didn't want to turn the accounts over to us."

"Yes, and this makes him a lot more interesting, doesn't it?

We've got a hell of a motive now. What do you think the chances are that it was him?"

"The chances of him killing them? Not too good. Yeah, he tried to put us off about the accounts, but in the end he let us have them, didn't he? What did it take, five minutes? If he thought there was something there that could help us finger him as a murderer, he'd have used every lawyer's trick he knew to keep us from *ever* getting them. No, I think he just didn't want it to come out that he was diddling the wife of his old friend and employer." He shivered. "Whoo. Now there's an image I'd like to get out of my mind."

"Hold it," Martignetti said when the switchboard buzzed him. "Let me see if this is anything." He listened a minute, then said "I'll take it," and replaced the receiver. "It's the guy who used to be Pietro's doctor—another possible lead from the account statement. There was a bill from him for a follow-up visit with the old man last August, a month before he went up to the mountains. I figured there might be something there."

"Right, go ahead and take it." Rocco stood up to leave.

Martignetti put his hand back on the phone but waited before picking it up. "Rocco, on this Severo thing . . . if it's all right with you, I'll go ahead and dig into it a little, see if there's anything there, but you're probably right; chances are this is a whole separate thing, no connection."

"No, I never said there wasn't any connection."

"You didn't?"

"No, I didn't." He smiled. "Tonino, did you ever hear of the Law of Interconnected Monkey Business?"

TWENTY-THREE

GIDEON spent the rest of the day working on the four-hundred-page dissertation but failing to make it all the way through. By the next morning, he was only three-quarters through, and it had been a teeth-grinding slog the entire way. Full professor of physical anthropology he might be, but physical anthropology had a great many subdisciplines these days, in some of which he was as much at sea as the rawest grad student. And one of those subdisciplines was the subject of Angela Stark's dissertation: *Assessing the Extent of Genetic Admixture Between Modern Populations of Tatars, Kazakhs, and Karakalpaks in Northern Uzbekistan by Means of the Analysis of mtDNA, Y-chromosome STRs, and Autosomal STR Markers.*

"Angela," he'd told her when she'd asked him to be on her advisory committee a year earlier, "I'd love to, but I really don't think this one is for me. If I can't understand what the title means, how am I going to understand the rest of it?"

"Professor Oliver," she'd said, "I already have Dr. Sherman and

Dr. Spatz on my committee, and they know the technical side forward and backward. What I'm really asking from you is to keep me honest on the overall rationale, the big picture. The scientific method. Do my conclusions follow from the data? That kind of thing. I mean, the two of them are great, just great, don't get me wrong; but . . . well, they're kind of, you know, not exactly 'with it,' if you know what I mean. Not that I'm criticizing . . ."

He'd known it was his duty to defend his colleagues, but she was right. "Oh, the guy's got a full six-pack, all right," he'd overheard a student say about one of them—he didn't remember which, but it fitted them both—"he's just missing that plastic thingy that ties them together." So he'd limited himself to a mild "Well, I wouldn't say that." And then a few minutes later he'd given in and taken her on. It was nice to have a student so concerned with proper scientific method. But now, sitting on the terrace with the thing on his laptop, he rued the day, as he'd known he would.

It wasn't that he thought the application of DNA research to anthropology wasn't a tremendous breakthrough—he knew it was— or even simply that he was a bit shaky on the technology, or that he had to take frequent breaks from reading the dissertation because his eyes glazed over every few paragraphs. More than that, the stuff made him feel like a fossil himself. Although he was on the young side for a full prof, he was an old-school, low-tech scientist. His field, as he saw it, comprised human variability, population movements and relationships, growth and aging, evolution, locomotion . . . it was, in other words, what the word *anthropology* literally meant: the science of *people*. But over the last decade or two, as in so much of science, there had been a reductionist revolution. The new bright lights of the field didn't seem to him to be people-studiers so much as chemists, physicists, geneticists, statisticians, mathematicians, and computer modelers, all more grounded and interested in these dry (to him) subjects than in human beings as such.

Or maybe the whole idea of DNA depressed him because he knew that it portended the end of the usefulness of the forensic anthropology that had become so central a part of his life. What he'd been doing with Rocco was out of the ordinary. What forensic anthropologists did, by and large, was to assist the police in the identification of skeletal remains. But who needed someone to tell them that a particular set of bones had belonged to a white female of twenty-five to thirty-five, right-handed, five feet three to five feet six in height, who had suffered a broken ulna in childhood, and who had gone through at least one period of malnutrition during adolescence, when all they had to do to find out who she was was to take a DNA sample and enter it into the vast data banks of DNA that would someday—someday soon—be as ubiquitous as fingerprint records?

It came as a relief when this gloomy line of thought was cut off a little before noon by the noisy return of Luca's group, back from their culinary travels. It had been the last event of the class, so there were hugs and good-byes and e-mail address exchanges all around. Gideon gratefully shut down the laptop and went out and found Julie and the Laus, who were talking longingly about taking a break from serious food and wine and finding someplace—a bar, maybe—where they could have a non-Italian lunch. Not that there was anything wrong with ambitious Italian food, of course, but enough was enough. They needed a little time off.

"Good luck finding someplace non-Italian around here," John said, then brightened. "But there's this great pizzeria—"

"Ah, but there is a place," Gideon said, breaking in. "I was taking a walk this morning"—on one of his frequent breaks from *Assessing the Extent of Genetic Admixture*—"and I went right by what claims to be an English-style pub and looked like one to me. Says they serve lunch, English beer—"

"Ploughman's lunch!" Marti cried, grabbing his arm and shaking it. "Take me there! At once, do you hear? At once, I say!"

"I could sure stand a shepherd's pie," Julie said dreamily. "And an English ale."

"They have hamburgers in pubs, don't they?" John asked.

AND so they headed off to the Gate House Pub on Piazza Serristori, a small square that fronted the Teatro Garibaldi, the town's nineteenth-century opera house. From the outside, it did indeed look vaguely like an English pub, and once through the door it smelled like one too: a cozy, comforting mix of old pipe and cigarette smoke, floor polish, and decades of spilled ale that permeated the splintery wooden floors and probably the chairs and tables as well. There was another aroma they couldn't place and didn't associate with pubs, but it was appetizing enough, and in they went.

Behind the bar were a broad-backed woman in a black, spaghetti-strap dress and a burly man with a black T-shirt and a dense but neatly trimmed black beard, both of them busy serving up beer. The burly guy looked up from pulling on one of a dozen pump handles, quickly marked them as Americans, and waved them in with a grin. "Hello, Yanks, what I can do for you?"

John happily took in the rows of quaint, colorful, indubitably English pump handles. "You can send over four pints of that Old Speckled Hen, *por favor*."

"Half pint for me," Marti amended.

"And some menus, please," said Gideon.

The place was only half full—everyone else was Italian, as far as they could tell—so they had no trouble finding a table. They chose one in a niche, under a wall hung with old ad posters for Pears' soaps and Triumph motorcycles, and scattered black-and-white photos of matronly Victorian ladies, including Victoria herself. They had barely sat down when the beers came, in traditional, dimpled glass mugs.

They all raised a silent toast and sipped, except for John, who glugged down a long contented swallow, then studied his glass. "Interesting. A toffee-and-forest-mold foundation supporting leathery after tones with a blackberry edge—"

"He's been at Villa Antica too long," Marti said. "We've got to get him home."

"I saw that once in England in a beer ad, and I memorized it," John confessed. "Been waiting forever for the chance to try it out."

"So what do you really think of it?" Julie asked.

"S'okay."

The day's menus were delivered by a second guy in a black T-shirt, not quite so burly, and with a slightly smaller black beard. Brothers, Gideon thought. One look at the menus explained the smell they couldn't place: it was a mixture of jalapeños, salsa, guacamole, and fried tortillas. No Scotch eggs, no shepherd's pie, no ploughman's lunch, neither in the air nor on the menu. They had come on a Monday, and Mondays were *il Pranzo Messicano* days. For English food, come back tomorrow.

Their disappointment lasted about two seconds before they started poring over the menus, which were in English and Italian.

"Anybody want to split a fantasy salad?" Marti asked. "Feta

cheese, olives, radicchio, tomatoes, cucumbers . . . sounds good, doesn't it?"

All she got back from the others were brief, contemptuous glances before they returned to their studies.

Gideon was deciding between a couple of dishes when his phone bipped. It was Rocco, starting out in high gear. "Hey, listen, I just got the damn—"

"Hold on a second, Rocco, I can hardly hear you. Let me take the phone outside." He stood up. "It's Rocco. Be back in a minute. Order me the beef burrito, will you?"

There was a raucous, impromptu, four-man-team soccer game going on in the piazza, but he found a relatively safe place at the edge of the square and stood in the scant shade of a lone tree, next to a marble-slab bench.

"Okay, Rocco, I'm back. You just got the damn what?"

"The lab report on Cesare, and also the—"

"Whoa, whoa, you got that two days ago. You already told me about it."

"No, not that report; the report on the cocaethamethawhatever. And they—"

"The cocaethylene report? How could you have that already? The request just went in yesterday."

"Yeah, you keep saying that. Look, what you gotta remember is that we don't have all those murders you got in the States, you know? Our lab isn't all booked up for weeks and weeks. They do a lot of sitting around. They appreciate it when we give them something."

"Still, it's unbelievable. In one day? I didn't even think it was possible. I thought it only happened on TV."

Rocco let go a noisy sigh. "Are you gonna shut up and let me say what I want to say? I don't have all day here."

"Speak. I'm all ears." The soccer ball had come rolling his way, and he gently kicked it back to the players.

"Thank you. Okay. Here's what it says. . . . Umm . . . I don't know, milligrams, kilograms . . . but the upshot is, now they're saying the primary cause of death isn't cocaine toxicity anymore, it's coca . . . coca . . . what you said."

"Cocaethylene toxicity. Son of a gun."

"Yeah. But the manner of death is still undetermined, no change. So I get them on the phone—this was, like, ten minutes ago—I get them on the phone, and I say, What am I supposed to do with this? What's it mean? Why did you send it to me instead of the public prosecutor? And they say, Hey, all we do is analyze the blood sample. You're the ones who figure out what it means. You ordered it, don't *you* know? Except that I didn't order it—"

"Uh, yeah, Rocco, that was me. I tried calling you yesterday—"

"I know, Tonino explained it to me."

"It wasn't his fault, Rocco, I—"

"I know, I know, he's not in any trouble; he does it all the time, don't worry. But he doesn't know why you wanted it either. So how about telling me now? Why did you ask for this particular test? What *does* it mean?"

Gideon sat down on the bench, his thoughts tumbling.

"Gid?"

"I think it means," he said slowly, "that you do have another murder on your hands, all right. And now we've got some solid evidence to back it up."

Cocaethylene, he explained, was a toxic metabolite that was formed in the liver when cocaine and alcohol were taken together and which subjected both the liver and the heart to enormous stress; many times more stress than was produced by alcohol or cocaine alone. Some studies indicated that the risk of death as a result of cocaethylene formation was twenty-five times greater than the risk of death from cocaine alone.

"So Cesare was drinking, along with snorting the coke, is that what you're saying?"

"As far as I know, that's the only way that cocaethylene gets made."

"So where did the alcohol come from, Gid? There wasn't any booze on the nightstand. There wasn't any in the whole apartment. No wine, no cordials, no bottles in the garbage, nothing."

"That's because he didn't drink, Rocco. Ever. He knew better. Linda told me he once had a friend who died from mixing the two. Which is why we can assume that if he had any alcohol in him—and the cocaethylene proves that he did—he didn't drink it knowingly."

"You're losing me again, buddy. If he was doing coke and alcohol at the same time, how could he not know it? And where did the alcohol come from? You're saying whoever did it took it away with him?"

"No, I'm saying it was right there on the nightstand."

"The nightstand?" Gideon could practically hear Rocco's forehead wrinkling. "What, the cough medicine? No, that was Giorniquilla. I know that stuff. No alcohol."

"Rocco, I also asked Martignetti to request an analysis of the contents of that bottle. That didn't come back yet?"

"I don't think so. Just a minute." A clatter indicated the phone had been put down, and Gideon heard just bits and pieces of what ensued. "Hey, Tonino . . . did we . . . ? Well, why the hell didn't you . . . ? Let me see. . . ." And then he was back, speaking directly into the mouthpiece again. "Gid, there *was* alcohol in it—twenty-five percent. You want to tell me what the hell is going on here, please? And how you knew about it?"

"I didn't know, Rocco; I guessed." But it was a masterful guess—a masterful series of guesses, really—and he was feeling highly satisfied with himself.

The idea had come to him the previous morning at breakfast, when the literal meaning of Giorniquilla had belatedly dawned on him. *Giorni,* of course, meant "days," and *quilla* was probably from *tranquilla,* so Giorniquilla was a medicine that would quiet your cough and give you "tranquil days." Well—and here was where the guesswork started—if there was a cough medicine for quiet days, might there not be a variant of that medicine for quiet nights? And if there was, might that variant contain alcohol, as some American nighttime cold medicines did? And, if luck was on his side, might that medicine taste much like the daytime version, or at least enough so that someone wigged out on cocaine might not notice the difference? Might it even look like the daytime version?

And it had all panned out; for once in his life, every guess had been right. Dormiquilla—"tranquil sleep"—was made by the same company; had very much the same tongue-curling, acrid taste (with a bit more "bite"); was the same color (the labels were sharply different); and had the same ingredients, in the same proportions, except for the addition of *etanolo*—ethanol; pure alcohol—which accounted for twenty-five percent in volume.

So how hard would it have been for someone with murder in mind to purchase a bottle of each, empty the Giorniquilla bottle, and pour into it instead the alcohol-laden Dormiquilla version? Answer: not very. And once in Cesare's apartment, switching it with Cesare's current bottle could have been accomplished in an instant. Once that was done, death wouldn't have been long in coming. Gideon himself had seen Cesare take long guzzles of the stuff twice inside ten minutes. Certainly, he'd downed a good six ounces in that time alone.

Assume he was going at it at anywhere near the same rate at home. Twenty-five percent of six was 1.5. And 1.5 ounces of pure, one-hundred percent alcohol was the equivalent of two one-ounce shots of eighty-proof whiskey; surely enough, when consumed in a short time in combination with the reckless ingestion of cocaine, to trigger a fatal cocaethylene explosion. Gideon was way out of his field here, so, to be certain, he had called his friend Dave Black, a clinical prof at Vanderbilt who was his go-to person in matters toxicological, and had been told that that much alcohol would create more than enough cocaethylene to do the trick, especially in someone whose constitution was already compromised by his drug habit. That had been good enough for Gideon.

"I don't get it," Rocco said. "Why get all tricky and futz around like that? Why not just shove the guy out of a window? He lived on the third floor—what you call the fourth floor. He'd have gone *splat* when he hit the piazza."

"I assume it was because whoever it was figured it might raise suspicions, what with the suit and everything else."

"And he didn't think a doctored bottle of cough medicine would raise suspicions?"

"Well, it didn't, did it?

"Well, no, not at the time, but—"

"And the reason it didn't is because everything—the circumstances, his history—pointed to a simple cocaine overdose. I mean, it was practically *expected*, sooner or later. And since cocaine toxicity and cocaethylene toxicity kill you in exactly the same way—the heart has to strain so much to pump blood that it decompensates; it just gives up and stops working; heart failure, in other words—well, on account of all of that, there was absolutely no reason to suspect anything other than a plain cocaine overdose. No reason to test the cough medicine any more than a carton of milk he might have had in his refrigerator."

Hearing something like a mutter from Rocco, he added: "Nobody did anything wrong here, Rocco. Not the doc, not the lab, not you. Anybody would have drawn the same conclusion: death by cocaine poisoning."

Rocco was unmollified. "Anybody but you, of course," he grumbled. "Nothing gets by the great Skeleton Detective, does it?"

"What can I say? What's true is true."

Rocco laughed, and his voice eased up. "You're really something, you know?"

"If that's a compliment, I accept it. What about your end of things? Anything interesting happening?"

"Nah. Well, yeah, a few things. For one, we turned up a two-page list of passwords that he had at the back of his freezer."

"Passwords? For Web sites?"

"You got it."

"So he *did* have a computer."

"Exactly. And whoever took it didn't know about it—more likely didn't think about it. He's got some kind of code for what they're for, but the passwords are clear enough, and Tonino's busy deciphering right now and putting in every single one. We got his e-mail address from Franco, so it's easy enough."

"And? Anything?"

"So far, no. Bank accounts, airlines, discount travel, that kind of thing. But he just got started, so we'll see. I have hopes. Oh, and he's been going over those account statements we got from Severo too—"

"You keep the guy kind of busy, don't you?"

"Sure. Idle hands, you know? Besides, I'd have to do it if he didn't. Anyway, one of the bills was from a private eye Pietro hired. Guess who Nola was screwing around with."

"It's somebody I know?"

"Oh, yeah."

Rocco couldn't see him, but Gideon shook his head anyway. "I can't think of anybody." He laughed. "Severo Quadrelli?"

"Now how the hell did you—?"

"It *was* Quadrelli? I was just kidding."

"No, it was him, Don Juan Quadrelli. Pietro hired the PI to keep an eye on her while he did his hermit thing in the mountains. The guy took less than forty-eight hours to get the goods on them. Called Pietro on his cell phone on September second, one day after he got up there."

"Huh. Are you going to inform the family?"

"Not unless there's a reason to. I'd appreciate it if you'd do the same. We told the PI we'd keep his name out of it."

"Sure. What purpose would it serve anyway?"

"That's the way I see it. Oh, and we also heard from Pietro's doc; there was a bill from him in the accounts. Now, this is interesting. Pietro had a heart condition."

The ball had rolled Gideon's way again, and he kicked it back, but he was processing what he'd just heard, and it wasn't a very accurate kick this time. The players had to chase it farther than they would have had he not interfered, and he took some verbal abuse for it. "Now that *is* interesting," he said. "A bad heart?"

"Yup. '*Patologia cardiaca coronarica*,' it says."

"Coronary heart disease. Hardening of the arteries."

"Right. Pietro himself kept it quiet, no big deal, but it was serious, and it's been serious for a while. That was why he started taking his sabbatical in early September a few years ago instead of at the end of the month. The doc wanted him away while all the craziness was going on. But, you know, Gid, this brings up a question. . . ."

"It sure does. Was it a heart attack that killed him? Did the call from the PI bring it on? September second; that would be about right for the time of death."

"Yup, I'm thinking it went down like this: Here's this old, sick guy with a bad heart. He gets a call from his PI telling him his wife is definitely cheating on him. He grabs his chest and falls down in a heap, and that's it. Never moves again."

"Could be."

"So, pardon me repeating myself for the thousandth time, but . . . why shoot his corpse in the head and throw the body off a cliff a month later?"

TWENTY-FOUR

"WHY . . . and who?" Marti asked when Gideon had finished telling them about the call and they were done expressing their astonishment at identifying Quadrelli as the lothario in question.

He'd returned to the table after hanging up and had found them finished with their meals and drinking coffee. His own food wasn't out yet. Julie had correctly assumed that his "Back in a minute" was more hopeful than realistic and asked them to hold his burrito until he returned.

She cut in now. "Can we forget about the *who* and stick with the *why* for a minute? I think . . ." She paused to order her thoughts. "I just wonder if it all might not go back to the will, the joint will."

"For which Severo was the executor," Marti said pointedly, still digesting the news about Quadrelli.

"No, forget about Severo too. I'm not thinking about Severo; I'm thinking about Pietro and Nola. Look, the will said whoever dies first, everything goes to the other one, isn't that right? Pietro says: If

I die first, everything goes to my wife. Nola says: If I die first, everything goes to my husband."

There were nods around the table.

"*But*," Julie continued, "Pietro also says: If she dies before I do, then I leave everything to Franco."

"Right," said John. "And *she* says: If *he* dies before I do, then I also leave everything to Franco."

"Meaning, one way or another, in the end Franco winds up with it?" Gideon said, turning it into a question. He was trying to figure out where she was heading.

Yes, in the *end*!" Julie said excitedly. "But first it would *necessarily* have to go to one of the two—Pietro or Nola."

All three of them were looking blankly at her.

"Don't you see? Pietro dies first—Nola gets it. Nola dies first—Pietro gets it."

"But they both died, so Franco gets it." Marti said. "What difference does it make which one died first?"

Gideon's order had arrived. The burrito turned out not to be beef, but tuna and bean, but he hardly noticed. He was beginning to get a glimmer of what Julie was driving at, and he liked it. She, however, was getting increasingly frustrated with her effort to explain.

"Julie," he said to help her out, "why don't you just try telling us exactly what it was that you think happened?"

"Okay. Good. Let's assume that Pietro did die of that heart attack. But of course, nobody knows about it. Well, one of the brothers—make it Franco—shows up at the cabin to see him about something—"

"I thought Pietro didn't want anybody coming up while he was there," Marti said.

"Yes, but that doesn't mean nobody ever did. Maybe it was a question about the winery, or something Pietro needed to know, or maybe it was just to check up on him—that bad heart, you know? Or to see if he needed anything? All it would have taken was a couple of hours' drive. Anyway, he finds Pietro dead, and—"

"When would this be?" John asked. "Early, just after he died, or near the end of the month?"

"I don't know that it would make any difference, John. It works either way. Anyway, he does some fast thinking, and what he thinks is: I've had it. Pietro's dead; Nola's still alive. She gets everything."

Marti shook her head in confusion. "But doesn't she eventually have to leave it to him, to Franco?"

"Eventually, but not *now*. Now she has full control of it all. Who knows how much will be left by the time she dies, or how long it'll be before she gets around to dying? Who knows whether or not she'll try and get that will changed so she can leave it all to Cesare?"

Now she got nods. It was starting to make sense.

"So he decides that Nola has to die too. And it has to look as if she died first—predeceased him—that's the key part. He knows when she's going to show up to pick up Pietro, so he goes back up there early that day, and he . . . well, he kills her."

Marti was looking befuddled. "Okay, but I'm still not quite getting the weird thing with Pietro. Why throw him off the cliff too? Why *shoot* him? Why make it seem—"

"Because the whole idea, if I'm right, was to make it look like Pietro killed her and then committed suicide himself. See?" She paused expectantly, encouragingly, waiting for some sign that she'd gotten through to them.

"Yes," Marti said, "but I still don't quite—"

"There was one absolutely sure way to make it look as if he definitely outlived her, Marti, and that was to make everybody think he killed her. So he . . . I don't know . . . he hides Pietro's body somewhere, and then when Nola shows up, he gets her out on that path somehow and pushes her off the cliff and then goes and gets Pietro's body, takes it up to the cliff, puts a bullet in his head, so it looks like he shot himself, and throws him off the cliff too. And then—I'm kind of making this part up as I go along—then he goes down below and arranges the bodies so it's clear that Pietro came down after she did—"

"And probably sticks the gun in his jacket," said Gideon.

"Probably."

"But why did he shoot Nola *then*?" Marti asked after a moment. "She was already dead, wasn't she? If he was going to shoot her, wouldn't it have made more sense to shoot her up above?"

"I haven't gotten that far yet. I guess he just wanted to be positive she was dead."

"That's what I thought too," Gideon said, "but now I'm thinking—and this seems more likely, given what you've been saying—that he needed for her to be shot with Pietro's gun so that there was no question about what supposedly happened, but he didn't have the nerve to do it up above, so he pushed her off and did it down below."

That puzzled Marti even more. "What, it takes less nerve to push somebody off a cliff than to shoot them?"

"Sure," John said. "Think about it. If you're going to shoot somebody, especially with someone else's gun—a seventy-year-old gun—you have to worry about what'll happen if it jams, or if the charge is too weak, or if your hand shakes and you only wound them, or if they turn around just before you pull the trigger and you panic. But to push them off a cliff? A quick shove when they're not looking—on the back, the shoulder—it doesn't matter where—and over they go. It's done. You can shoot them later."

"I see," Marti said. "Yes, that makes sense. But wasn't he afraid that when the bodies were found, it'd be obvious that Pietro'd died a long time before her? I mean, changes in the corpse—well, you know more than I do about that, Gideon."

"Yes, it would have been obvious for the first few months," he agreed, "but not if the bodies were someplace where they wouldn't be found for a year—which is probably why he pushed them off the cliff and into a difficult-to-find area in the first place, rather than just shooting them and leaving them where they were, up on the path. By that time, in that climate, the soft tissue would be gone. They'd both be nothing but beat-up, chewed-on skeletons—as they were. And I doubt very much that he'd think those bones would give away anything about who died first. Or when."

"The bones and the jacket," John pointed out. "The fact that Pietro's body had been gnawed on *under* the jacket. That was also something he wouldn't have thought of."

"I wouldn't have either," Julie said. "But what *about* the jacket? What was the point of putting it on him at all? That, I can't figure out."

"My guess," Gideon said, "is that it's something he didn't think about when he first found Pietro. It would have been summertime, Pietro wouldn't have been wearing a leather jacket. But when it came to doing the final deed, the weather would have gotten colder, and he realized it would have raised questions for Pietro to be out on a forest trail in his shirtsleeves—Nola was wearing a leather jacket, remember—so he slipped it on him then. After the animals had been at him."

They looked at each other, trying to figure out if they'd covered all the bases. It was John who said, "I like it, I like it, *except* . . . how did he know the bodies would ever be found? Because if they weren't . . . oh, wait, of course! *He* was the guy who called about them, who supposedly didn't want to get involved, who just happened to have the exact coordinates on his GPS."

"Wouldn't be surprised," Gideon said.

Julie returned to her coffee. "So—you think I might be right? That that's what happened?"

"I think you *are* right," Gideon said. He'd finished his burrito now, and he too waved for a cup of coffee. "I have to say, nothing like that ever crossed my mind, but now that you've laid it out, it sure answers a lot of questions."

"Sure didn't cross mine," John said. "Good job, kid!"

"Hey, she's blushing!" Marti said delightedly.

"That's the hot sauce," Julie declared.

"Julie," Gideon said, "you used Franco as your example. Do you think it was him?"

She thought about that. "He *seems* like the most likely one, because he had the most to lose, but I don't know. They all had a lot to lose. Not just those stipends, but their jobs at the winery, and their free living arrangements. So . . . I don't know. What do you think?"

"Same as you do. Could be any of them."

"Franco," said John.

"Franco," said Marti.

"Do you think you ought to pass the idea to Rocco?" Julie asked Gideon. "Something for him to think about?"

"No, I think *you* ought to pass the idea to Rocco. You came up with it, you should get full credit." He got out his phone. "He must be still in his office. Give him a call. The number's in there."

"Well, I think I just might do that," Julie said, taking the phone and flipping it open. She was very visibly pleased.

"You'll want to be outside to do it," Gideon told her. He swallowed half the coffee and set the cup down. "Everybody's finished, right? Let's all go outside."

"*Muchas gracias, amigos*," the bigger of the two burly guys called to them as they left.

"And *gracias a tu, signores*," John called smilingly back.

ROCCO was unavailable, so Julie left a message.

"Well," Marti said, "we might as well get back to the villa, pack, say our good-byes—"

"Nope," said Gideon firmly. "We've been in Tuscany for more than a week, this is our final day out in the country, and I have never once visited an archaeological site. This is unacceptable. I'm going to spend at least one afternoon at an archaeological site. You are welcome to join me. Or not."

"Are you kidding us?" Marti said, laughing. "We just came from Florence. The whole place is one big archaeological site. The Duomo, the Uffizi—"

"The Duomo was built in the fourteenth century, the Uffizi in the sixteenth. I'm talking about someplace *old*."

"How old is old?" John asked.

"For Gideon?" Julie said. "Ten thousand years would be about right."

"No, I was thinking of a place called Sovana. It's not that far south of here. There's an Etruscan necropolis there. Rock-carved tombs going back over two thousand years. We could see it and be back here by six or seven, and in Florence at what passes for dinnertime in Italy."

John burst out laughing. "Tombs! Skeletons! Whoa, that'll be something different, won't it? Real change of pace."

But both Marti and Julie indicated interest, and Marti poked John with an elbow. "Come on, sport. It'll be fun."

"Yeah, maybe, but . . ."

Gideon put his hand on John's shoulder. "Dinner will be on me, how's that?"

"Well, now we're getting someplace," John said.

BY five o'clock that afternoon, all of the *Vino e Cucina* attendees had cleared out of the villa, with the exception of Julie and Marti, and they were off somewhere with their husbands. So, for the first time in days, the Cubbiddus felt that they could sit on their own terrace and discuss private matters without being overheard. They were at the largest of the tables: Franco, Nico, Luca, Linda, and Quadrelli. All of them except Nico had a glass of 2008 Villa Antica Sangiovese Riserva in front of them. Nico was drinking Cinzano from a highball glass.

The subjects under discussion were the death of Cesare and its implications for the suit. Was it ended now? Or did signora Batelli have something else up her sleeve? They had more than that on their minds, though. It escaped none of them that, if suspicions of homicide arose, they would all be high on the suspect list, with Franco, who had the most at stake, at the very top. Franco himself understood it best of all. But no one talked about it. It was the suit they concentrated on.

"I myself spoke with signora Batelli again a few hours ago," Quadrelli was saying solemnly, "and I am happy to report that I anticipate no continued threat from that quarter. I believe I can safely say that I set the lady straight on— Ah, gentlemen."

Three uniformed *carabinieri* had come out onto the terrace from the main building: *Tenente* Gardella, *Maresciallo* Martignetti, and a lower-ranking *brigadiere* they hadn't seen before.

"Gentlemen," said Franco with air of austere resignation, "how may we help you?"

The newcomers didn't reply. There was something about them—a reserve, a formality—that sent a ripple of uneasiness around the table.

After a moment's stony silence, the *tenente* pointed. "Him."

The *brigadiere* stepped smartly forward, reaching for his handcuffs.

TWENTY-FIVE

"AREN'T those *Carabinieri* cars?" Marti asked as they got out of their own rental car in the Villa Antica's main parking lot. She was looking at a midnight-blue Fiat hatchback and an Alfa Romeo compact parked in the far corner, each decorated with a slashing red stripe from front to back.

"Ya think?" John said. "Could be. Hey, maybe that's what that big '*Carabinieri*' on the sides means."

Marti bared her teeth at him. "How amusing. I couldn't see that from where I was sitting."

"Did you know they were coming here?" Julie asked Gideon. "Do you know what's going on?"

"Not a clue," Gideon said.

The question was answered before they reached the entrance. The door swung open, and five men emerged, walking quickly. Three of them were stone-faced *carabinieri*: Rocco, Martignetti, and a brigadier. Directly in front of them and being more or less frog-marched by the brigadier was a shambling man with his head down, his feet stubbornly dragging, and his wrists cuffed behind him. The fourth man, trailing behind and babbling at Rocco, who wasn't paying attention, was Severo Quadrelli.

The group strode by them without word or glance. And, even if there had been a glance, they wouldn't have noticed. They were staring at the man in handcuffs, and once he'd gone by, they looked at each other.

"Well, that's a surprise," Marti said.

"Yeah, it is," John agreed. "I figured if it was any of them, it had to be Franco. Or maybe Quadrelli."

"I'm just glad it wasn't Luca," Julie said.

Gideon was as surprised as any of them, although the pieces were already beginning to fall into place. "What do you know about that?" he said softly.

Nico.

NICO was stowed in the caged-in back seat of the hatchback with Martignetti beside him. The brigadier took the driver's seat, and Quadrelli stuffed himself, with some effort, into the front passenger seat. Rocco, who was apparently going to drive the compact back to Florence on his own, had a few words with Martignetti through the window, saw them off, and walked back to where the Laus and Olivers had stood watching.

"Surprised?" he said.

"A little," John said. "What exactly is he being arrested for?"

"Cesare's murder."

"But not Pietro's and Nola's?" asked Gideon.

"Hey, I'm not, you know, Superman. I can't do everything at once."

"Rocco, take it easy," Gideon said, laughing. "That wasn't a criticism. Jeez, you're sensitive. You guys are doing great. An arrest in *one* day. Congratulations. Do you have time to tell us how you—?"

"No, I better get back to the city with them. Maybe tomorrow sometime we could go get a cup of coffee somewhere."

"Can't. We're flying out in the morning."

"Oh. Hey, I'm sorry to hear that. Maybe give me a call, then?"

"Rocco, you don't look as pleased with yourself as you ought to be," Gideon said. "Are you expecting problems with the arrest?"

"Oh no, I'm good there. It's just . . ." He seemed to decide he had a little time after all, lit up a Marlboro, and took a drag. "It's just that we're still not getting anywhere on what happened up in the mountains. Nola and Pietro. I mean, I *know* Nico did them too, but I sure can't prove it. Hell, I can't even understand it."

"Well, you've got him now," John said. "You'll have plenty of questions for him."

"Yeah, sure, John, but you know how it is. When you're asking them questions, it goes a lot better if you already know the answers, and I don't have any answers for the way it went down up there. Throwing them off a cliff, shooting Pietro . . . I've run it through my mind a hundred ways, and it just doesn't make any sense. I mean, what's the rationale?" He shook his head, took another drag, and studied the cigarette the way smokers do, as if it held the answer to this and many other deep and ineffable mysteries.

"Oh well, we can help you there," Gideon said. "Julie can, anyway. She's come up with a pretty good rationale for what happened up there. It answers every single question we had."

"Oh, it's not that great," Julie mumbled. "I just . . ."

"Look, she's blushing again," Marti said.

Rocco smiled. "That's good, Julie, and I want to hear it, but right now I really have to get back. There's a lot of paperwork that needs doing, let alone—"

"Take the time, Rocco," Gideon said. "You need to listen to this."

Rocco reared back a little, surprised at Gideon's assertiveness. "Well, okay, sure. Shoot, Julie."

"It'll take a few minutes," Gideon said. "Let's go sit down somewhere."

They went to the deserted tasting room, and twenty minutes and one more Marlboro later, Rocco sat back in his chair, slowly nodding. "Julie, I have to say, that is f—absolutely brilliant."

"Oh, look," Marti said, "she's—"

But Julie silenced her with a growl and a look that would have stopped a charging rhino.

THEY had anticipated spending some farewell time alone with Luca and Linda that evening, perhaps going out to dinner with them, but Nico's arrest had naturally enough subdued the family—what was left of them—and pulled them closer together, and the Laus and Olivers had thought it was best to leave them to themselves. They went to dinner on their own, to the pizzeria John and Gideon had been to, then came back to make their good-byes, went to their apartments to pack, and left early the next morning for Florence Airport. There, Gideon's attempt to reach Rocco was unsuccessful, but a few hours later, during a layover at Amsterdam's Airport Schiphol, he got through to him.

Thus far, Nico had admitted to nothing yet, Rocco told him, but thanks to the bumbling, pontificating Quadrelli butting in all over the place, Nico had stumbled repeatedly, contradicting himself time after time, and Rocco was convinced that Julie's reconstruction of events was correct—that Gideon's cocaethylene hypothesis also had it right, and that Nico had killed both Nola and Cesare.

"But how did you settle on Nico in the first place, Rocco? I'm glad we were helpful, but nothing that Julie or I came up with had anything to say about *who* did it."

"That's a long story, buddy. Police work at its finest. Deductive reasoning—"

"We have to board in ten minutes. Can you make it short?"

He could and did. Admittedly, there was no direct evidence that Nico had killed anyone, but the circumstantial evidence was overwhelming. First of all, Nico, being Pietro's favorite, was the one most likely by far to break his father's rule and drop in on him in the mountains—

" 'Circumstantial' is putting it mildly," Gideon observed. In fact, by his definition, it wasn't even circumstantial, not in the legal sense. Circumstantial evidence is indirect evidence, a fact of some kind from which another fact can be logically inferred. Jane testifies under oath that she heard Jack and Mary fighting in an adjoining apartment. She heard Mary scream, "I'm going to kill you!" followed by a shot. When the police arrived, John was found on the floor, shot dead, and Mary was gone. Inferred conclusion: Mary shot John and ran off.

But where was Rocco's "fact" in the first place? This was nothing more than opinion and conjecture.

"Hear me out," Rocco said. "It gets better. Okay, second, Nico was the only one of them who still had a relationship with Cesare and would have been the *only* one to have been welcome in Cesare's apartment, where he could have switched the cough medicines."

Gideon didn't think too much of that either and began to wonder just how solid Rocco's case was, or whether he even had a case. But Rocco'd been saving the best for last. "It turns out that Nico's getting rid of the computer and printer and the rest wasn't good enough. Remember, I told you Tonino was checking out Cesare's list of passwords? Well, he struck gold. One of them was for an outfit called Ricordare that backs up everything on your computer in the cloud. Including e-mail."

And in Cesare's e-mail history was a sequence of exchanges with Nico, among which was one in which Cesare told him that he had made a big mistake accepting the new job, and he desperately wanted to return to Villa Antica. He asked Nico's advice about going to see Pietro at the cabin, hat in hand, to express his regret for what he'd done and to plead with the old man to take him back. Without Luca and Franco around to poison Pietro's mind, he thought there might be a better chance.

Nico advised against it: Pietro was still furious with his stepson, and a visit from him would only make matters worse. But Cesare wouldn't take this for an answer. He was determined to do it, and he begged Nico to go and talk to Pietro first to try to soften him up for the visit. Nico had always been the favorite son, the one most able to talk Pietro into changing his mind about anything. Besides, if anybody could get away with dropping in on Pietro during his retreat, he was the one.

At first Nico declined, but Cesare was persistent, and after a few more e-mails he gave in. He told Cesare he would go up to the Casentinese toward the end of Pietro's *mese sabatico*, when his father would be at his most relaxed, and he would do his best to set the stage for him. He said he would do it on September 26.

Late that day, Nico e-mailed Cesare that he had made the trip and reasoned with Pietro, and that he had gotten him to agree to leave Cesare's stipend in the will, and perhaps in time even to welcome him back to the villa, so there was no need for Cesare to go up on his own after all.

"Which couldn't possibly have happened," Gideon said. "Pietro'd been dead by then for almost a month."

"Exactly. It couldn't have. But Nico claimed it had. Why? There's more, listen."

Cesare was ecstatic. He e-mailed Nico that he would go up to the cabin the very next morning to express his sincere gratitude and to extend his promise to live up to Pietro's expectations in the future and so on. Nico's response came back in less than two minutes, and was just this side of hysterical: Don't go, *don't under any circumstances go* (it was in italics in the e-mail) to see him. Yes, Pietro had changed his mind about the will, but it was a delicate situation. His feelings toward Cesare were still bitter in the extreme. For Cesare to show up at the cabin was sure to set off an explosion. No, better—much better—to let time take its course, to wait for Pietro himself to decide when the time was right for his errant stepson to make an appearance. Anything else would be a disaster. And then Nico sent two follow-up e-mails saying pretty much the same thing.

"And so, your conclusion," Gideon said, summing up for him when Rocco seemed to have finished, "is that, having gone to the cabin at Cesare's request, and having found Pietro's body, he'd already made up his mind to kill Nola and make it look as if she were the one who died first. So he had to lie like crazy—*Pietro was there, sure, but don't go near him, you'll ruin everything!*—to keep Cesare away."

"Right. And then, as for killing Cesare, you know, I wondered at first why he took so long to get around to that. But then I realized there was no reason for him to do it, not until, well—"

"Yeah, I know. Not until we blabbed to everybody that Pietro had died long before Nola did—which suddenly made Cesare a threat to him, on account of those exchanges. Until then, there was nothing in them that contradicted the Pietro-killed-Nola fairy tale."

"Yup. We broke the news to them—including our boy Nico—on Friday afternoon. Saturday morning, Cesare was dead. So . . . that's the story. What do you think?"

"Rocco, I think you've nailed it."

"Me too, buddy," Rocco said happily. "And the public prosecutor says it's a go. Thanks a million for your help. And thank Julie!"

"THAT wasn't Betty," Julie said, coming back outside after answering the phone.

It had been two weeks since they'd returned home to Port Angeles. It was late September now, so the gloomy rainy season couldn't be far behind, and they'd been taking advantage of what might be the last of the sunny, golden evenings of fall and sitting out on their deck before dinner, watching the big Black Ball auto ferry from Victoria do its usual smooth, impressive job of pulling—backward and sideways—up to the ferry dock, when they'd heard the phone ring inside the house.

"I'll get it," Julie had said, getting up. "I'm pretty sure it's my sister."

Gideon had been more than content to continue to remain outside in the mild breeze, sipping his martini on the rocks and munching on an occasional shrimp or little wedge of Gorgonzola from the plate of appetizers they'd brought out with them. The call had taken a surprisingly long time—twenty minutes—and as he'd just learned, it hadn't been from Julie's sister Betty.

Julie dropped into the deck chair she'd been sitting in before and dipped a shrimp into the cocktail sauce. "That," she said, chewing, "was Linda."

"And what did she have to say? I can tell from the look on your face that it was something interesting. Something about the trial?"

"No, nothing about that. Gideon, that night at the *Vino e Cucina* reception—do you remember a woman we were talking to? Tall, kind of imposing . . ."

He raised his voice to an imperious mezzo-soprano " 'So what is it that a Skeleton Doctor does exactly, anyway?' Was she somebody important? She seemed to think so."

"She *is* important. She's a TV producer, and she works with the Food Network. She was there to look Luca over as the host for a possible cooking show."

"Was she? He'd be great at that."

"That's what she thought. Luca's got himself a show. Guess what it's called?"

"I have no idea."

"Sure you do. Take a guess."

He thought for a moment. "*La Cucina di Nonna Gina?*"

"That's it. *La Cucina di Nonna Gina with Chef Luca Cubbiddu.*"

"Well, good for him. He'll love it. And they'll love him. Here's to Luca and Grandma Gina." He raised his glass and they clinked.

"They've been filming right there at Villa Antica since yesterday. First show airs here October 19. He's starting with a tricky dish to make right; I messed up when he tried to teach us in the class. But I'll record the program this time. He says it's one dish you can freeze—*if* you do it at the right stage—so I can make enough for a few meals. It'll be a wonderful one-dish dinner on cold winter nights."

"Sounds good. What is it?"

"*Ossobuco*. I'll make a ton of it."

Gideon downed the rest of his martini, choking just a little, and rose with his glass. "You know, I believe I'll have another."